DIARY OF AN INNOCENT

SEMIOTEXT(E) NATIVE AGENTS SERIES

"Cet ouvrage publié dans le cadre du programme d'aide à la publication bénéficie du soutien du Ministère des Affaires Etrangères et du Service Culturel de l'Ambassade de France représenté aux Etats-Unis."

This work, published as part of the program of aid for publication, received support from the French Ministry of Foreign Affairs and the Cultural Service of the French Embassy in the United States.

Published by Semiotext(e)
2007 Wilshire Blvd., Suite 427, Los Angeles, CA 90057
www.semiotexte.com

The translator is profoundly thankful to Carole Sabas and Laurence Viallet for their help.

Special thanks to Dennis Cooper, Marc Lowenthal, Abdellah Taïa, Robert Dewhurst and Alice Tassel.

Cover art by Stan Douglas, *Rooftops, Habana Vieja*, 2004.
C-Print mounted on 1/4 inch honeycomb aluminum, 31 x 38 3/4 inches.
Courtesy of the artist and David Zwirner Gallery.
Design: Hedi El Kholti

ISBN: 978-1-58435-077-4
Distributed by The MIT Press, Cambridge, Mass. and London, England
Printed in the United States of America

DIARY OF AN INNOCENT

Tony Duvert

Translated from the French and with
an introduction by Bruce Benderson

Bruce Benderson

Innocence on Trial: The Politics of Tony Duvert

Literally, the "innocent" to whom the title of this novel refers only makes an appearance at the very end of the book. He's a sweet, dimwitted street boy who is fascinated by the narrator's typewriter and spends long periods of time typing every letter of the keyboard in order, over and over. Jokingly, the narrator considers handing in the boy's work, rather than his own, as the manuscript for the book but realizes that few would read it. Nevertheless, he asks himself, "Is there a law that is so different in the series of words that I put down?" Such comparisons and contrasts between the illiterate and the literate, the amoral and the moral, the impoverished and the well-to-do, and the individual and the family are the mechanisms that drive this narrative. But the real "innocent" to whom the title of this novel refers is the narrator himself, an unnamed lover of boys living temporarily in an unnamed southern city that suggests North Africa of the 1970s. This shouldn't, however, lead to the conclusion that the word "innocent" is being used ironically. Or rather, if it is, that irony is at our expense, rather than that of the protagonist's or author's.

Those familiar with the other writings of Tony Duvert (1945–2008) or his public reputation are bound to conflate the fictional experiences recounted in *Diary of an Innocent* with his own. However, during the years in which he enjoyed notoriety as a literary figure (1969–1989), he never publicly clarified his own sexuality, despite the fact that he made his politics surrounding the issue of sexuality absolutely clear. His critique of French bourgeois life seen through the lens of sexuality was as acerbic as it was tireless, and much of it targeted initial repressions and exploitations of sexual energy during the period of childhood. As he explained at length in his nonfiction book, *Good Sex Illustrated*, those cultural institutions we sanctify the most—the rearing of children, education, the family, our legal and medical systems, the clergy, marriage—are actually accomplishing the very opposite of what they claim. The raising of children, as he sees it, is a ruthless commandeering of their impulses and the capitalization of their bodies by an enslaving process of marketability. In this system, mothers are no more than low-level meat factory managers, who serve as the overseers of the sacrifice of childhood to the capitalist packaging conglomerate we call decency; fathers are trained to take out their frustrations through oedipal vectors in order to geld their children before they have become fully aware of their own capacity for pleasure; teachers are hypocritical lackeys whose sole occupation is to rein in children's polymorphous creativity and to provide convincing rationalizations for its reshaping into obligation; doctors, psychiatrists and priests are there to stamp such processes with legitimacy. And finally, the sole purpose of marriage is to repeat this inescapable cycle by creating more upholders and defenders of it. The narrator in *Diary of an Innocent* serves quite obviously as a mouthpiece for these politics. For Duvert, the promiscuous boy lover has become the most convenient device for taking pot shots at our social order.

So much for the narrator, but what about the succession of street boys in the novel who serve as his love objects? Almost all of them are wayward prepubescent panhandlers or child laborers from the petit bourgeoisie and working classes. Most tend to enjoy a high degree of autonomy in the streets outside the family circle. All have relationships with parents or elder siblings that are characterized by neglect or violence. Certainly, we expect the author to be calling attention to their plight. However, Duvert demonstrates quite convincingly that—even given such conditions—these boys are in a position that any French middle-class child should consider enviable. This is because the street boys enjoy full ownership of their bodies and their time whereas the average protected French child is taught to be a robotic tool of parents, teachers and priests.

This is not to claim that, when the novel enters the homes of some of these street boys, their parents and older siblings aren't portrayed as frankly tyrannical. But Duvert goes out of his way to attach such behavior to the reality of poverty and to the rigid, simplistic, traditional codes of the culture he is describing. What mitigates the bad behavior of these particular caregivers is their directness, the fact that their actions lack the hypocrisy and hidden motives of the same kind of treatment when it occurs in a bourgeois context. In taking these positions, Duvert's radical project essentially involves turning our moral code upside down, so that the alienation and sexual tastes of the narrator resemble innocence and sincerity whenever they are compared to those of the normal bourgeois literary audience who will become his readers and whom he is attacking.

The narrator in *Diary of an Innocent* functions as a test case for someone who attempts to avoid—however abjectly—the oppression of social institutions. His position is one of complete alienation from every element of society that Duvert has defined as hypocritical. He lives without family, without concern for his own safety or health, without allegiance to his own country and without the sexual orientation and sobriety we would expect from someone of his level of education and class. He is "innocent" of all those things and thus completely at odds with the social order. Rather than being a member of a political group or movement, he is single-handedly opposed to the capitalist cultural machine that produced him. This does not imply, however, that he is a firebrand, fighting for justice and attempting to convince others that he is in the right. As an "innocent," he seeks merely to live his life in as unfettered a way as possible.

Despite all of this, one is occasionally—and erroneously—led to believe that Duvert is a kind of activist. One of the most striking devices in this complicated narrative is a section that fantasizes obsessively about what it would be like if homosexual pedophiles were considered the norm and heterosexuals were treated the way homosexuals were in the era of pre-Stonewall. So fastidious is Duvert in covering every element of reversed oppression that could occur that this section becomes a hilarious send-up of the child protection schemes and exclusion of homosexuality from daily life that prevailed in Western society in the middle of the twentieth century. As each prohibition and each prejudice is piled on, all of them begin to seem more and more absurd, producing delightful satirical effects. But once this reverse dialectic is accomplished, Duvert deflates it immediately by pointing to a central flaw in his argument: no homosexual, he explains, would ever oppress another group to the level of exclusion and isolation to which the homosexual himself has been pushed. Thus, the purpose of this upside-down narrative is not to produce change, but merely to sharpen our consciousness of the mechanisms of the social order, and such a process of analysis promises to lead most of us into a profound state of uneasiness.

What American readers will find most repulsive about this novel is the fact that it isn't redemptive. In order to understand the importance of the theme of redemption to the American scene, we must first briefly discuss the influence of seventeenth-century Puritan literature on the roots of the Anglo-Saxon literary tradition, and the about-to-be-born novel of the century that followed. Especially in its early stages, the novel in Anglo-Saxon cultures was deeply influenced by the spiritual autobiography, which had already become a favorite form of reading. Perhaps the best known of these spiritual autobiographies is John Bunyan's *Grace Abounding to the Chief of Sinners* (1666), in which Bunyan recounts his lapses into sin that lead eventually to his epiphany and conversion. In such a book, the journey from point A to point B—from damnation to grace—created a ready-made linear narrative that always enjoyed the same structure. It is a movement from error toward conversion and the proverbial "happy ending." And it suggests that no story is worth its salt, or perhaps, no story could be called a story at all, unless the protagonist is brought back into the fold. Although this fold may have originally denoted a relationship only to God, it has taken on more banal and conformist parameters in modern times. One could almost substitute "family" for "fold."

Today there are thousands of fiction and nonfiction books that are constrained by the pattern established by narratives like *Grace Abounding*. Depictions of transgressions may be limitless, accounts of sensuality and appetite luridly graphic, the altered states of drug abuse described to a T, but we always end up in a recovery meeting, which we then realize is our perspective for looking back, and which wins us, hopefully—if we are authors—a guest spot on Oprah.

By saying this, I am not claiming that we do not also enjoy narratives that end in tragedy rather than in a happy ending. But these tragic narratives are, as well, adapted to the mold of redemption. In every case, the tragedy serves as a kind of punishment, and since the book is being written from a post-punishment perspective, the narrator is finally established as "good," having gone beyond error (even if it was too late in his or her particular case) and therefore worthy of our attention. As an extreme but relevant example, I must point out that our literary tradition has no narratives about pedophiles who avowedly enjoy behaving in a manner they admit we would see as having bad intentions. They are either confessing an illness to us or trying to prove that their orientation really is well meaning and socially constructive, usually in the sense most accepted by the middle-class mind.

Duvert, on the other hand, who remains very close to his narrator in this novel, doesn't wish to be thought of as contributing to the well-being of society, which he sees as a machine of speciousness. He makes a strong claim of being absolutely irredeemable in our eyes, salting this negation with a brazen claim to innocence. And indeed, in a way that may seem perverse to some readers, he locates the moral superiority of his text in its absolute *irredeemableness*. He forsakes the only two possible approaches to this subject that an Anglo-Saxon might choose: "coming to his senses" and realizing the error of his orientation, with the narrative representing the journey to that realization; or settling on a way to convince us that his life-style is for the betterment of society. Duvert's character, on the other hand, is "lost" to our notion of what is good or right, and he chooses to stay that way for the very purpose of declaring himself innocent. He may be "lost," but if that is the case, it's not because he has chosen the wrong path and is lost to himself, but because he has been abandoned by the social order, something he has little hope of changing.

Duvert belongs, of course, to a well-known tradition of French *poètes maudits*, who aligned themselves with variations of the notion of evil and who include Sade, Baudelaire, Bataille, Huysmans and Genet. The fact that many passages of *Diary of an Innocent* were repulsive to me and that I identified that repulsion as much more than a matter of taste is merely proof of the efficacy of Duvert's purpose. Several scenes are there mostly to ensure a portrait of the protagonist as someone who is plainly repugnant to the normal reader. In one, he removes a tiny worm from his anus with the tip of a knife as if it were light comedy; in another, he devotes almost an entire page to describing a cat munching on a giant cockroach as he speculates about how it might taste and compares that taste to elements of French cuisine; in a third, he recounts an attempt to have coitus with a dog during a camping trip when he ended up in a French town that felt alien and rejecting to him.

Even in France, discussions about or with Duvert have tended to touch upon the startling amount of aggression and alienation in his texts. In both his writing and the interviews with him, it is almost as if he were jumping the gun and expressing his disgust for those who would express theirs for him—as if he has left any call for inclusion by the wayside long ago and has made himself a sacrificial victim of social rejection. But for what purpose? One could say he has chosen to lie down with the Devil in order to escape the narrow boundaries of social experience—and thus achieve an unusual kind of transcendence. As I have tried to show, such a stance probably could not be more foreign and more distasteful to the American mind, which tends to function on the assumption of conformity and inclusion. (There's room for everybody, if only we can learn to understand!)

There may also be one other purpose of Duvert's narrative, though evidence for it is subtle. I would call this *de-idealization*. Idealization of human behavior is a tactic all of us use to survive. A most obvious example of this is our reluctance in almost any discourse (excluding vulgar satire) to discuss or provide examples of certain activities we engage in regularly, such as defecation. When we see a beauty queen on television gushing over the receipt of a rhinestone crown and a bouquet of long-stemmed roses, it is true that some of us may in our minds subject her to a prurient sexual objectification, but the furthest thing from our thoughts is what she looks like on the toilet or menstruating. Why? Not only does the frequency of both make them an integral part of human life, they also preoccupy all of us to a high degree at moments when we're alone.

As a child, I remember a transgressive game I would play compulsively with myself: I would think of friends of my parents, teachers, politicians, alluring actresses or any individual who encouraged idealization and radiated social power; and then I would try to visualize the same person on the toilet. After questioning friends, I have come to the conclusion that such perverse fantasizing is far from original. To see authority, beauty or other social currency suddenly disappear the moment one adds certain universal but private behavior to the repertoire of the imagination can become positive exploration for a child who has just begun to confront the world and its intimidating institutions.

Duvert's intention in this text may be analogous. Not only is he forcing the grotesqueries of his own libido upon us; he is also calling for a de-idealization of our experience and human experience in general. Hidden behind his rather boastful descriptions of situations that threaten to turn our stomachs is the challenging question: *And how pretty would you look with your soul bared to this extent?*

If this aspect of Duvert's texts truly exists, it presents one of the hardest of his lessons for us to take in. Our initial and defensive reaction will obviously be: *Well, I don't sleep with little boys!* But anyone who has the inclination, the mind and the stamina to absorb a larger part of Duvert's oeuvre will eventually be subjected to his careful and detailed inversion of our system of values, obsessively and meticulously worked out according to the most stringent rules of reasoning, with the help of Marxist theory. His worldview certainly is audacious but never lacks rigor. I would go so far as to say that its repercussions are as inescapable as the oppressive systems he is unraveling. They support his claim that our intimate and private lives are just as wicked—indeed, more so, because of their hypocrisy—than the disturbing descriptions in this book.

This allows the dialectic of the book to justify the narrator's plea: he is *innocent*. According to Duvert's reasoning, it is an innocence that approaches sainthood (in the sense of Sartre's *Saint Genet*) because the protagonist chooses to suffer (and, in fact, there are even passages in this book in which he chooses to live for several days on bread and water, because he finds this preferable to confronting the social networks of the outside world). By his "sins," he is critiquing, or even neutralizing, all of ours, which are not only oppressive but entangled in exploitive social functions that have constructed themselves as incontrovertible and reach far beyond us. And though it may be true that the protagonist's life-style is helping no one, we—as cowards and upholders of the very order that oppresses and exploits us—are harming many. Into the libidinal, alternative, alienated world which this narrator so categorically invites us, it inevitably becomes our shit that stinks, not his.

I wanted to talk about birds, but the time for that has passed. In spring there were storks; they were gray and scrawny, like the dead branches of the nests they built on some of the embankments, far away to the south. Later, they stretched pitiful wings, fanned them disjointedly with an ancient sound and slowly soared off.

In this city it was the time for fasting, and I began writing. Call it winter in this world without seasons; my friends desert me; living weighs more heavily. Sunny days go by without celebration. Then, at twilight, life can begin again. People are already sitting down to eat at the cheap open-air restaurants and getting their bowls of chickpea soup. It's a loose, spicy purée mixed with lentils and fairly acidic tomatoes, swimming with beans and vermicelli; it tastes good, smells of roasted grain; it's starchy and hearty and it burns. I don't feel comfortable in this house. A widow and her daughter are sitting to my left, almost on the ground, on a straw-and-dried-flower mattress. I'm on the edge of an iron box spring, which another straw mattress has converted into a couch; the two women are leaning back against the edge of a similar bed; the older brothers, who are on stools, complete the circle. In the middle is a low table. The mother has placed the soup pot next to her, in one corner. She's sitting cross-legged with her dress and apron hiked up to her knees, and she has large tits, a flat, square face, smooth white skin, and a narrow mouth and eyes; she's slurping soup from a small wooden ladle, glancing up at me briefly with a touch of suspicion, mixed with contempt and amiability. I feel like one of those arthritic old dogs that the women pet because it belongs to a crony. I'm having sex with one of her older sons, and maybe she's aware of it; the forced smiles that form creases and dimples in her chubby face make her hard little eyes seem colder.

For my admiration, she's offering the two little boys in the family, sitting on some rag cushions below a bare wall. They have on worn, but still spotless and untorn, athletic suits that also serve as pajamas; they aren't eating, just staring at us silently. I hardly know them. The seven-year-old has a doll's grin, you'd say he was pretty, he's the youngest; he has curly hair, a long face with a heavy jaw, eyes like a girl, a touch of wickedness to his cheeks and on his lips; he keeps grabbing me by the shoulders and kissing me, looking for flattery; I push him away.

I like the other one, who has a round face and short hair, a flat nose that can wrinkle. His eyes are steady, serious, at times a little absent; he acts terse, out of politeness; he doesn't speak and has touched me only once, to bite my hand while they were taking our picture. He's nine or ten. Between two gulps of soup, the woman of the house asks me which I prefer. I choose the little surly one. They're surprised, make a joke of it, insist he's not good-looking, ask me again and I answer the same. There's a moment of shock, as well as rancor under the laughter, which I don't understand. We start again, I'm supposed to redeem myself; visitors have always adored the youngest and been turned off by the other, the mother insists.

Afterward, it's made clear to me why my answer induced such a bad reaction. When the father was alive, he preferred the boy I like, and disregarding the other five, considered him the best son. There was nothing advantageous in it for the kid, nor did it appeal to his vanity. Then the father died, his spouse became boss, and the serious little fellow who'd once been the preferred was cast aside, while the youngest son got put in first position, and the eldest, a hardworking numbskull, took the old man's role. The account is as blatant as a children's story. The night they question me, I have to incarnate the father himself, back from a long war or trip to put right the injustices of a cruel mother. We're in the time of kings and fairies, simple, straight-forward ordeals; the little boy's tragedy is as clear as the big typeface in the books kids read on vacation.

I don't give in. The mother consoles her little cipher, and I wonder which of the two are looking more angrily at me. It's the little one who scares me, he's going to choke: his brows are knit, his skin yellow with bile, his cheeks swollen, his mouth trembling, his nostrils pinched, pulling his nose into an eagle's beak, and he's picking fiercely at little black boogers and forgetting to respond to the flustered fondling of the old woman, who's beginning to look whiny.

The boy I've chosen is studying me, his face lit up with sur-prise, as if I'd just kept him from being hit. He stays sitting on the ground with thighs spread, knee to chin; and he's bare-foot, scratching between his toes with a finger, shifting gently from one buttock to the other and sending me playful little winks mixed with laughter that opens up his face. They let him have his day. Then he falls back into his usual reserve, and his eyes get their faraway look. The men have begun to talk about other things; but now and then, on his own, he still breaks into the surprised smiles of someone having a good dream.

It would be better to think of a name for certain boys. I'll take them from a novel by Quevedo; I have hardly any books here, and that will do. I just need to follow the order of the first chapter: I come to Francesco, the author's first name, then Pablos, Pedro, Diego, Andrès and a few others. For the moment I only need the first two. Let's call Francesco the teenager who brought me to his family and Pablos the little brother I preferred.

I don't know if these first names are a good match; some people would think they are, others wouldn't. But choosing accurate or attractive ones isn't important; it's enough for chance to decide, the way it does in the case of real births, depending on people, languages, matings, here or there, for no particular reason. Besides, Francesco, who's probably about seventeen, has manufactured a legend about how he came into the world. Around that time his father was serving a three-year prison sentence for concealing weapons, though he didn't know that he was. His family put up with sneers, suspicion and hunger. So, when the father got out of prison, it was like a resurrection; they feasted all night, sang, cried out of pleasure with reunited friends, women, neighbors, rich parents, it was a celebration; and Francesco was born two days later.

At first I reacted the way I was expected to; the story had been told well, he'd used his most astute speaking voice, complete with innocent eyes and some very nice expressions. Really, a lovely story, with Dad as God and the nativity of Francesco.

"But since your father was in prison, how did he make you?"

"What do you mean, *make* me?"

Then he understood and blushed a little, his face changed, his voice fell. I felt ashamed. He said, "Uh, I dunno. That's how they told it to me. I was too little!"

We're at the table at my place. He's picking at some raw vegetables that he's prepared, tomatoes with salt, green peppers, olives, radishes split crosswise and salted, kind of bland, like the taste of cold water. He holds back, looking shamefaced and vaguely hostile: I've deprived him of his family legend, all he's got left is an orphan's face.

The book by Quevedo that I walk around with is *The Life of the Adventurer Don Pablos de Segovia, Ideal Tramp and Image of the Swindler*. I like this novel a lot, despite the fact that I haven't read it. The child that I dubbed Pablos isn't a swindler, nor even a rascal. But he seemed to have a great appetite for living when we talked. A quiet, determined student, he didn't brag about school; laughing delightedly, he shows me an assignment he scored an A on, in a notebook filled with praise and good grades. He gets up at five in the morning to read his notebooks and books; sunlight trickles silently onto the patio of the house; he studies in a low voice; nothing distracts him. He doesn't say anything about this work, but in the evening, before nine, he gets dazed, lies down wherever he happens to be, withdraws and falls asleep. He doesn't get a lot of it.

He's unaware of the first time I saw him because he was already asleep, in the most deeply recessed of the beds, which form a tower of flowered bleachers in the room I came back into. They put me next to him. His head is on the other side, which I can't see because it's facing down; and right beside me are the bottoms of his smooth, dainty feet, the curled toes forming two pinkish rosary beads. Then they lift him up to put him to bed in another location. He doesn't wake up. I can see the somewhat coarse sweetness of his handsome, impenetrable face; his four pale, sturdy, naked limbs dangling limply; and in the gape of his briefs, his little boy's prick, mischievous in a glint of light that tongues it furtively as they carry him off. This plump sex, exposed in its shell of creased fabric, looks like a fleshy face, chortling for no reason, the kind you'd discover by parting the edges of swaddling inside a crib. Pablos's other face: less innocent than his shameless slumber would make you think, but more naïve than I'm hoping when—gripping his dick and balls through his underpants to demonstrate what he's saying—he calls them my *loaf of bread* and my *grapes*.

This imagery has an origin. On a photo that was just taken, Pablos was wearing an old pair of wrinkled cotton trousers that were too short for him, to go play in the dirt alley where his family lives; the fly and the entire front, tight along his stomach and struck by the slanting sun, were full of weird bulges, knots, worn, raised areas, one of which looked kind of obscene, long and stiff like the member of a faun. We had a good time with it; and when the kid saw the photo, he laughed, too, but explained that it was only because there was some bread in his pocket that day. And the word migrated from this conspicuous crust to the invisible thing it had suggested.

As for the *grapes*, on my table I have some chocolate with raisins, Pablos ate some of it and, as he retold the bread joke, found a better way to describe himself: with the word *grape* on his lips, his eyes and his finger on the gilded bunch decorating the wrapper, his other hand tugging between his legs at his two balls to verify the resemblance.

Long months passed between the evening of the chickpea soup and that pleasant afternoon of the *loaf of bread*; then a lot of gloomy days that I don't see any end to. A little twelve-year-old boy, Pedro, who used to come by a year ago, used a piece of fruit another way. During his first visit, he stays by himself for a while, frozen on his chair, or rather, slumped on it with slack shoulders, the back of his head sunk into his neck and chin high, his eyes sluggish, white and vacant the way they are during a medical exam. I'm talking to his brother in the next room because I haven't understood if they're going to have sex together or one by one. This older brother, Diego, who's sixteen, is small and looks somewhat childlike, but he has a big prick and doesn't take kindly to little brats. When we come back, I've decided to wait until later to go to bed with Pedro; but even so, I'd like to kiss him, touch him before he leaves today. Standing behind his chair, I slip a hand into his clothing, without undoing it, until I've reached between his legs, and immediately regret choosing his brother, whom I've known.

Notwithstanding, under Pedro's clammy, lightweight "scrotumette" is a large, hard and rather cold ball. Taken aback as if I'd discovered some disgusting infirmity, I palpate it. And then I understand what it is: an apple. The boy had grabbed it and hidden it while he was alone. His older brother, who sometimes flaunts his principles to me, wouldn't mess around with such stealing. So I keep quiet and search for the child's eyes in the mirror opposite; they meet mine, he suppresses a smile, then gives into it but avoids my glance. Now he's blushing; a wave of pride, even a certain preening, floods his face. I keep my hand where it was. Standing next to us, Diego probably thinks his little brother is getting hard, and that I like his dick.

Apples are expensive in spring, and so are bananas. I keep these fruits for guests, who eat a lot of them and often arrange them into red-and-green cocks and balls, ready to crunch into. Not many boys like boys; but they like being a boy, showing it, being it together.

One of them mockingly put a bizarre-looking, disgustingly purplish plum on his fly, made of two asymmetrical fruits stuck together unevenly, the first lower than the other, like testicles. He used a vegetable for the penis, a carrot, maybe; there were some odd ones that were smooth and thin, hairless baldies. One of those carrots was forked, making a bifid prick against I forget which belly, and it was like jerking off times two.

I was living in a run-of-the-mill part of town, two furnished rooms in a small building with a garden, a new neighborhood, where it was easier for foreigners to stay than in the immense old quarter. It was expensive, bright, sterile, modern. The boys liked coming there; they ate, smoked, had cold drinks, hung out on the balcony, took baths, gabbed, slept. To them I seemed easy to be around, the fact that I'm twenty-nine didn't put them off. So I was happy to let it go on.

A teenage friend of Francesco criticized me; he'd offered to buy me a beer in an old columned café as vaulted and as dirty as an entrance lobby. He said that I was wrong to waste my money on boys, I should have been saving it to buy serious things. I said that I'd rather have sex and be nice to those who said yes. He shrugged, and as if recommending a recipe for tea or some syrup as a laxative, described his remedy: get hold of some weekly magazine with pictures of women; and when I felt like fucking, open it, look at a photo and satisfy myself with my hand.

"While thinking of a woman, understand?" he insisted heatedly, his voice emphatic, saddened by my obstinacy. Among these boys, jerking off is called *Mrs. Five Finger*. It's a more easy-going term than the French slang, *la veuve Poignet*, or the *Widow Fist*. Pablos said they did it under desks at school, and mentioned a buddy who was older than him and came in the inkwell; then once this concoction was discovered, he accused Pablos, who was still too young to have any jism, of doing it. It's a made-up spiel, part of the international routine of *Mrs. Five Finger*. In another version, the inkwell is filled with piss, and Pablos lets it be believed that it could be his. Ever since Madame Clot's cooking-pot, the utensil in which Jean-Jacques Rousseau claims he pissed (there aren't any to be found in Geneva, just as you don't find any chamber pots that smell of asparagus in Combray, either), baptizing all containers with an orifice that appeals to their willy is the trivial pursuit of little boys.

Holding up his thumb and forefinger, Pablos shows how he rubs his member. I call it *Mrs. Two Finger*, and he immediately takes the ball by inventing *Mrs. Three Finger*, fingers making a hat floating in the wind.

The boy who gives me advice about polluting magazines is earning a little money as a bird-catcher. In the olive tree gardens surrounding the city, or in the nearest country woods, he uses birdlime to trap tiny sparrows; the males bring forty francs, and the females, which there are more of, or which are easier to catch, go for only two, because they don't sing. But in the wicker cages the merchants carry around, they're all mute, bristly, starving tremblers. This must make it possible to sell the females at a high price by pretending they're frightened males. The boy swears it isn't true.

In this modern neighborhood, I didn't have many chores to do. Paltry furniture, bare walls and a clean sky. I like breathing the air here; in the evening it spreads the odor of flowers and trees over a large distance. There aren't many flies. No mosquitoes. The sun is strong, the nights mild, it rarely rains except for brisk, heavy showers. My windows were always open; under the table, there was a worn raffia mat that caught the crumbs from meals; but I'd always find it clean. The birds moved so quickly that I only caught sight of them one time when they thought I was dead. On the balcony their cry was composed of two joyless, gratuitous notes, vibrant, like the whistle signaling that hoodlums are assembling. From the balcony, the birds would dart under the table. I run to close the window, but they're faster than me, except for one.

I walk toward it with a vague bullying desire. Animals make me feel like a boy in his prime; as soon as I'm alone with one of them, even a vicious one, I get ideas. It would be touching to catch this bird, hold it in my hand and jerk off with the other hand, to wet its beak. But either I'm not mean or depraved enough, or I'm lazy, with a philosophical mind, and a mania for listening to the preposterous thoughts that pop into my head, like little good-for-nothings do, before they're capable of reasoning, and some giggly old fogies.

But let's not call what I have thoughts. The acts they inspire fill them out, deceive me about them. The words make them evasive.

My captive took refuge under the little bed that serves as a couch. I lie down on it suddenly, and the bird flutters away along the tiled floor, rises and, like a bumblebee, crashes against the mirror several times. The collisions are brutal, really loud. Later it's clinging to a curtain. I hope I can touch it, but it takes off. Yet it seemed to have come to a halt, hovering in front of my head to get a look at me. Its eye is cold, intense, black: the eye of a lizard or iguana. Because its ancestors were reptiles; its gray feathers, scales; and its wings, pudgy paws.

It lets out a harsh, full cry. It perches on the sideboard; creeps under the bed; comes back at top speed to crash against the mirror. When it falls, it remains a little out of it, hides under something, comes out in tiny hops, takes off, gets knocked out, goes to hide or comes immediately back to the attack. For a moment I think it's idiotic for laying siege to the mirror as if the sky were behind it; but if it flies into the window where the sky really is, it won't get to it that way, either; its only mistake is making the wrong mistake. They call you a heretic for less, but this is just a bird.

It flies some more, shrieks in my face, slams against the mirror again, doesn't shit. I open the window; the sky comes in, and the bird flies off into it. In a sparrow's head, this is the proof that you can pass through mirrors. Afterward, other birds came to peck away at the crumbs. I shut myself up in the room in order to leave them in peace.

The bird-catcher rarely came to my place. He liked to drink beer, wine, but hid it because of his age, though he was tall.

One time he came over drunk, plopped himself down with a grin, then looked trounced, nodded his head, was silent for a long time; his eyes dulled, then they closed, were wide open, flashed with anger to deny the fact that he'd drunk. I liked it. I opened a bottle; he watched me, grimaced, fell back into his mindless state. Then he decided to go vomit.

He couldn't hold it back all the way to the toilet and projectile-vomited an enormous, winey spurt onto the white wall. He'd eaten some bright-colored raw vegetables; I really liked the way he'd chewed, because the vegetables were delicate, graceful filigrees, like those paper chains little children cut out. I put the boy in an armchair by the window. He takes a breath, lets out his stomach, sees the setting sun and the trees, hears the games being played in the avenue lined with orange trees. He started to feel better, got control of his expressions again, joked, excused himself, cleaned up. The filigree strands were building up in the bidet, we forced them down. He stayed for dinner and to sleep, something that usually never happened.

He has a pleasant face, intense eyes, a big noiseless laugh, a long, muscular, satin-smooth body, very tempting. But we don't have sex together. Despite the fact that he goes with an old guy from time to time, with me he's embarrassed to; he sees us as too alike, feels like I can see through him.

He chuckles as he's getting undressed. When we brush against each other under the sheet (we had to cover up and turn the light out), he stifles his hiccups in the pillow, against his shoulder. And that laugh of a little girl upset about being tickled, a fem little guy with awkward curves and a hollow voice, shows that he's dying of embarrassment. Kiss me? He gently takes hold of my neck but bursts out laughing when he touches my mouth. Get fucked? He feels me up, tries it out, claims it's too big. I grab his prick, which is as hard and straight as a chair leg, long enough to put two hands on it, if not more—but it's shaking from hilarity as are his stomach and ribs. Nobody knows how to uphold his propriety so affably. We settle down, rest on our laurels, pull apart, sleep.

Later on, he was forced to work in a garage and had a hard time doing it. He was covered with black grease right to his eyes, he'd grown eight inches, had hollow cheeks and looked worn out, a defeated expression. Out of depression he started drinking, stopped going home with foreigners.

Soon after school had started again, Pedro, the boy with the apple, stopped coming over, too. I wasn't seeing any other kids and didn't know how to find them. Eight to ten gloomy days went by. I'd liked his visits.

In the afternoon when school got out, I'd often be coming back from the market. I'd take a quiet avenue, which was divided by a median strip planted with very short palm trees. There were a lot of well-dressed passersby, but not many cars. Everybody looked indifferent, respectable, was going for a walk, taking his time.

I saw a few little kids at the foot of a palm tree, catching a hail of yellow fruits being tossed down by another who'd climbed up to the center of the tree; they were unripe dates that tasted bad, rather sour. They greeted me casually, and I glanced at the kid in the tree. He had nice calves with a summer tan that had already faded on his forearms as a result of his washing up; he was pretty stocky, in mismatched clothing, his pants covered with patches, with the bearing of someone playing hooky from school, a look no longer admired in France except in illustrations engraved a hundred years ago. Finally, the imp's face is revealed— it's Pedro. He was far from outgoing, but today his entire face is convulsed in laughter, and he calls out to me, lets go and slides down the trunk. He grabs his schoolbag, gathers some of the fruits, dumps his friends and comes over to have sex.

He says he stopped going to my place out of fear of his brother Diego, whose relation with me was strained. I told him there was nothing to worry about.

Plucking a little boy perched high on a tree, in the lovely late afternoon sun; freedoms of another world. I wasn't comparing my climber to a bird, we would have despised each other. Because, though people may see birds as lovey-dovey little things, for me they seem tough and flighty. As for children, I don't know anything about them—except for Pedro, a pigheaded little beast with a tough hide, clutching his tree like a peasant, a stubborn donkey.

Around two in the morning, I left Francesco and Pablos's place, then went even further south to hang out under the ramparts. Down there, when the night is deserted, immaculate bellies soar around you in long, white-winged arcs—barn owls, crossing from one wall to the other in the series of courtyards you go past. Farther on, I took some unfamiliar alleyways inside this maze, which led me to my place a mile or so later, after I'd gotten my bearings. The meager lights, a vivid orange dotting the broken line of facades at unequal heights, twinkled like country lanterns. No one. Everything was silent, a pure kind of silence.

Lost in these images of low houses and stars, I suddenly noticed an airplane—a boy with his arms spread like wings, roaring like a supersonic jet, which spun, twirled, landed and turned into a car; it rumbled as he activated the gear shift, grabbed the steering wheel, and in a booming voice that cracked, revved up the engine, then used his fists as fenders and braked suddenly against another car, to pee on it.

I went up to him. He was fourteen or fifteen, not hideous given the moron he was, with the strong, simpleminded expressionless mug I was expecting. In this place, idiots often go around freely, as do nutcases who aren't violent; people put up with them. The moron's pee-pee tool was a colossal sausage, a fresh pink. He looks at me looking at it, and when he's finished pissing, leaves his fat piece hanging to concentrate on better seeing what I'm seeing. I'd like him to fuck me. But we don't say a word, won't move. I point to his penis with a gesture of my chin. He doesn't understand. I do it again. He doesn't understand. Again. He doesn't understand. Again, and he thinks he understands and points to it himself. I nod. Yes. He grabs hold of it, looks at me, at it, at me, strokes it, looks at me, pumps it up to an enormous size. Suddenly he stops, knits his brow, puts the wilted thing back in his pants, and as if he were remembering how the world is made, raises the finger of a visionary and gravely indicates the night sky, to show me that God was looking down on his innocent prick.

Francesco lives with other guileless types. He'd spent three days in a neighboring town, with some friends and some girls. They go down there regularly to have some fun where things are slower; they drink, dance, have sex, for a few francs they rent the back part of a house from the villagers, who tolerate these adolescent escapades. When he got back, he told me about something he happened to see one morning. On an out-of-the-way street, two kids were glued together standing up against a tree, their shorts around their ankles. Francesco (because he likes boys) was turned on but indignant, and told them, "Hey! Aren't you embarrassed to do that outside?"

And the little pipsqueak who was plowing the other answered furiously, "Leave us alone! In the first place, he's my brother!"

Francesco respects family; he shut up and walked away. The little couple went back to work right away.

Because Francesco's the biggest liar I know, his story, which is almost formulaic, may not be true. True, however, to what I know about some children and their turn-ons, which are as old as the human race.

In a village in France, I'd tried to rape a dog, and I was no little scalawag anymore, but an adult. I was biking and camping alone. At sunset, I found this picturesque village with sun-dappled stones and houses on a slope. And waiting for me was an empty fenced-off meadow, equipped with some pay toilets. I was feeling sociable. Unfortunately, this was no town like Francesco's, but a village in our country. There was no one but a stray dog who wanted to speak to me. You take what you get. I would have had to go to the tobacco–convenience store, a café-grocery, which you'll find in every village, just as you will monuments to the dead. And in such establishments you'll find grannies and grandpas doing business and chatting with the inhabitants. Or maybe go knocking on the church door? I don't know what to do to meet some fellow creatures.

The dog, who'd seen me, was as frustrated as I was, and had begun following me. He was an ugly little bastard, timid, as stupid as they come, he'd look at you briefly like an animal that isn't petted. I lured him into my tent with chocolate. He was distrustful but finally came in. He had quite a meager dick, limp to the touch, poor little thing. He didn't bite, was a giggler, acted nervous, reluctant to sit down. I took down my briefs, and he sniffed me in front and behind, without much enthusiasm. He didn't like chocolate very much, either. I tried what else I had, and he chose the bread. Then I let him go. Next I jerked off while imagining that the bastard was pounding me hard. I'd gotten off, vaguely, but couldn't stay alone in my meadow, so I went walking through the village again. Untouchable children, teenagers with dodgy eyes, old people whose averted faces were spying on you, groups that closed rank as they passed by. Not even a public urinal. Soon, some warmhearted country TV series had emptied the streets. It was curfew. I walked for a long time past these beautiful, lifeless houses; sinking colors, fresh smells, the rustling of trees, the limpid shadows of night had a tenderness that tore right through you. Those are life's saddest evenings; and it's not the dog's fault—nor mine.

If this memory, or others that are older and less abstinent, filled me with a sense of shame, Francesco's stories relieved me of it, because so many involved relations with animals. One of his brothers was drinking wine with two buddies; they caught a dog, shut her up in a little room, kept her in there and fucked her; but when it was the third gang-banger's turn, the others let her out and she fled at skidding and pulling behind her the one who was banging her, his member stuck so that he had to follow her on his hands and knees. Several years after it happened, the practical jokers were still laughing to the point of tears.

Francesco claims that he caused a poultry holocaust at a tiny religious school—a kind of kennel into which poor parents tossed their children to get God and the alphabet drummed into them. The teacher (or should we say keeper, since he's paid by tips) was a torturer, which was the rule among these parochial equivalents of the greasy spoon; he spent less time teaching reading than whipping his charges and trying out punishments from which they emerged with bleeding skulls, unless it was their hands, or the soles of their feet. And Francesco got his revenge for this abuse by pummeling the old priest's farmyard with his dick: chickens, pigeons, ducks and even one goose.

Now, if he was this victim, he still may not have been this torturer. As I've said, bringing up the subject of Francesco certainly involves quoting his lies, which form the essential part of my memory of him. And at five or six, your rod is too thin to choke a goose, and even a simple pigeon. If it happened when his cock was as big as it is today, I'd believe him; given the two or three times in the space of a year that we hooked up and I wanted to get poked by him, I can guess what a small biped without a backside must have been feeling. And some diarrhea that he described as yellow, red and greenish after having buggered a chicken one day has, dare I say, the color of truth to it.

The best was a steer. The boy was thirteen; he'd been given the animal to lead it to an open-air area where they were going to slaughter it to eat for a celebration. He ended up alone with the steer in the shade of a tree. A young, attractive steer. But its hole is too high for the boy. He goes to get some stones, a stump, builds a step, grabs hold of the steer's loins, pushes away the tail and slips in like a puff of air. The steer didn't even deign to feel the jab, but Francesco got caught by a man and was beaten for having seasoned the beef for the festivities while it was still alive.

I'm less curious when it comes to intercourse with goats; everything has been said about that shepherds' companion, its fiery vulva, its graceful ways, its sensitive face. I'd rather go back under the trees for a pastoral lyric in which there are no animals, just the affectionate gesture of a child that I found touching. Francesco was ten. Between two pranks, he'd often do *Mrs. Five Finger* with another brat in the olive gardens. But it was his habit to wet his hand before stroking his penis. So our little fellows sat side by side, each concentrating on himself to produce some thrills. But it was hot. Francesco's mouth was dry; soon he couldn't keep going, through lack of saliva. So the other child quite obligingly spit a thick, frothy jet into Francesco's palm, rescuing his chance for pleasure.

Love between boys is prohibited, but the morals of the common folk allow a few remnants of it; they hook up a little when there are no girls or women available. Small boys aren't considered any different than men, they aren't taught to be innocent, they're attracted to the bodies of adults, and if they're the forward type, they want to have sex like anyone else; even prepubescents seem to think it's completely natural for people to be interested in their little penis, of which they're more than half proud.

Sex acts are simplistic, whittled down to the essential, and sometimes brutal. Butt-fucking comes close to being a feather in your cap, but being the one on the bottom makes you a degenerate, though less so at a young age. Nevertheless, even among my most reluctant partners, I rarely encountered a tensed-up anus as happens in our country: the interdiction is in their minds rather than their organs.

Coldness when it comes to masculine sex is proof that it's punished yet indulged in at the same time; you keep from being a homosexual by mistreating those whom you're with. You're supposed to keep it strictly secret, which is an illusion, since everybody likes to talk about it. Those who do the act with virility or venality don't hide it much; those who have a real desire for it hide it fearfully. You're not afraid to be queer, you're afraid to be associated with the name; as if the dominant form of eroticism had one part that was forbidden but couldn't be given up, which you persecuted in those who embodied it openly.

Foreigners are less subject to these constraints, and when you're with them, you are, too. What these foreigners think of you doesn't count, which works in their favor. And since they seem free of their negative mores when you meet them, it's often assumed that such is the way it is in their country. You go out of your way to look for them, because you can go out with them without too much of a risk and simultaneously look down on them for agreeing to it. You might also make a few bucks, but it's usually not about prostitution.

A lot of these boys, when I was alone with them, were friendly, sensual, good-tempered and sweet, very free with their bodies. In a situation that they saw as shameful, they could have acted cynical, nasty, dishonest, but I saw almost none of that. They were, instead, rather defenseless, brimming with innocent warmth, politeness, cheerfully content, friendly and soft in a way that they weren't with women. Like daydreamers, AWOL for a night in a secret land in which they did not live; they were only half there. The presence of a woman would have elicited the sense of duty, the role-playing, the kinds of aggressions and anxieties that boys are trained to have; with me, on the other hand (a queer and a subhuman about whose opinion they didn't care a fig), there was nothing to gain, to prove, to test. They became good boys despite themselves.

Then, once they returned to ordinary life, they came back to their senses and the laws by which they lived. They denied the strange pleasures their bodies had experienced, rejected me because I'd been satisfied by it. Without the freedom to disown what they'd done, none of these boys would have come over to see me; without the right to dismiss me, none of them would have touched me. I saw almost no exception to this rule; it was the only thing that let so many boys from the lower classes dare—heterosexual though they considered themselves to be—indulge in forbidden love on a regular basis.

Being rejected like this put me in a kind of isolation that was new for me. In France, social life is so hideous that I don't mind being on the margins or being subject to it. Exclusion has the same value as those who enforce it; the disgust my country often inspires in me protects me from its judgments. Here I was suddenly deprived of such a freedom, because I passionately admired this city, its inhabitants, the customs of its common people, the street, the elements of daily life; everything we'd lost was still alive here. Unfortunately, I'd be accepted only to the extent that a queer can be. I'd be a piece of shit for some boys, a whore for others, innocence for some; I'd be kept apart like a bad scene.

Because each person exploits the rules of society differently, I was at least hoping to meet those who didn't apply them to me to a high degree. It's not something easy to assess, and it's determined to a great degree by the situation. I avoided the flashy ones, with their gift for gab and their mediocre performance in bed. As a rule I stayed away from homosexuals, who seemed to me to be fearful, hounded, possessive and underhanded. I didn't know any adult—I'm enough of that for my purposes. Lastly, my needs and habits kept me away from the upper and lower-middle classes, as well as from students and other foreigners. But I was able to enjoy some pleasant company now and then; not all of it was short-lived.

My life, then, consisted of living the intermissions of others, their brief lapses from being normal. Here is where I shed my identity as a homo; those who came over weren't, and they didn't want to be; myself, even less. I stopped feeling any difference between us since they didn't bother establishing one; I felt like I was with my kind of people. Just an illusion, to which this book is dedicated. I wouldn't be able to explain who these boys or their city were; I can only gather up what slipped out of them, collect what they cast out of their existence like an excrement, which is the best of my life.

As for the wilder pleasures, I obviously wasn't giving them up. Night and quiet alleyways favored these furtive couplings. I took them the same way anyone does: as nasty, exciting, coarse, puritanical, inevitable. Moreover, I had a liking for them. When it came to morals, diversity—from the brusquest to the softest, from the purest to the most far out—worked better for me than a single rule for living, no matter how perfect it was considered. And since I approve of a hundred different ways of being, the only thing that works for me is to adopt a little of all of them, based on the company I seek.

Pedro went to school on a regular basis but wasn't interested in studying. He did it to avoid being beaten. I don't know what he liked. He didn't talk very much about himself or anything else and seemed to possess no perceptions, opinions or feelings. I saw him once or twice a week, irregularly, for several months. He never stayed more than an hour. From beginning to end, he was a crude, undecipherable object, sixty-five pounds of child-like flesh piloted by a mulish mind, lacking both meanness and affection. He often brought his schoolbag and let me look inside it. But the notebooks, besmirched as they were by the ink of a ballpoint, were as uncommunicative as he was: collections of chores, a testimony to the boredom of going to school. When adults were around, Pedro, who envied their power, was like one of those unsocial kids who hide their face if a photographer approaches. He refused to be commandeered, handed over to another, captured in effigy; the injustice of a photo comes from its author being able to look at you in it without your being able to look at him.

When it came to our pleasures, there was nothing to discover; he smugly put his restrained good will into them, and I didn't push it. No fantasy, no embarrassment, just a rather clumsy sensuality that had conviction and was kindly, solid and cold-blooded.

He had good understanding and judgment; and though his movements were a bit sluggish, he'd warm up when the time came. Nevertheless, on that day with the apple, when Pedro's theft was hidden under his balls, it surprised me that he hadn't stopped me from sliding a hand down there. When he was with his brother, playing it circumspect became an invincible ostentation. But he wasn't worried, stayed calm and didn't even press his thighs together, which other children would have done out of simple embarrassment about someone wanting to touch their anus.

In blue fountain pen ink, he once drew me a man, a woman and a little boy, each on a half sheet of stationery. The figures were laid out on the page so evenly that it was almost shocking, given how instantaneously he did it: centered exactly, neither too large nor too small, in frontal view, broad and square like the figures on a deck of cards, left and right sides completely symmetrical.

First he made the man, which he liked doing. The lines are spare, emphatic, carefully executed; the drawings are so frankly oversimplified that they don't seem awkward. The man has curly hair on an oval head; an elegant mustache ending in curlicues; attractive, almond-shaped eyes; round, clear pupils; a sweet look.

A U with long, curved serifs forms the eyebrows and nose, pierced by two small nostrils that give him a mischievous expression. The even mouth is closed, unsmiling; a fat cigarette hangs crookedly from it with the smoke rising in an oblique tendril. His trunk is a square, decorated with buttons between two vertical lines. Appropriately large tentacles form the arms; one of those rubbery arms has been raised to the height of his head to wave hello, in a gesture that's a bit patronizing, indifferent.

When Pedro had to draw the hands, he hesitated; he looked for a moment at his before doing the man's. A tube for the wrist, a circle for the palm and very well-proportioned little sausages for fingers. The man has a weird pair of trousers: the hips are triangular like a simplified pair of briefs, placed on two parallel, fairly long cylinders, spread far apart from each other, with shoes pointing to the left. Later, when Pedro had drawn the woman, he added genitals to the guy, on top of his briefs: a straight rod with no balls, hanging at a slant. The hair at its base is indicated by a bold ring of ink; a circle on the other end represents the head. That rod has been drawn and positioned exactly like the cigarette, but the cigarette is fatter, and the circle at the end stands for the ash.

I wanted the woman to be nude. He reduced her to the essentials: long hair with a middle part, blank eyes, a lipless mouth, dangling arms, cursory fingers. A square for her torso, the inevitable line that separates the top and bottom of the body at the waist, then the triangle of the hips, with no feminine outward curve; however, between her thighs, the apex is rounded to the shape of a donkey's belly. In its middle is an oval hole surrounded by some playful hairs that radiate out like a hedgehog's when it's rolled up into a ball. Her bare feet have three and four toes.

At that point, I told Pedro that he'd left something out of his woman. He didn't agree, but looked for it anyway, in vain. I pointed to her chest—there wasn't anything there. He let out a scatterbrained laugh and began drawing the bosom. It started with two round spirals; then, hanging from each, a kind of pocket or pear or sock, which he finished with a long nipple end. It called to mind a limp version of those drooping one-scoop ice-cream cones, rather graceful-looking in their fashion as breasts.

A lot of boys older than him who came to my place had scrawled pictures of naked women and had also left out the breasts, which seemed to be banished from their graphic tradition. Pedro had to make an effort at being inventive, and without getting distressed; because it left him cold, he overdid his bright idea that much more; he had to do his best with the details to be sure of reproducing what I was asking for.

He doesn't want to draw a child, but I insist. The woman was fun, the man flattered him, the little boy means nothing, except perhaps an unpleasant flashback to the time when he was one. Pedro's aware of social norms, puts up with them, applies them rigorously; he's still at the age where you think you only need to grow up to escape outside control; like almost every child, he's sacrificing himself to the adult he wants to be, without imagining that such renouncing is destroying in advance the man he'll become.

He had no experience drawing boys, no stereotype for it. But after much hesitation, he unearthed a memory from a schoolbook that guided him—the image of a schoolboy in a beret, the type you don't see around here, which he interpreted in his own way. The beret is immensely enlarged, the sides enormous, a stem sticking up from the middle like a felt tassel; it looks like a clog with two feet. The hair is swallowed up by this hat, the ears sticking out; the man and woman had none. These ears are beautifully drawn, like half-daisies, with a small hole in the middle. Pedro added the very extended U that represents the nose and eyebrows, botched a crooked mouth and lifeless arms, then called up his memory of school again to draw the bottom part of the body, trousers with a fly, placed over hips that aren't a triangle this time but loins, wearing rather realistic briefs of loose material over a concave crotch.

I told him to draw the boy again, but naked. This new piece of work, drawn in a corner of the sheet of paper, was composed, obliging, assiduous. Pedro looked at and touched himself for reference, perhaps a sign that he'd accepted identifying with what he was depicting; it wasn't like the sullen discomfort evinced while drawing the schoolboy in underpants.

Since his own pectorals were quite pronounced, he gave the little boy a bosom by drawing two C's, the opening of which pointed downward, whereas the curve faced up; according to Pedro, therefore, the difference between the breasts of a man and the breasts of a woman were that the former rise and the latter fall. But I've seen the same detail in the graffiti of my other visitors. And since they put nothing where a woman's breast should be, the males seem to incarnate the organs of both sexes at the same time, and the females to be nothing but boards with a hole.

I also find the insistence on pectorals striking because the teenagers I knew had muscular, wiry bodies, which weren't skinny but were without significant volume. Chests like a flattened cylinder, very narrow hips; smooth, beautifully shaped limbs; slender hands; exquisite hairless skin shaped by the most delicate contours of the flesh, as if by Cellini. But they wanted to be thickset, heavy, solid. Despite this, I'd never seen boys as good-looking, or so many of them, combining so much grace, looseness and ease with perfect stature and such attractive faces—with very dark brows, harmonious bone structures, smooth cheeks, flawless chins; daydreamers with defined lips and pearly white teeth as transparent as those in childhood; hazel, ebony, steel-gray eyes with thick eyelashes, curly eyelashes, beaming with vivacity and sweetness, characteristic of a lower class type that's almost universal and can also be found in Paris among teenagers from poor neighborhoods who are too well put together, handsome without wanting to be, and thrown into a rage if a queer looks at them. What they fleetingly possess is that archaic beauty, just as their language—in its incorrect constructions, slang, accent, rhythms and inventions without rules—conserves traces of periods when French was a living language that was created communally and served the art of speaking in a real way. And in the same way that their listening to the radio and watching television makes them correct this bountiful way of speaking into stammering malapropisms, into an ignorant, hoity-toity, petit-bourgeois *mass media* style that is hackneyed, curt, bled dry, maimed, and stuttering, so do they repress that part of their attractiveness that makes them feel inferior, deriving from it a mask of servility, triviality and spite.

Nothing like that here. However, the boys never think they're manly enough and spurn their own perfection because they see no sign of power in it.

Therefore, when they drew, they gave themselves an emphatic chest and went to lift weights in the grimy gyms in their neighborhood. As soon as they had hair on their body and face, they shaved it off, hoping this would make it grow more, that it would get blacker, thicker, straighter. After a few years, the most determined, now hairy and mustachioed, with a hardened jaw, cold expression, rugged shoulders and an arrogant walk, would take on the unsettling appearance of a plainclothes cop; all they lacked to make them look like they belonged in a bad film was a trench coat. They were adults now, made up to look like a lout to get their place in the sun and control their wives and brats.

Still groping himself under his sweater, Pedro added a few random lines to represent the stomach muscles. He forgot the navel. He managed to create the clear face of a dreamer, left out the ears (but not the enormous beret) and centered the dick precisely, making it identical to the man's—dangling straight but without balls. A circle of ink sketched out the pubic hair. Pedro didn't have any yet, but he liked to show me what he had by plucking out seven or eight brown hairs curved like the ringlets at the nape of a little girl's neck, which lay there dormant without producing a shadow.

He signed the sheets of paper solemnly and emphatically, in firm, round horizontal writing, the letters slanting slightly backward, full of curlicues, in a deft, sufficiently pleasant, important-looking, placid hand.

These drawings offered an image of Pedro he didn't project as a person. And into the perception I had of this child I would have liked to introduce the honest, emotionally moving view that his work revealed, which was shot through with nuances in spite of its caliber. It was like seeing a frozen tree in winter, an unimaginative plant with uniform branches and a geometry that is far from remarkable, which bloomed into beautiful, wholesome foliage, like an apple tree's when spring came. Pedro, who was crazy for apples, was expressing something about himself when he hid one between his thighs. But I hadn't known how to use it to discover the wonderful roundness he was made of, hearty and affable, bathed in a scent of fresh, plump flowerings, fleshly with a pulp that held no mystery, the ample flavor of a little peasant farmer.

It was when we first knew each other that he did his drawings. The following fall he disappeared, a short time after our reunion at the palm tree, when he was approaching thirteen and beginning to be able to produce some come. His family moved to another city, and I stopped getting news.

But around the same time, Francesco finally decided to invite me to his home, and I saw Pablos asleep, as I've described.

Obviously, I didn't know it was Pablos. I went back the next day, they were inviting me to lunch. They showed me a little boy with a round, pretty face, energetic and dark, quite thin and very short (his mouth or chin must have been on a level with my navel). Then we left; it was the men who ate together. In the afternoon, he reappeared, sat down near me for a moment. He had a smilingly open face. And I heard his first and only words of that day, pronounced slowly and diligently, with a voice buried lower in his throat than is natural: "*Are you happy?*"

"Yes."

He shakes his head, laughs. "Very, very happy?"

So, he was the one who had been asleep. He was so young that I didn't dare realize how attracted I was to him. Instead, without result I teased one of his older brothers, who was thirteen and had large, flapping ears, a nice funny face; he was a little ugly, the rascal of the village under the dark cloud of puberty. His status in the family was disadvantaged; he was everybody's servant and reacted awkwardly to signs of interest.

I didn't really discover Pablos until later, when they were reckless enough after the soup to start pointing out the charms of the little ones. I let myself be tempted all the way; but I thought he was too young, was being brought up too strictly, was well-behaved and serious, I was only half-thinking about it.

Then a term went by without my seeing him. In Paris several times I shared a bed, some fooling around and some walks to school with a French lad of six or seven, which was something that had never happened to me. After that experience, Pablos would seem like a very big boy to me.

In fact, he'd hardly gotten any taller; but his willowy look had become more thickset and square, with a short neck, too much of a swayback and a belly that stuck out. You noticed it most in profile. A lot of little boys go through that phase of growth, during which they increase in width without the length catching up. All you can do is be patient.

From then on, Pablos looked vaguely like his mother, who had a low center of gravity and was nimble and as broad as a barrel, with her own brand of being a shrew. Those of her children who'd become adults were at least two heads taller than her, and as slender and nicely put together as she was round and midget-like. Furthermore, Francesco and Pablos had snatched some attractive features from her moon-face, which looked a bit Mongol, with wrinkly dewlaps and little sow's eyes.

Pablos hadn't gotten fat, it was just his frame. However, they made fun of his oversized belly and heavy behind. That was because he'd been thickened by a dozen undershirts, tee shirts, shirts, sweaters, shorts and pants that they put on him once winter came. He got cold easily.

One afternoon, I'd come over unexpectedly. They were stripping the child down for his bath. They pulled off innumerable articles of clothing of ill-assorted sizes and colors, more or less worn out but still clean, and perhaps once attractive. Their mother, who was rather lazy, except when it came to cooking and eating, never mended anything; her sons' wardrobes were a spectacular collection of rips and tears that the big sister drowned in bleach every eight days. Francesco had a friend, a boy tailor, living in a little room, where he went to get things mended. The little kids stayed unpatched, like a lot of children from poor neighborhoods; but that kind of neglect kept them from being harassed about their clothes; they could make a mess of them, tear them without having to worry.

Soon there was a mountain of rags, and a little man in boxers appeared, his shoulders bulging, his muscles gnarled, with skin pale and white like a cave-dwelling larva put under the light, and wide, flat abdominals that were as cut as the scales of a reptile; a slim bottom with a prominent crack; straight, muscular back and cute legs. They had him go into another room to take off his underpants. He'd been blasé in my presence, neither upset nor calculating; in vain I searched his eyes for a sign that he'd noticed I'd been looking. I was surprised that he still let himself be dressed and undressed. But piling up his rags was a really complicated task; once it had been done, he kept it day and night for a week.

Three months later, Pablos thinks of himself as quite grown up; that fall he was nine, that winter he said he was eleven—I think he's ten. A real change must have inspired him to exaggerate like that; in fact, he isn't at all wild or brooding any more. The boy that's blooming in him, which I'll get the chance to know, who'll be him on a daily basis, had only appeared in my sleeping boy of autumn like a promise or a passing fancy; he's the one who'd asked me, Are you happy?

Pablos's conversation was often highly interrogatory. And when he questioned me, he seemed to be imitating a schoolmistress busy with a tot with a boo-boo who doesn't know how to answer: she worries about him in a very reassuring tone. Sometimes, however, his face expressed an astonished rapture as if, in listening to himself speak, he'd discovered a stupendous pleasant surprise; it was like he wanted to mimic his curiosity and conscientious good intentions and at the same time anticipate the pleasure I was feeling, savor it, demonstrate it before I did. This approach to miming both roles reminded me of the playacting kids who begged at the old market. I liked them, got involved with the little rascals from time to time—but more about that later. To get a handout when a stranger came along, they'd quell the mischievousness in their eyes, extinguish the cheerful health in their cheeks and strike a sad, afflicted pose, their head tilted to the side, a fake look of suffering in their eyes—as if you were the beggar who had aroused enormous pity in them. In a pithy, ironic way (since passersby shot back an icy look), this method combined the outstretched hand of someone in need with the tender face of someone who gives.

Francesco swore to me that his house had no windows. It was easy for him to moan about his lot, but I didn't really believe him. It turns out that he was telling the truth—all the while lying, of course. The first evening we took a long dirt alleyway under two dark rows of buildings, walked through a low door, crossed an unlit hallway and ended up in a large, tiled, barely lit room with a very low ceiling and several double-shuttered doors. Women were seated in the back of this cavern, and there were brats everywhere (his uncle's, some neighbor's). The room where we huddled with the older brothers was narrow and elongated and really was deprived of windows. Other than the flowered benches, there was a dark wooden armoire and a television with little curtains in blue gauze. I was hot, there were too many unknown people, you had to listen to the men's boring platitudes, they'd carried away the kid, who was asleep, I felt like I was suffocating, was full of angst and would have liked to leave.

When I got back the following noon, the big central room that was like a vaulted tomb revealed the entire sky—because it was a patio. I'd mistaken the night sky for a ceiling because there were no stars and the women in the courtyard had placed their lamps on the ground; with the light at ground level, so the edge of the darkness was very low. Besides, I'd thought that only the rich had houses with a patio surrounded by rooms, which got their light through the door and sometimes also through one or two small windows that were often left shuttered. So Francesco's dungeon, teeming with females and kids, became a cool, tranquil, lovely, nearly uninhabited place, full of sunlight, once the neighbors were gone and it was day again.

The image of Pablos asleep remained associated with my first impression of a sepulchral house, like the pose he'd assumed in the arms that carried him when he'd looked like a pietà. The crypt that held us, the round shadows on the bare plaster walls and the child being carried formed a scene in my memory that kept getting more and more intense, and false; I could have framed it, made it into a religious painting in grisaille like the kind that hung gloomily over the beds of the sick.

If they were a good catch, Francesco sometimes brought his queers back to the house. With me he hesitated because he knew about my taste for children. My questions about his brothers got on his nerves, and after five or six months together, when he finally invited me into the sheepfold, he gave me fierce looks every time I showed interest in the little kids. He was afraid it would jeopardize him and that the freedoms I took would compromise the role he was playing. Since the age of twelve it had been understood that Francesco would have encounters with strangers in the street because they'd ask him to help them find their way; he was pleasant, personable, intelligent, honest; they loved him like a son, and presents would follow. One of these men (two or three were invited before me) became good friends with his aging, and then dying, father.

Francesco's family, or at least his older brother, must have suspected that he was, in a sense, hustling—that he fucked men, which was a venial sin. But this revealed secret was hiding another, which my carelessness risked revealing: his homosexuality. All people would have to do was think of my relationship with Pablos as dubious, and the clear-cut sexual categories of the population would take a clumsy turnabout. If I liked boys, I couldn't be on the bottom. I'd be a boy fucker, and that would mean I was using Francesco as a woman. My desire for Pablos, once it was revealed, would make me more manly and feminize Francesco; as far as he was concerned, this was the danger.

I wasn't worried about it. They let me approach the little boy precisely because they were absolutely certain that I was big time—one of those gentlemen whose wallet is like a strainer and whose butt has holes in it and whom certain sly young foxes in the city so willingly bring back to the family lair. Such a conviction was useful to me, as was their belief in Francesco's virility; they'd hesitate a long time before placing a fine young son into the degrading role in which it made so much sense to stick his foreign friend. Since these false notions allowed them to protect the nature of things, they stuck with them; it was up to me to draw some advantage from this; after all, maybe they were loaning me an imaginary costume, but it was better than having to walk around butt naked. And could I wait, to try out certain opportunities, offered by human tolerance? I'd kick the bucket as a hundred-year-old before having lived. It's better to reckon with stupidity, the baseness of humans, when you want what there is no point in hoping to get from their intelligence or their heart. What individual, what nation has ever survived by any other means? Moreover, it's not infallible, at least when you mix a bit of humanity in, or make it serve less repugnant ends—as I rapidly saw.

Since Francesco only knew how to save himself by hiding, he didn't understand that I saved myself by revealing. That's why I'd give Pablos long caresses, kisses in front of his close relations; and as long as he didn't see anyone disapproving, the child would respond with delight. His mom would offer me the fake smiles of a mother-in-law, and everyone else grimaced their version of a sympathetic expression; the older brother would tell me the story of his life, feeling sorry for himself and lying with every word (and his smooth-talking felt like gentle claws scratching at the tear in my pocket to make it larger so that the money would fall out); but Francesco was in agony.

However, as time went by, he saw that my tactic was a good one. During the last weeks we knew each other he even helped me with the very difficult task of getting Pablos out of the house, inviting him to my place. A strange tenderness made him do it; our relationship had weakened, was coming to an end; he was unhappy and jealous that I liked his little brother and was trying to revamp himself into an accomplice, to make himself indispensable. It wasn't able to salvage anything; when he'd understood this, at the first pretext, he stopped coming. Such a wordless breakup depressed me, yet I appreciated it.

The fear that he'd had about the suspicions of his family had turned out to be too simple. They saw that the least kiss from Pablos made the money rain from my fingers in a way that no decorum, courtesy, pressure had been able to. It made them think, and they forgot about Francesco and his morals.

The big brother, however, had read my mind. He didn't show any of it directly. He had no scruples. For years he'd been emptying Francesco's pockets, filching from his brother, using or reselling the gifts Francesco got. My affair with Pablos didn't bother him, and when he understood the intensity of my strange ways, he drafted some plans based on it. He supported the entire household by himself and would have liked to get out of it, even if it meant my appropriating Pablos. Unfortunately, he had to handle his mother and the others carefully because they were less radical and had been distressed by a similar trans- action. It was impossible to sacrifice the child to me without his mother knowing about it; so there needed to be a more moderate solution. He hoped that a harmless flirtation would be enough, and he already saw me covering the house with elec- trical appliances, the women with dresses and the children with chances for study. But the real difficulty came from elsewhere. Pablos wouldn't have responded to me if he hadn't had permission to; as soon as it was granted, he believed that it completely justified an intimacy that—as I've pointed out—was only superficially condemned among the working classes. If the boys feared others' opinions, they turned it down; if they weren't afraid of it or if by any chance it was favorable, they opted for it. After being allowed his first kisses, Pablos began acting very forward, looking for ways for us to be alone together, getting flirtatious, lying down against me, returning each and every caress, trying tricks out in the open whose message was crystal-clear. Then it became necessary to put him off. They cruelly poked fun at him for the suspect devotion being shown to him by a man; they derided him, made insulting insinuations. Very sensitive to majority opinion, and unable to be cunning, he turned to the favorable camp. Now the only choice was reestablishing that trivial bit of license that was useful to the intrigue; Pablos wouldn't go beyond it, or would very slowly. They tried not to leave him alone with me, as a further precaution. But if the one watching was Francesco, the result was unusual; then we only respected appearances. The two brothers had begun to trust each other a little, without saying anything. So, for example, I'd have the child on my knees with Francesco sitting opposite, and I'd be masturbating the little one through his trousers. Completely hard, his breath a little shortened, he'd pretend to be telling something to his brother, who'd avoid looking at my hand and would answer Pablos with a more understanding and serious expression than was usual. Not the slightest thing on our faces at all showed that we were in cahoots: what was the point, since nothing was happening?

Apart from these very rare examples of misbehavior, the arrangements that now involved the child were unbearable, and so complicated that they failed all the time—the older brother was heavy-handed, he set up his dupes with mind-boggling tactlessness. Without my inordinate interest in Pablos and his receptiveness to it, nothing would have lasted eight days. Even so, I thought a great deal about withdrawing. I did it several times, ridiculously hoping that it would help clarify the situation. These rebellions took them by surprise, and they'd quickly send an ambassador: one of the older brothers with Pablos under his arm. It was to give me the scent again, to make me remember and return to the fold. And I would. They'd offer me dinner to celebrate the reunion. But the time for invitations had passed; they'd make me pay four to five times more than the family meal was worth. And I was to bring wine, whiskey, expensive cigarettes, medicines; and then there was that overdue electric bill, a new pair of trousers the tailor was holding back, two dresses at the dry cleaner's, the doors of the house that needed painting, and next, an urgent affair: that pitiful moped belonging to the older brother, whereas he'd seen an enormous motorcycle on sale, it barely cost six months of his salary, it would get him to work so much more quickly, he'd be able to sleep in mornings; and the second oldest brother would definitely be able to find a good job if he had new clothes and a train ticket for the other side of the country; and now that I'd given Pablos those new clothes the other children were jealous, they'd had to buy some for them, too, and they couldn't pay the salesman, and let's not forget the ladies (when were they getting their perfume, slippers, coat?), and that friend whom they'd bet a watch—and I don't know how many other pretexts, until the middle of the night. I gave in as much as necessary, for a few minutes they'd surrender Pablos, whom such a scramble for the spoils was making morose and who'd slipped away, and then they'd fawn on me with all the Cheshire cat smiles that put an uncle in the mood to leave an inheritance. They were pleased with themselves, saw me as hooked, and now I was supposed to come every day. I was surprised that they didn't guess over time the only reason for my compliance, the fact that Pablos was worth more than them. But he didn't show it in front of his family any more, now he waited to be at my place with Francesco.

When Francesco split up with me, an essential piece of the game was lost for all the players. After a slack period, they tried to patch things up by sending me a lot of people. This new mission didn't thrive. I'd decided I was done with it; I said that I wouldn't go over there any more, but that I'd welcome the little one as much as he liked, with or without accompaniment. They took the suggestion. Pablos came several times; his chaperone was the small older brother with the floppy ears, whom I liked a lot. They'd given the boys some commissions to carry out: mention the words studies, clothes, perfume, Frigidaire, invite me to the house. They performed their duty quite unenthusiastically, then got back to the three of us. These times—which were more chaste than when Francesco had been chaperoning us—were happy ones. The checkmating of the little legations soon put an end to them; nobody came any more, the chess pieces were tucked back into each of their boxes, the checkerboard stayed empty. For how long?

This affair had made me sick, and I was suspicious of everything near or far that called itself friendship. However, the adventure had brought me a change of scene, a benefit: it came from a situation that was, all in all, heterosexual. I'd been yanked out of my cave, illicit desires had been admitted, life had been arranged around them; I'd been made to look like a rich old fart who was infatuated with an innocent virgin, I was being given a filly from a poor family who'd decided to charge a lot for her underage cherry, and presto, I was becoming normal. Up to this point, no one had ever tolerated my love affairs. With emotion, I watched this attempt to tie puppet strings to my limbs, and I actually wanted them, if they'd free me. For a moment I believed this had happened, hoped the boy would come over often to eat, or sleep some days, like Francesco had been able to do. But it's because I was imagining that family as either naïve or depraved; instead, they were only a bit perverted, and too lily-livered. Not to mention that, contrary to my old fart disguise, I wasn't rich. In a few months of plenty, I'd used up the part of my royalties that my debts hadn't devoured. Now I was spending an amount barely equal to what an ultra-shabby, stuttering, novice French teacher—to scrape the bottom of the barrel—gets, one whose teaching, which comes packaged with slaps, stinks of cavities, a bachelor's asshole or a cafeteria. It was still a lot of money, because the standard of living in this city is low, and Pablos's family had nothing but the eldest's salary— nearly three times less than my own resources. Still, I was too parsimonious to buy motorcycles; I wasn't going to be any son-in-law, and playing old farts was too challenging, so I became abnormal again.

When I stopped promoting this fake social identity of mine, all that were left were some ruined friendships and an outlook on things that was more frigid than it had ever been. Strange penalties for my having spent three or four months striving to live as if I weren't marginal.

I went back to the sterile, isolated existence I'd had before, littered with anonymous encounters, enlivened by moments of savage thrills: gorging on huge pricks, shooting loads in nice backsides, gobbling up every bit of these brats. I stopped speaking because there was nobody to listen, heard very little of what others said. Went out as little as possible, and slept during the day so I could stay up at night—something I hadn't done for a long time; the time for sharing was over.

But I'm exaggerating. Because it's also empty pockets and writing this book that keeps me shut up inside. The unfettered life of a single man is just as costly as the sheltered life of a family, maybe more, since there are no established limits beyond which you can refuse to have others around. You spend in order to enjoy your peace and independence, to have friendships without ulterior motives, not to guard your prison or possessions. But if your income's too small, you're still under the thumb of family rules, desires, prohibitions; you live in the wake of their values, at the mercy of their reprisals; that's when you become miserable, dirty, torn to pieces.

Having no children, wife, salary or fellow workers; no boss, career, TV or car, no business card or voter registration card, social security or alarm clock, no radio or newspapers, no Saturday bargain hunting or Sunday picnic, no songs or sports records in your head, no movie or horse-racing tickets in your pocket means a slew of opportunities for freedom and a lot of risk of being alone. Money decides between the two; the slightest action performed outside the usual hours, places, circumstances, institutions or approved persons costs a fortune. Unless you subscribe to "the fringe," which I can't bring myself to do. It means rejoining the same world by another door. Middle-class hangers-on in beards and worn dungarees disgust and repel me in the same way that their kinsmen in ties and cars do. A different style of speech, ideas that are against the grain, different threads equal the same civilization, limits, dependencies, pretenses. And neither revolution, drugs nor pop turns me on. Frankly I'd rather be a nasty, puritanical, self-satisfied, imbecilic, withdrawn, hypocritical, despotic, intolerant, marriage-advocating, illiterate, sunken-eyed, deaf-as-a-doornail flabby-mouth than be all of it with a coating of libertarian mega-bullshit.

Besides, one side is just as oppressive to me as the other. Whether it comes from clean-shaven faces, whose treasures don't impress me enough, or from pious mugs, because I don't take communion, or whether I'm eating with families or *chowing down* with the *guys*, they can spot me. Usually I don't say a word, make a gesture that would reveal the disgust and distress I'm feeling, so I'm more likely to be judged for being halfhearted. Like a skeptic at a séance who ruins the perfect circle. They root out the guilty one, come down him, ask him one more time to obey and approve, show he's like the others, one of the guys. But I don't know how.

Occasionally, it turns bad. The *guys*, especially, can get really vicious, offensive when you question their religion and their wholesomeness. I don't react; but if it really gets on my nerves, I only know how to respond physically. My rages are extremely rare but very sudden. I'm likely to grab the bastard, shake, slap, pound on him. It's a drag, and I'm not proud of myself afterward. But you can't make due with words since every single one of them is rotten to the core when it's a matter of these geniuses of self-deception. In a language surprising for someone who is nonviolent, my body transcribes what they really are, were really saying and doing. It would probably be better to stomach it; but I'm not that community-minded; as soon as it gets too bad and smells too awful, I send it back where it came from—minus its evangelical gift wrapping.

On the other hand, I can put up with a lot; if I responded as willingly to the hoaxes of the "fringe" element as they react to the slightest doubt about their perfection, I'd be fighting morning and night. But it almost never comes to that, and it would actually require the pious mugs to dare way beyond the average cheats of their peers.

With time, my indignation dies down. For example, without grimacing, I put up with three *guys*, aged eighteen to twenty, whom I met here one evening. It was raining and they didn't know where to sleep, so they spoke to me, and I put them up. Disgusting, hunched-up little Frenchmen mouthing left-wing clichés; they must have had their hair done to look like mops because they couldn't—for the life of them—find any haloes in the hip boutiques. They talked a lot, and our "discussion" went on until dawn. They made it abundantly clear to me that my beds, shower, short hair, age, income, wine, heaps of food, and street kids meant I wasn't part of their crew. Then they told about their experiences hanging out as hippies at the homes of some Mediterranean *lunatics* (because not only do *those people*, as they called them, suffer from poverty, they also think only about money and—height of insanity—about yours). This mixture of fine sentiments and racist garbage would have been enough for me to kick them out. But how could I blame them? If a man who was eight or ten years older than them made them so hostile, all they deserved was pity for having to rub shoulders with the people around here, who differ widely in ages and are even a little brown. I won't have the energy to recount the filth I heard. I should, though, given what perfect examples they were of how naturally three and a half ounces of long hair, a virtuously flat wallet, three third-world necklaces and dirty feet allow a rebel to cultivate to the hundredth power those same intellectual and social vices he reproaches his middle-class parents for. But it's too exhausting.

These pages flatter me the easy way, set me off in a nice clear category. However, the life I lead doesn't really prevent me from telling myself lies that are as big, or as little, as those who disgust me. It's that I'm alone, nobody's watching; and I do have my vices. Devoting myself to them would be too dangerous if I didn't maintain enough lucidity; the slightest illusion has tiresome consequences, mistakes harm me too quickly and for too long a time. That's what keeps me from petting my own navel at every chance. So I'd be intransigent despite myself—the same way I'm a writer without choosing to be; I haven't seen any other viable identity that's available, any less destructive compromise. This is enough of one.

It's impossible for me to write without cutting myself off from the outside world for long periods; walks, visits disconcert me for several days, during which my text vacillates, gets repulsive, superficial, unrecognizable. Writing is so unhealthy; playing the crook with words, controlling them the way that's required is hell when you like to live a little. I don't want to come to the conclusion that an art form that needs to torture and isolate those who practice it does so because it's too old, too implacably policed by a narrow network of requirements. Or believe that today's modest successes are achieved at the expense of more sacrifices and more trauma than required for the masterpieces of the past. But when it comes down to creating a serious work, there's no other form of art in which the result is constantly so imperfect, so debatable and so often ignored or hated: it's like draining all your blood from your body in order to dye a worthless rag. Obviously, literature is in a bad way if it survives only in flat parodies pulled together the way you make a phone call, or a few books that half destroy those who create them. In any case, I have this archaic profession, and I like it and don't want any other.

So the sadness and anguish of these last months couldn't alone have pushed me into a withdrawal that is as difficult as it now is. I go to sleep at dawn. From a high window comes the delicate light of the sun and the shouts of children passing by. The sky is as pure blue as it is on mountaintops. Some mornings, the cool, fragrant air and transparent shapes, the limitless mildness that welcomes the new day, the laughing, vivid, multicolored music produced by boys everywhere they walk, offer me as much emotion and desire as awakening on an island of dream and coming to life for the first time. But I close the shutters and go to bed.

Well, almost a year has passed since I began this book. During the months when I lived normally, and sometimes happily, I covered whole pages with black and tore up a lot of them. All that withstood were the first sentences that proved I'd begun; I doggedly destroyed the rest. And it is only when my life found itself stripped bare, in suspension, that I was able to hold onto my texts—which such a life would doubtlessly have continued to delete for a long time and chain them to that beginning that nothing followed.

If I want to remember the year I knew Francesco and had other friendly visitors day after day (and tore up so much paper), those months when I was trying not to get Pablos, who was in favor of it, but to be alone with him, I no longer think about the way it ended. Instead I think about those boys as if an accident had suddenly killed them. The idea that, as I write, they're alive and unchanged and a few minutes away from here doesn't bother me. Now I have their doubles, and if they reappeared in front of me, I'd no longer confuse the two versions, mine and the other. I wouldn't even try to establish a connection between the two, which would be a detriment to what I'm writing. I like to evoke autonomous images, brief scenes, sensations, obscenities, words; they come from them, but that isn't important; I participated in all of it, but it's as if I'd been an invisible witness. There was cowardice, fear of suffering, in my need to incorporate in real beings these fragments of existence passing through me. It wasn't me, wasn't them. These images can hover without ever pertaining to anyone or linking to an outside source, a place in the world that can be named. And it's only because, in my memory, they're composed of each other that my narrative lends a name to each group of fragments, the way you assemble three phalanxes in a reliquary, half a jaw, two vertebrae and the splinter of a tibia, which are enough to represent the body of a saint; that's how I can easily create boys with a smile, a nice set of balls, a sentence hovering in the air, a sunlit morning and three pairs of eyes, without worrying about the living from whom these relics have fallen.

Francesco wasn't really a prostitute. He became attached to his customers and was endlessly saying goodbye to the street. He made fun of himself and said he was the biggest whore in the city, because it wasn't true. He was very touchy about money; his face became a grimace, it was a horrible embarrassment that made him edgy if he had to ask for something. Homosexuality and poverty were a double misfortune, a double humiliation. He would have been mortified if he knew that the people with whom he hooked up actually considered him a whore. But he was a penniless boy of the streets with a quick mind and fine features who liked men.

That's why his family welcomed his foreign friends, without being impatient for gifts, despite what I've said. Their hold on you only tightened gradually; Francesco let it happen without taking part in it. Besides, in most cases they were only hoping for trinkets. The mom was especially fond of pharmaceuticals; in a wall niche she'd put together a collection for herself—with an emphasis on syrups—forming a disgusting little liqueur cabinet. That's why, when I arrived, she pretended to cough every once in a while, or to have stomach trouble, or whatever. She performed her little ruse like a child, quickly launching into her act to show that she was sick, rubbing her belly, coming out with sighs and doleful looks, stopping for a moment to see if I was reacting, then quickly starting up again and drowning me in grins as soon as I put on a serious expression and talked about buying some medicine. I'd annoy the pharmacist because I wanted to choose a syrup she didn't have. She'd forget that she was sick, greedily examine the packaging, exchange some opinions with her daughter and, planted comfortably on her cushions, begin her tasty ritual: open it, a small spoonful, taste it, mmm, mmm, is it OK? Her eyes would stray for a long time as I waited for the result: yes, it's good. A little later I'd find the syrup next to the other little bottles that had barely been started. The last time that I got some for her, she was worn out, had trouble walking and shot me an expression that would move mountains. I discovered a new one (it was written on the box): a cherry syrup for bronchitis. It made her much better.

She also had social security and went to the doctor whenever she wanted to. Since her real medical treatment was free, they managed without me—except for one time when she rubbed her belly and moaned louder than usual, and handed me an empty tube of tranquilizers that cost a lot; I bought them without considering that she actually only wanted to save herself a wait at the clinic. Despite all this, her kids could have the flu for three days without her giving them an aspirin. If Francesco told me about it, I took care of it; but deep down I preferred fake medicine. There was nothing immoral about the small pleasures they expected from their hosts; a father comes home to more demands than I endured, and I think the eldest put up with some, which helped me to tolerate his. After all, getting a few treats from a guest who's richer than you goes without saying. Only the children had nothing to hope for. All acts of kindness that would have favored them over the adults were discouraged. The presents I gave Pablos (clothes, shoes, books, a pen, the movies, sweets) upset priorities, were taken badly, and were considered too expensive or nonessential. Even Francesco, whom such a thing deprived of nothing, was vexed by it. As for Pablos, he'd amiably show his satisfaction to everybody: his brothers—despite the fact that I'd slip them pocket money— would look darts at me and the adults, judging my wealth by what I was wasting on a brat, and they'd step up their requests. Soon I discover a solution: the eldest likes alcohol, so I bring him a bottle whenever I give Pablos something. A tax on the pleasure of giving against the grain. Once the head of the family was appeased, the others kept quiet. The little ones remained glum: I think they took the money back from them, or else the little ones *turned it over* themselves. Only Pablos's gifts were irretrievable—and they were very careful to show me that they still existed, hadn't been sold.

These complications and tributes didn't embarrass me. In France, when I want to see a child, I'm obliged to go by way of his owners and pay the piper his exorbitant rights: giving it almost every time I stay with them. They know I'm coming for the little one, who's waiting for me; but they can't get used to it. To be neglected in favor of a kid makes for an upside-down world. Since I have to play the game to keep from being suspect, the parents take advantage of it, monopolize me, unload their mental garbage cans, secrets and opinions on me, a fetid stream of friendship and problems. I leave so worn out, so nauseous that I don't start again for ten days. An original method of child protection.

Of course, they love the children; it provides an inexhaustible source of themes for conversation.

"Look at this drawing *he* made, what do you think it's saying? Terrible, isn't it?"

In middle-class families, manners have barely changed since the time when they had bachelors to admire the watercolors of their daughter; today, they invariably show you the little ones' drawings and psychoanalyze them. They make aghast commentary if the images the brat produced are conformist; his duty is primitive art, not imitating big people. I dodge the requests for Freudian drivel; evolved parents don't need any help discovering the daddy-mommy syndrome all by themselves and inventing a case history around it. As for the conformist drawings, I say that if a child copies adults it's because he'd rather be in their situation:

pictures by children who are free are quite nice, but the parents don't do any while they have the right to do everything else. One explains the other.

"But why are you getting hostile?" they answer. My blunders accumulate; what a lousy teacher I'd be. In my country, I'm not a good conversationalist, especially with intellectual conversations or the ones pretending to be (because that's also something that creates a facsimile of itself: the frog that comes on like a toad, the pest that becomes the pox). Everything I say in front of somebody immediately launches into orbit around his navel-gazing, and his answer will be a reaction to that kind of gravitation. He doesn't see what I name, be it a poor smoked herring: he contemplates only the landscape of himself complemented by the new moon that I've launched. And depending on the light it affords his navel-gazing, he approves, critiques, touches up or, most often, eliminates: the moon sets. His navel is sad, and I don't know how to have a dialogue.

I've never seen an adult who finds me with a child (I'm talking about the ones who don't know about or disapprove of my ways) hesitate to bother or interrupt us, not pull me over, or kick the kid out for a walk without asking anyone—something he'd never dare do if the other person were my age. Their disdain for children makes them view my interest in them as trivial, my connection with them as insignificant, the conversation that they're interrupting as derisory. What they'd see instead is an obsession or exaggeration, a pose, and they'd try to fix it in me, bring me over to the correct side among people of the same stock—meaning, adults. They can't conceive of the fact that between two humans I'd choose the one that seems to them the lesser, when in reality he's the only one I'd choose.

I liked to be with Pablos to make up for the intermittent and crippled nature of my relations with other children: I sampled the bodies of one, the company of the other. Two forbidden things, and it's almost impossible for them to exist together, because not the same kind of child permits each. On some days, when Pablos was brought over, I'd had sex the night before with one kid or another of the same age and, occasionally, better looking, but whom I wouldn't be able to see again and whom I knew nothing about: we had too much to hide, it was left there. Pablos brought the half that was missing; by looking at him I'd evoke the other.

Likewise, in Pablos' family, they figured he and those like him were too skinny to interest me. Popular custom dictated that brats were to be revered, petted, spoiled, favored; but only until the age when they could outrun their mother. From then on it's all over in a poor family. They're the last, the last in line. The eldest, who's singled out from the others, escapes part of that. At home, the boys help with the housework (as adults they won't lift a finger); outside, if they don't stay in school, they're rented out to anyone at all, and they'll be under the thumb of any boss who denounces them to their parents for laziness or supposed thefts so he can cut back on their salary. They say they're sorry, slap him around, take next to no money, and the kid only obeys more. That's how the children become the standard workforce for all the cottage industries, tiny penitentiaries where a lot of families get rid of excess baggage. The countless workshops and stall of the city, tailors or carpenters, plumbers, electricians, masons, painters, grocers and every trade, blacksmiths, garage and bicycle mechanics, locksmiths, greasy spoon owners, and a thousand other petty professions—there are almost as many of them as there are human objects or actions—present an invariable spectacle: kids at work, some of them teenagers, an idle adult who gives the orders. The workdays are very long but relaxed; few places give Sunday off. Apparently, in this place, half the inhabitants are younger than twenty; and since it's to the advantage of the small-time bosses to exploit the population of underclass children, you end up working more often before you're an adult than after.

Francesco's family, which isn't as poor under the eldest's rule as it was under the father's, was lenient enough with the later children, who were well treated and well fed, quiet schoolboys raised with lower-middle-class virtues, in contrast to the childhood of the older ones. Looking at Pablos's fine notebooks and his chaste belly, I thought how Francesco, at the same age, in between school and work with the bosses, would take off in a thousand different directions for a dose of male sex organs. He says that he'd squeeze them between his thighs and wouldn't agree to any more; I believe him, more or less. He didn't feel good about his former exploits, and to his other friends he preferred telling stories about far-fetched challenges when—returning from jaunts—he came close to bringing home treasures and crowns. He finds a lot of wallets. The photos of him as a child show a sad, hard, hopeless face.

Now his little brothers couldn't go thirty feet from the house without being thrashed. The eldest performed the beatings. He was doing a bad job with that brood inflicted on him by his father's death; he terrorized his younger brothers and wouldn't put up with anything from them. However, he looked down on them too much to harass them; he liked wine, whores, stayed home as little as possible. But his mother, as fond of drama as she was of potions, insisted he torture. She ordained punishments while whining that her sons didn't respect her, then begged for it to stop while whining that she'd never asked for anything like that, although the consequence of her denouncing was always the same. Good at his role, the eldest kept smacking right to the end; his own violence excited him, and although the thrashings were rare, they were dreadful. That's how he took on all the hate, and the old lady shrewdly maintained her maternal power and the love they bore for her. To me, that way of taking charge seems common among mothers; their double game is in proportion to their calling for being loved.

Before being a torturer, this son had been victim, at a time when his father was tough enough to lay down the law; he added the chilly cruelty of the virtuous to it. One day, when the eldest hadn't gone to school (he isn't the one who told me about it), his mom denounced him; tears, moans, hysterics. Today she's less dramatic, because she has become too fat; but she still rolls around on the floor, which she's nicely shaped to do. Her husband believed in public school as he did in God himself. He found a way to punish his son. He undressed him, tied him to a railing on the street, hit him with an army belt until his back, shoulders, waist and calves were bleeding. Then he bound the little boy's hands, attached the rope to his bicycle and yanked the staggering, bleeding kid into a run all over the city. No passersby intervened: he was a father. After this torture, the mother had another fit because her little boy had been torn to pieces; according to her, his father was only supposed to hit the soles of his feet with a stick.

This father's harshness didn't prevent Francesco from describing him to me as good, friendly and fair; but it's because he was talking about a dead man. Besides, Francesco himself was rarely beaten—his father was too old, his brother too young. As for the mom, during the twenty years that her ploy lasted, nothing could exhaust the flood of tears and hysterical convulsions torn out of her by the punishments that she herself had required. You can tell that the poor woman isn't in it for nothing; it's obvious how she suffers; during one of these sessions, the shrieks make the neighbors come running and feel sorry for her. Then the kid who's been beaten comes out of the room in which the eldest was locked up with him. His limbs may be striped with wallops or his face bloated by bruises, but these ladies are too involved in their calamity to pour just a little water over them. This is the hour of motherly triumph, and they don't need children now. Moreover, being accustomed to the order of things makes the boys consider it humiliating to receive any aftercare.

Brutal punishments are the rule, and teachers and bosses are as devil-may-care about it as the parents. One evening I took a very gentle, well-behaved child I knew to the clinic to get stitches. He was working for a shopkeeper, a fat man with crooked legs, and accidentally bumped into an oil lamp, without knocking it over. The shopkeeper felt afraid and cured himself of it by chasing and hitting the kid with an iron bar, and then, yanking him by the hair, hammered his face with his own skull, which burst open one eyebrow and a cheek.

The theme of my friends' reproaches about my tastes weren't about small boys being asexual creatures that had to be protected from desire, but about their being too little of anything to be loved. The kindness I showed the little ones was disconcerting, as if I'd been seen giving up my bed to a dog, pouring it champagne and covering it with gold. Even those who felt a little affection for the children treated them despite themselves like an inferior race, something below the rank of women and above the donkey, or should I say below. They had the same disdain for their childhood and remained astonished, for example, that I saw great value in some old photo that they'd indifferently left for me.

Francesco tried in vain to take part in some little get-togethers I'd have. At my place children felt at ease; it was all about pleasure, and visits left them satisfied; they drank, ate, left with round stomachs and full pockets. They told their buddies that I had a *great ass*. But when Francesco was with me, they no longer allowed the slightest touch. Shame about getting it on with a local boy and fear of the older ones were mixed up in this refusal; no sweet talk could convince them; the long, pleasurable conversations with Francesco, his lack of defensiveness, seemed more suspect than anything to them; they remained convinced that you only wanted to catch them off guard and rape them.

"You see, they're stupid," Francesco would remark sourly. I suggested he give them a smack to make them intelligent. He'd hang his head, but it was only to please me that he showed disapproval he didn't feel in the face of such bad treatment.

Children's ordeal—temporary, of course—came instead from the fact that they had nobody to put under them. Cats run fast, dogs are few and far between, mothers protect the littlest ones. Going one-on-one with each other is dangerous; it's better to join forces. There were gangs of them everywhere, and it wasn't always for playing football or protecting themselves from the older ones. I got a kick out of a fight with stones that I once saw (among boys eight to ten years old), because after a few throws hit their mark and caused tears, the warriors lined up far enough away to keep them from reaching one another. But the fight went on for a long time. The stones were only insults, a volley of bad intentions that were lost in the dust.

I found that even the softest of the adolescents had contempt for the little ones. His name was Andrès, he was a friend of Francesco, sixteen, rather skinny and short, who dressed like a little pretty boy: sharp clothes, long, beautiful black hair falling down to his shoulders along a pleasant, bony face; with the gangly look of a runt trying to act like a man without having the build for it. He was crazy for men. He was too shy to look for them and preferred to rely on chance or the lovers of his friends. If you paid for it, he did it for the money; if you didn't pay, he just did it. He was attracted to me and I less to him; he didn't ask for money or presents. He was overflowing with silly virtues and with vices that were even cuter. I met him one morning at a square. He'd spent the money order he got from an old friend who was very generous. He was extremely well dressed, had on good shoes and every hair was miraculously in place; with shoulders thrown back, he was nonchalantly exhibiting a new tape recorder to two or three dirty, slovenly children covered in black pieces of cloth that were in tatters; with their heads shaved and their feet bare, they looked like convicts a month after their escape. I went up to him, the kids in rags took off, we went for a drink and I asked him who the little ones were. He shrugged.

"Oh, they're my brothers."

Obviously, he was the eldest. I never understood why the kids were in such a state, since his family wasn't as poor as Francesco's, none of whose brothers were dirty or wore clothes in shreds.

There was a thirteen-year-old kid from the streets who was crude but pleasant and whom I liked a lot and sometimes invited home, though it wasn't at all easy. He had a heavy, fleshy prick with large balls, an attractive, welcoming tush, a long scar on his forearm. I wanted to know what it was. He said that a big guy had fought with him to get a few pennies and had ended up using a knife. Obviously, the boy wasn't very happy about it. When I asked him, without dwelling on it, whether he'd be capable of doing the same thing later to a little kid, he took his time, stared off into space, scratched his knee, lit up with a happy smile as if he were dreaming and said: yes.

He also had several short, jagged older scars on his shins; once his father, who was a bricklayer, had punished him with a trowel. That man was dead; the new father, a very poor man who sold vegetables, was so gentle that the three boys who were the other's sons (mine was the eldest) were now totally at their liberty, were truant from school, panhandled, misbehaved, hung out in the city until midnight and after.

I should also lose my illusions about the severe conditions I've been describing. In the prison-like life of a child in our country, they're hair-raising; but here the context is completely different. First of all, life is hard on the body. Eating, sleeping, working, getting from place to place, performing daily tasks— these are typically uncomfortable and full of trouble. You develop a resistance to illness, to accidental injuries. You communicate, express yourself with very intense physicality; but even so, there's nothing vicious or excessive about ordinary relations. Outbursts of violence occur within a world hardened to suffering, but causing very little anguish.

Besides, these violent incidences are rare. Long periods without any cruelty follow. Defying certain taboos provokes fierce reprisals, but people aren't ever guilty of the thousands of offences at home with which prejudice and repression poison every hour of the lives of children in our country.

In the street, the cafés, movie theaters, shops, little kids are treated as equals. They go out on their own, hang out where they want like everybody else. They spend their time off with one another, meet up, laugh, run, bicker, tell what's going on with them, study in small groups, have fun with everything and nothing, never being forced to confine themselves to places reserved for children; they live outside freely, and there's no adult keeping his eye on them to "emcee" or control their pleasures, leisure, friendships or bodies. They're not afraid of strangers, go out at night alone or in groups, are as curious as cats, love to blab, to be surprised, to create situations that are fun or a turn-on or that put them in a good light; and since putting them to work at a young age leads to their rubbing shoulders with adults, they spread their vitality, happy-go-lucky attitude and mischievousness to those places, brightening up the most morbid workshops and filling them with their explosive laughter.

When I first came to the city, I got a kick out of a little show. In an attractively kept traffic circle in a new neighborhood full of shade and flowers, a policeman was directing some light traffic. Two little boys come to a stop under his eyes and piss on the flowers. These are school kids with their book bags; they're laughing, messing around, and one of them aims a thick spray of urine at the other. The one who gets sprayed pulls away, splatters himself; the sprayer holds back the last of it and scampers after him as he finishes pissing. People passing by don't say a word or do a thing; neither does the policeman. The prankster has gotten his clothes too undone; he arches his back, pushes everything down to his thighs and carefully puts his trousers back on. Then they leave, as merry as they'd come. Nothing there that's anything to see or describe.

In a French family that lived for a while in my building, a thirteen-year-old boy was slapped and locked in for the day because his father had seen him from the balcony running on the sidewalk for about twenty feet along a garden fence. I told you not to run, he shouted, get up here. This child and his little brothers were nice, energetic boys. But this is how they were being raised, and everything I noticed about it made me turn purple with rage. A normal upbringing and an ordinary father. Nothing here, either, to say or describe.

During heat spells, the crews splash around in the fountains of the old city the whole day; the boys set their shoes afloat, splash about, splatter the streets with water. Thirsty, they eye the outdoor cafés as they pass by, and if they see a carafe on the table they go up to it and are given a glass of water. They gulp it down, and off they go. They also drink from the water faucets at gas stations or from sprinklers.

Living around everyone makes the children considerate of others; they're calm and can show restraint, but without repressing their physicality and anything that pops out of it that is out of the ordinary, fast-moving and loud.

The street and city space belong to them. They sail through it so well and are so thoroughly familiar with it that they turn it into a village. It's not a uniform bunch; but the poor kids possess the same dignity as others; the old people here impose themselves in their way just as the children do in theirs; no one bothers the disabled, they're involved in everything, no pointless consideration is shown them, nor is any revulsion; all day long the beggar population walk around without the slightest embarrassment. But there are so many children and adolescents, and they are so good-looking, that when I'm there as a people watcher,

I start believing there's no one else but them; it's even too much to take in. They're beaming with health, and have few bodily defects—squinting, limping, obesity, bad proportions, skin-and-bones physiques, rotten teeth—are very rare.

Small businesses are ready for little people; they cater to their tiny resources with packages of chewing gum, cigarettes, etc. The grocer slits loaves of bread and fills them with jam, hands out glasses of milk and a thousand sweet or salty treats priced low; everything possible is laid out in a child's proportions. In the parks, they walk everywhere, sit down and lie everywhere, climb trees, move as much and make as much noise as they want (a few of the guarded parks are calmer). Even school has this easy quality about it since it isn't too mandatory.

Thus, the harshness, the inferiorities that impact the life of a child have their compensations. Tranquility, respect, pleasures, considerable tolerance mitigate them. Family life and community are interdependent; you share the two and circulate between them to the benefit of the latter, from the youngest age. You set right in one what causes you pain in the other, creating a balance between pleasure and suffering. In this way, the contempt suffered by kids doesn't harm them or cut back on their freedom; they're not kept apart from the life of the collective; their misdeeds, or what are considered to be such, are punished, but their autonomy is accepted and anticipated everywhere; and the violence they endure at least has the advantage of reducing to a few brutal events that educational oppression that adults in our country inflict upon every aspect of their relationship with children.

I'm walking by a run-down movie theater. In the hallway that serves as the lobby is a young orange-and-gray cat with a long, slender neck. It's lying there but not asleep. The tile floor is extremely clean. An enormous cockroach is scurrying quickly around the place. The cat's attentive eyes open, it brings its snout closer, rises, drags the cockroach toward it with one dart of its paw and puts it gently into its mouth; it crunches into it with delicate movements of its jaw. The hindquarters of the insect wriggle at the very center of the cat's mouth, which looks like it is innocently sucking on a piece of black licorice. It gives me a surprised but unruffled look, finishes nibbling on the treat without spitting a crumb of it back out. Then the cat lies down again. I wonder if cockroaches taste good, because cats are dainty eaters. Unless it's rancid. Maybe the cockroach smells like an old fish, an unwashed prick, stale pussy. We like those odors on ourselves well enough, less often on others. As for eating it, shrimps and smoked herring are a bit like that, as are some cheeses, which smell like decomposing urine, and tripe or andouille sausage, which are macerated in shit. We don't deny ourselves anything.

Cats around here are happy, as far as cats go. They multiply rapidly. The old city is overrun with them. You see them at night in deserted alleys, roaming quietly in packs, looking for food among the trash dumped in front of the houses, which the garbage collectors pick up at dawn. If it weren't done that way, there'd be no more cats. They're beautiful, healthy-looking animals of various colors, and none of them are emaciated. Bold, wild, they barely let themselves be touched, but they like it when you look at them and they study you for a long time. Sometimes people carry off one of their kittens for the amusement of a young child at home. These kittens are puny and seem less well fed where they're given meals than they are where garbage is dumped. When the kitty has grown a little, they put it back outdoors, if it hasn't bit the dust—because they aren't placed where they are for the purpose of teaching children to be gentle. These playthings become as unsociable as the other cats and are probably more so.

I had no intention of talking about cats, but it came into my mind all by itself. However, I ought to stay away from animals, the human race and general concepts; this is a pornographic book I'm writing, all it needs is cocks.

Andrès the pretty boy's was mediocre or average, and something about it turned me off for some unexplained reason; if it got hard, what I saw was a turd without details, molded straight, and as hard as a meal of pebbles. I wouldn't go so far as to say it was ugly, but individual tastes about such things are sometimes subjective. I was so little interested in it that it might as well have not existed; happily, Andrès took care of it himself with a great deal of affection; he was always stroking it.

Like the bird-catcher, he narrates his pleasures with images. At his place he keeps an old issue of *Paris Match* in which there's an ad for underpants and an article on sports, rugby or something like that (it reminds me of the pornography I was already trying to get hold of when I was barely a teenager). If he feels lonely, he slips it under his sweater, goes to the john, locks himself in and looks at the good pages while he jerks off. I ask him what he thinks of. Innocently, he reports that he imagines meeting that good-looking athlete, or the man in the underpants; and they talk and kiss and touch each other and then go where they need to and do such and such—he doesn't like to tell the details.

Andrès's solitary ritual impresses me; his homosexual fantasies in the toilet are quite exotic for the mentality of a boy from the city. These are bourgeois morals. When he told me about them, he was in confidential mode; he'd never admit directly that he liked to look at men, those made of flesh and blood.

His reputation was bad enough already. His friends made fun of him and looked down on him; homosexuals who were like him but more hidden, such as Franceso, crushed him with sarcasm and were happy to spread the worst gossip to make themselves look innocent. Friendship doesn't hold up when it's a matter of saving face, because here, seeming and living are one and the same thing. The cruelty displayed by the poor teenagers around here, the feeling of inferiority that makes them sacrifice everything to social conformity, is horrible to witness. Andrès was the dumping ground for the vices others were absolved of; putting him down was an orthodox duty.

So they claimed that he'd play bottom for the men of the city, the ultimate degeneracy. He wasn't the only one, but he must not have made enough of a secret of it. It seems that, to punish him, one day a hunky young man invited him to step away with him; Andrès says OK and ends up getting pronged.

Then the hunk's buddies show up, and each of them fucks Andrés so that he'll understand once and for all that it was taboo. There were forty of them. I obviously don't believe the figure, but it's a commonplace kind of thing: a butt that's been had attracts the young bachelor crowd like a honey pot draws flies. The guilty one gets named, talked about, they go to him when they need to get off, and sometimes they don't take no for an answer; it would be dreadful if he refused, since he's already broken in. Foreign fags have the same status, but since they're adults, well off, and since they're hoping to get money from them, they're shown some consideration.

I figure that, as a kid, his friends would climb on top of him (they probably chose him because of some weakness, a pleasure he'd given or looked for, and the story spread). Starting then, he told convenient lies, acted like he was being forced; if not he'd have been nothing more than a homo, rubbish at the curb. Every day it had to be against his will when a few little suspicious horndogs came to check that he'd put up a fight while they whittled away at his cherry.

A boy becomes the group's faggot because he looked, wanted, sought before another decided to. They don't see desire (they're learning how to expel it), they catch sight of a hole and make use of it. An obedient child closes up his anus; the one who keeps his open becomes the whore of the other boys and in that way helps them save their own hole. It's like an educational game: together you squeeze your ass closed, and the first to let go is a faggot. The heterosexual order that condemns him and behind which the little horndogs take refuge is constructed on his yawning ass.

Andrés claims that a foreigner raped him at twelve, in a hotel room, after having gotten him drunk. It's impossible. Kids are totally repulsed by alcohol; of those who sampled it at my place, only one managed to swallow a mouthful of whiskey, heavily cut and sweetened with Coca-Cola; the others spit out all of it, whether it was liquor, beer or wine, and went to wash out their mouth vigorously, like they would have if it had been sperm. Moreover, pedophiles don't rape, especially at a hotel.

Andrès, like a lot of guilt-ridden homosexuals I've met in France, used a few remnants of his past to invent an event that pushed the responsibility for what he was onto someone else. The process is barely conscious, and it gives expression to something real. Andrès wanted boys, in a way that was neither innocent nor guilty, nor thought out, nor provocative; it was something he wanted to experience and preserve, because it suited him. So the laws of the group transformed him into a "faggot" because they were fabricated from heterosexuality—a system of values based on the exclusion of almost all pleasure connected to loving, and on the establishment of inequalities, falsifications and the physical and mental mutilation of men, women and children. It makes sense that the story of rape invented by Andrès would expel this "homosexuality" outward, where it came from. In reality, he was subjected to the violence of a normalizing group, not a pervert, it came not from a man but from a word. In both cases, it certainly was against his will that he "became queer."

Even today when he gets screwed, he plays at being hesitant, winces, squeezes shut, lets out sighs of distress, exasperation, pain; but a minute after, you can pound him like a lumberjack, he lounges on the pillow like a small well-fed child. Accordingly, he begins by showing that he doesn't like it; then he enjoys it discreetly; and when it's finished, if he meets any accusations, he holds up the proofs of displeasure he exhibited. With people he doesn't know, it's enough; but others aren't duped for very long. Teenagers blab more than gossips, they make you keep their secret and then don't respect it themselves, they know everything about everybody else and think that no one knows anything about them. They pool their information and rapidly unmask a boy like Andrès, that weird straight boy who so willingly accepts what hurts him and looks so often for what he loathes. He's not even clever enough to give it up to the rich and get paid each time; he deprives himself of his last alibi. He steers his way between the risk-taking imposed by his desire and his fear of the group, he makes blunder after blunder and ends up naked as a jaybird, ready to be squashed. The others grow stronger by stomping on him, and none of those like him (because several have the same life, but live it better) help him to his feet; that would be admitting that they're like him, which is too dangerous.

I'd only known Francesco for a week when he brought over Andrès. The pretty boy wasn't too experienced yet. They had dinner at my place. Andrès was sweet, attentive, cheerful, very childish, proud of his spelling and the sleights of hand he knew. It became clear that he was staying over. Not in the little bed out front, but in the big one, with us. While we were getting undressed, he snuck a look at us and said distractedly, as if he were speaking to his feet, "Mine's little."

And he hid it with his hand as he got into bed. Francesco and he weren't as much of a team as I'd been hoping. They were a little distrustful of each other. They kissed, hugged, but prudishly. They didn't touch each other's pricks and didn't do any fucking. They felt each other up while they were lying down, and when they were standing they fought. Even with the lights off I can't fuck Francesco, who's hiding from Andrès the fact that he enjoys the passive role and plays it superiorly. Besides, it's the pretty boy's cute behind that turns me on. He's on his side, with me lying along his back; I try—no reaction; I go back in—no reaction; I get off without his even having taken a breath. He wanted to be fucked and didn't have the patience to wait for us to see each other alone. But he'll be able to use his way of silently making no big deal out of it to counter any mockery that could come from Francesco tomorrow by saying that I'd only stuck it between his thighs, something that's fairly innocent, at least for them. Francesco touches me, pounds me with his big prick and senses that it's getting to me, but he doesn't try to probe the meaning of it too deeply.

That's how it went every night that the three of us spent together. I didn't know such precautions, hypocrisies were necessary, and they exasperated me. Later, I found out that the lewdest young boys I could meet become a senseless lump the moment one of their peers is there to watch, even if he's as queer as they are and waiting in the next room. A sense of propriety isn't the issue, they barely have any and have no problem watching each other fucking a boy or a girl—that's a masculine thing to do and nothing to worry about. But anything else is dangerous to their image. So they'll do with me what they'd never do together—except maybe when they're grown up and certain kinds of conformism mean less.

Nevertheless, Franceso and Andrés gradually started to have a good time, to warm up. It was fun watching them fool around. It started with a ruckus, some joking around, they tickled and provoked each other, if one of them went to take a dump, the other snuck up to surprise him, they competed with each other in tests of strength, using the furniture, the doors, me. To show off their abdominals, they lay flat on their backs at the edge of the bed and you were supposed to fall, fists forward, with all your weight on their stomach. They held up very well, but it didn't go on for long.

After this foolishness and the lights were turned off, with me in the middle, they shared me. I felt as if I were putting up two schoolboys who were pretending not to like men and then were snickering with excitement under the sheets as they lost their innocence to one and hid it from each other.

Officially, I'm for Francesco, so Andrès fakes disinterest when he comes from time to time to see if I'm alone and he can sleep over. Otherwise he comes with Francesco. But I prefer him and don't pay any attention to Andrès. In bed he's resigned to it, takes me by the arm and says, in his deep, amorous voice, a little breathlessly, as if he'd been slapped, "Yes ... yes ... stay with Francesco ... Only, this is for me."

What he does with my arm is startling. He puts it around his neck, folds my forearm against his chest and begins to make love to it. He murmurs to my forearm that it's beautiful, that it's good; he sighs, rubs himself, trembles, writhes, gives it every possible compliment, as if I weren't attached to it. My forearm has a normal amount of hair; he adores it (and all the hairs on a man), kisses it again and again, grazes it with closed lips, caresses it smoothly, delicately, quickly with his hand and whispers how much it turns him on. At the same time, he jerks off, without trying to come. I can feel some perplexing shivers in the nape of my neck, the hollows of my shoulders, my loins. It's more intensely gratifying then my run-of-the-mill games with

Francesco. Such over-the-top enthusiasm, that puny fondling, those little monologues and such obstinate passion get to me. As for the shivers, I quickly realize what they are; not that I've ever had them during sex, but they're very familiar. The ones I had when I was child were often like that. For example, when you've accomplished something good and the adults compliment you cannily, pressing just the right buttons; it's when you're all alone and think of it, anticipate it, remember it. In other words, shivers of flattered pride. Vanity, maybe. Their physical appeal is in the innocent sensual delight they provide; and how strange they feel at being the intense physical effect of a contractual, abstract gratification.

The fact that Andrès can express his affection on a part of me to which I accord no attention, that he himself is a boy who doesn't interest me much, adds to the peculiarity of my pleasure, to its animal transparency. As a matter of fact, I'm used to opposite situations, in which I'm expecting nothing that feels good and in which the pleasure comes from the boy and what he agrees to put up with. I don't feel any disappointment about the fact that most of the boys I'm with barely touch me, adhere to their heterosexual code, neglect my cock and take no initiative, except to fuck me occasionally. But they often put up with a lot, and that's what suits me.

In some vague way, Andrès took me to heart as a friend or as a big brother. Evenings with him were sweet. There was no company more peaceful or more well-intentioned than his. He's helpful, subdued, conscientious, I feel like a sick old man whom a little scout's come to take care of. However, he bores me, and I don't show him much consideration. But for him that's part of my role as an elder, a good match for the one he plays so merrily.

When he's alone with me, nothing bothers him anymore. He knows I don't gossip about boys, and spontaneously he has shown me his least allowable talents. The only rule is that I don't take advantage of them in order to tell him that he's a faggot. He'd never come back again. As long as that condition's respected, he acts very freely.

But despite what a nice body he has, his muscles, how smooth his skin is, I had no desire to touch him. I lay down like a despot and waited. We'd leave the light on. His routines with face and hands on my body hair lasted a very long time. I wouldn't get hard. He'd slide his hand through it, exploring, fondling it deftly, delectably. His fingers seemed to sense minute reactions in my skin that told him where to touch, squeeze, press, dwell. He'd lower his head, suck me sensuously and would no longer get tired of eating my cock. Then he'd go lower, his nose rubbing against my balls, inhaling them, smooching them. I'd spread my legs, and he'd rim me. His tongue was as ingenious as his hand; it spiraled, flattened out, plunged, became limp, pointed, wide, narrow, pecking or solid.

After that go-round with my body, I was aroused, on edge; I'd push Andrès flat on his stomach and fuck him selfishly. Then I'd resume my role as a despot. He'd go off to shit out the come, comb his hair, would come back relaxed and a bit fatigued, then smoke, sit in a chair, tell a few anecdotes, never talking about himself unless I questioned him. Then he'd lie down again, begin worshiping my chest or my arm again, etcetera. His flaccid, suction-cup kisses on my mouth disgusted me; but they felt great in other places. Often his lips were warm and his tongue cool. On my cock or anus, the effect got the better of me. If he kissed me, I'd soon turn his face away and pull his head toward my crotch.

Such coarse macho gestures were OK with him. Obviously, he was seeing me for that. I wouldn't have thought that as I neared thirty, I'd be seeing a teenager—a handsome one, no less—who was crazy about me, and that I'd be turning up my nose at him. To be worshiped by someone and not return it is rather refreshing. But it's only by accident that I can be that kind of man, a master with a devoted servant. Not that I prefer the opposite.

One night when I'd used him in an especially rough way, he asked to fuck me, and instead of refusing as I usually did, I said OK. I don't even know where he'd been climaxing on the other occasions; in the bathroom, I suppose. He lay down on my back, shoved it in, his entire body began trembling and he came right away, then pulled it out. He'd almost never had a chance to be on top, and the simple sensation of starting to be got him off. He didn't fuck me, he nicked me. If I'd imagined it would be like that, I would have said yes more often. But his little stone pestle did hurt.

Francesco came up with the idea of raping Andrès one morning. We run after him, catch up to him, yank him forcefully onto the bed, and Francesco gets on top of him. Andrès laughs as much as he struggles, but also seems to be crying; he slobbers, yells, goes into a panic; but Francesco isn't going to stick it in, there'd be too big a fuss. He fucks the crack. I watch. The two crotches in one heap turn me on, but Andrès's is lurching so roughly that I don't dare come as close to the sight of it as I'd like. Francesco has a nicely shaped butt, shapely thighs and, between them, a largely, powerfully rooted cock that either arches upward or twists toward the right when it gets hard. In that position, his smooth, heavy balls, as large as a couple of lovely eggs, have the laughable, healthy volume of a donkey or horse's scrotum. The two boys wrestle for a long enough time, then the crack of Andrès's ass gets soiled. Released, he runs to the toilet as the sperm trickles out of him all the way to the hollow of a knee. He's not angry.

On another morning, on the same little bed, I'm feeling up Francesco. Andrès, who's already dressed, is watching and lets out a sigh, then rubs the flat of his hand against his fly and smiles sadly. He decides to jerk off standing up, takes out his cock and kneads it, an absent look on his face, eyes closed. He's in front of the mirror (the one where I'll see Pedro a few days later as I discover his theft), and I tell him to watch himself in it, it'll be better that way. He gets closer, but keeps closing his eyes. I tell him, as well, that he'd better not come on the floor, or I'll rub his nose in it. He keeps going, gets worked up, sucks air through his clenched teeth, pulling the lips away from them, jerks off at top speed with his left hand under his balls, and comes. I keep an eye on him; grab him by his clothing, twist his arm, knock him down and shove his nose in his come; he laughs and protests so much that he gets it in his mouth. I let go of him, he rushes to a towel and complains that he hadn't even finished.

When we're alone together, he covers me with compliments. When I go to comb my hair, he follows me, studies me in the mirror and expresses pleasure in what he sees. When we eat, what he's eating is the best dish on earth, I'm a fantastic cook. The most ordinary bottle of soda is the most refreshing he has drunk, and I have the best cigarettes. I get undressed, each piece of meat extracts an expression of adulation from him. I open a closet, the clothes in it are the most beautiful. If I rough him up for a laugh, he admires my strength, and when it's over, he comes up to me to touch the source of it. He doesn't utter these compliments like someone in love, but as if he were alone, busy with some manual task and commenting about what he was doing: "… yes, this piece of wood is nicely cut, sure is, good … it holds up … it'll look great … works well, this saw"—he says it casually, his hands already busy with the next task. He's expressing himself not for me but for himself. A way of behaving that disconcerts me as much as his remote fondling of my arm. The compliments have hardly any effect on me, despite the fact that they're a rare thing for me to hear; I've had a reliable idea of myself for a long time, nobody's going to change it like that. It's made me indifferent to how I look, and with a boy, I forget quickly that I'm visible. But Andrès's admiration, the excited, disjointed monologues he murmurs, for which I'm the object yet not the person being addressed, offer me—despite myself—that animal pleasure I've described. A thousand times I've loved thinking of them again and trembling. It's only when I write about them (as I'm now discovering) that they do nothing for me.

When invited, he helps with everything, sets the table, humbly gazes at my pots and pans, even if there's nothing cooking in them but noodles. My opening a jar of jam fascinates him; when it's empty, he picks it up again with a respectful gesture to throw it in the garbage, as if he were the assistant of a great magician. In the morning, he won't leave without doing the housework. He makes the bed, washes the dishes, puts them away, sweeps, dusts the furniture, all of it calmly and skillfully, more or less in the nude, while whistling inane songs from the radio, because there's always a tune on his lips. His graceful form moves across the kitchen with such delight that you'd think he'd only been flattering me for the last twelve hours so that he could finally satisfy his real vice: the art of housekeeping.

After he stopped coming with Francesco, his visits got less frequent. I'd run into him in the street, and we'd share some news. He'd come over for a little while, have a drink, primp in front of the mirror. His life was taking its toll on him. In five or six months, his face got thinner, more wizened, his features hollowed, drained, the eyes ringed by circles, his complexion yellowed and sickly. People maintained that it was his lifestyle of depravity, in view of the brutality of the boys who kept an eye on him, but I think it was the state of nervous tension in which they kept him.

A casual friend had left a box of condoms in the bathroom. I almost never use those things, except as entertainment. Francesco wanted me to put one on and fuck him with it. He liked the feeling, I didn't at all; it felt like I was being inflated by my sperm rather than discharging it. But these were luxury condoms, with reservoir ends. Andrès inflated them. By moistening and twisting the end, you can tie them closed. You end up with balloons as big as your thigh, which float sluggishly in the air. Andrès would keep up two at a time, running from one to the other like a volleyball player to send them back up to the ceiling. With my cigarette, I popped one that sounded like a gunshot. It was night. Frightened, Andrès stopped moving. He started juggling again soon after, but cautiously, as if he was afraid of being caught in a dormitory by a student supervisor.

He began seeing a very old Frenchman who was enormous and terribly ugly, and he was hoping for a lot from him. It was said that he did to this appalling old man what no other boy would have agreed to do: for example, blowjobs. I talked to him about it without any unkindness, and he weakly denied it. His blind admiration for me no longer surprised me. He wouldn't say anything bad about the old fellow, nor about anybody else. I don't know if it was because of a naïve moral sense, sensitivity about the malicious talk he himself had to endure, or fear that it would get back to the ears of the injured party. At any rate, if he was just as accommodating to that man as he was with me, he was preparing a happy death for him. From what I could see afterward, he got nothing out of it, and the old man is still alive.

Whereas Andrès looked at photos of men in secret, Francesco kept a diary. More bourgeois in terms of values, and more unusual, too, because he had very little education. But the inwardness homosexuality requires produces such miracles. He'd described this diary to me entertainingly, but with pride. He'd been keeping it for three years. Every day, he puts down what he's seen and done. I would have liked to have read the story of his life at fourteen. When it came to his love life, he divided up the information: his encounters were written in words; what he did erotically in symbols. A cross if he got fucked, a circle if he was on top. Concerning the different ways of reaching an orgasm, he listed only penetrations; the rest was offensive or insignificant; he wasn't as sexually uninhibited as Andrès. At the very end of our relations, he decided to blow me and take the come. Before that, some nights when he was drunk, he'd on occasion agree to sixty-nine, but not very whole-heartedly, and I'd only come in his hand. He tells me that once an old man made him suck him; he does an impression of himself as a child with his little head bending from the force, and he describes a forest of white and yellowish hairs that stink of urine. Also, he sticks a finger in and out of his mouth when he's explaining that he'd like to suck a little boy. One night, he claims, he was in bed lying against his younger brother, who must have been around five; he felt him up, found out he was hard, put his mouth on it and masturbated while the kid was sleeping. He puts such nice details about touching and position into it that you'd believe it happened.

Our nights usually consisted of "fornicateries," but combined with other kinds of stroking that got our come all over. It didn't bother him, and when he spoke to me about his diary (we'd spent four or five months together), he merely counted out seventy-three crosses and four circles. Those figures surprised me; I've never shot my load so many times in the same hole, so it must have happened without my realizing it.

He was in late adolescence: his strong, slender, rather tall body wasn't as thick or hairy as an adult's, but he had nothing of what appeals to me about boys. I loved him as a friend; as a lover, I wasn't too interested. On the other hand, the morals of the city and his anxieties made him fall back on me, a foreigner he could count on. I was more generous and less shabby than what he'd been able to come up with in the past; that was the reason for his immoderate interest in me. All in all, our natures that year were so similar that we synched without trying, or noticing, or saying.

I argued about the four circles in his diary; he made it clear that he'd fucked twice inside me and twice against me. I would have thought it was three times inside and a lot of times against. We discussed it heatedly. It became clear that he was only counting intercourse from which he'd come—and he'd break it off often. Mornings, I liked to feel him pressed against my back; he'd cram it against my rear end without penetrating and get aroused. When he was really hot, I'd turn around to fuck him. He rarely asked for the opposite; and when he went inside me,

I'm the one who did all the work, sitting with difficulty on his erect cock. I didn't keep a flexible enough hole for swallowing a member like his; I liked getting fucked, but when it came to big cocks, my eyes were bigger than my stomach. My resistance would make him go soft. I don't like difficult anuses, either; and if the boy I'm inside doesn't attract me enough, or if his rear end is a little hairy, I lose my hard-on quickly. Moreover, the end of my dick has always been more vulnerable than a little dog's, so tensed assholes hurt too much; if I spot a condom to protect myself, I put it on; otherwise I forget about it. And I hate rubbers, as I've said. All these disabilities certainly are pathetic for a pornographer. Even so, I'm going to finish this book.

Sometimes Francesco comes between my thighs, without attaching any importance to it. Myself even less so, if I do it, because big boys' thighs aren't right for the cock. Children's, on the other hand, are white and worthy of esteem, they feel a lot better to be inside than the tail of someone older. The skin of children's crotches is smooth and humid, taut, smooth, elastic, it creates a velvety funnel below the anus when they lie on their side and press their thighs together while you stick it in from the back.

I stopped desiring Francesco quite rapidly. I'd fuck him like an old spouse, without thinking about it. I realized he was a handsome boy, pleasant to look at; I'd always grasp his large balls as I fucked him, like a kid taking hold of a teddy bear to sleep; but it was becoming abstract. I wasn't having sex, I was stroking my cock less deftly than with my hand, and that was it.

A particular feature contributed to this dispassion. When I'd fuck Francesco, his physiognomy would change completely: that laughing, attractive, impertinent clear face would become an empty-headed star's playing her big love scene. The boy I wanted to fuck would vanish and leave me alone with this Hollywood rubbish. It was such a complete metamorphosis that the first time it happened I thought the lighting was distorting his features. But no. That smile of faded elegance enticing a pretty boy, that slightly crooked mouth, that veiled glance of an aging streetwalker soaked in champagne—were actually his.

And he was doing this on purpose. If he's on his side while I'm pounding him, he turns his back to me; and his face, which I see in half profile, doesn't change. One morning he's washing at the sink as I walk by; his backside gets me excited and I put it in right then and there. At first, his reflection in the mirror is unchanged, I'm admiring it and thrilled to be fucking Francesco in that way. Suddenly, he remembers the mirror, sees that I'm watching him in it; his face immediately transforms, starting with the mouth, going right back to that ghastly smile, and then the entire mask.

He showed me a color photo of him from about a year or two ago: he was stretched out in the sun, his arms behind his head, eyes closed, his face that same star's with her false, doomed, dissolute, alcoholic smile. And yet, he adored it and thought it was the best portrait that had ever been taken of him. What films or magazines had furnished him with this model, and why did he identify with the mug of a vamp, a stupid cunt's kisser—that I do not know. But his transformation into a parody of a woman as soon as he was being sodomized, the choice of a face that he thought matched the situation were deliberate. "I'm still beautiful and you're what I need, my big darling stud," that stale Hollywood mask would say again to me.

So I took Francesco by the back-end whenever he was willing. But he didn't like it very much because he couldn't get hard at the same time. His favorite position was flat on his back, with me curled next to him, my thighs under his, which were raised. It was simple and not tiring. When this was the way he was penetrated, he'd go into his routine full throttle. His face would be taken over by the proverbial *l'heure exquise*, his eyes veiled as he jerked himself off. He masturbates in large, calm strokes, kneads his cock with a lot of energy like heavy batter that has to be softened and shoots in several spasms all over his stomach and chest with thick, creamy, extremely white ooze that's a bit sweet; his hole contracts to the same rhythms, as if it's swallowing. It's almost as if he's sucking in with his buttocks what he's discharging with his cock.

He told me a popular joke that expresses that notion of communicating vessels. If a boy boasts about having a big dick, the others answer, "When the grape is good, it's because the vine is being watered."

In other words, if you've got a lot in front, it's because you're getting a lot in back. Such a way of putting pretentious machos in their place is nice; but it's also a reference to something that we're taught not to take advantage of: the unity of cock and ass. As everyone knows, that area belongs to a single occupant; a cock isn't an isolated piece of flesh that sticks out, but a long pipe that you straddle; it begins at the anus and goes all the way to the end of the prick; it has a small hole on one end, a big hole on the other. Every imaginable connection (muscular, nervous, spatial) links the rectal cavity to the penis, which makes the cavity serve as its own internal space. Root of member and hollow orifice are one and the same location, the anus. Thus, Nature, more mischievous than those who claim to reference her to impose their order of things, has given boys two sex organs, which are one.

She didn't divide the two, but we're obliged to. If they're interested in belonging to the stronger sex and possessing, dominating, ruling females, males need one sex organ for display (the little pissy one) and another for elimination (a little shit). To become straight, you have to transform your cock into a phallus, that well-washed instrument of power. The asshole can remain dirty, but you've got to sew it up, forget the half of the penis that joins it, favor the external part and confine orgasm to that part.

Such a selective localization is accomplished at the price of endless training: years of frustration in love and of masturbation in families endured by children and adolescents. Their hand, which is repulsed as much as obstinate, and their fantasies of daddy-style intercourse accustom them to having flesh whose pleasure zones are limited to a few ounces of tubular meat that they can send out on an orgasmic mission, far away from them, without even having to strip their abstract body of the male subject. You forbid—and you're forbidden—sensations, curiosities, experiences that would lead to discovering the twinned nature of the organs that make up your groin. Every possible method is used to suppress this "feminine" cavity, which is too closely combined with boys' penises and the pleasure they receive from them—because its effect makes the male enjoy being penetrated and creates an intolerable similarity between the erotic possibilities of the two genders.

This is why we butcher this cock into two ends and two functions so that only the allowable fragment—the phallus— survives. Even many fags (because we receive heterosexual conditioning like anyone else) impose upon themselves the erotic divisions demanded by society. If a phallus has been manufactured for them, they keep their hole shut and refuse to let anyone bypass its stitching; if their anus is open, they refuse to penetrate anyone at all.

For Francesco, this division is expressed by a conflict between two attitudes. When he chooses the phallus, he condemns his habits and talks about going back to girls (to become the worst type of male and master). When he chooses his rear end, on the other hand, his cock is just a toy and he's declaring himself to be homosexual, meaning liable to be penetrated. But being penetrable, enjoying orgasms thanks to another cock, turns him into a pariah; a sewn-up anus allows him to become part of the life of the collective and be protected from the fears, loneliness, persecution common to the other state.

The mechanics of his responses to social pressures are like a barometer to character; and every time that Francesco gets rid of one of these identities rather than the other, according to the days, pleasures, ordeals he has just experienced, I know that the one he claims to be eliminating is only being held at bay. The solution that would reconcile these opposites makes no sense. Individually, unity has already been accomplished, provided by the human body and the freedom to make use of it as it is. Socially, on the other hand, such a thing is impossible for Francesco: his only options are to remain whole but be excluded, or to be accepted but become mutilated. And yet, he doesn't want to be deprived of the securities offered by the group any more than he wants to sacrifice the pleasures that his sexual honesty allows him.

In both cases, however, he is denying the part of his body that is taboo according to common law. If he's with his straight friends, he has a phallus that has no ass; if he's away from them and being penetrated, he has a hole without a cock. This latter denial seems superfluous. As is expected, Francesco emerges from it as a reproducer of social norms.

On occasion, he also becomes an intense top—but with boys who won't fuck him; the situation is then merely a variation of hetero intercourse, because Francesco approaches it as a purely phallic partner, suppresses his other tastes and fucks a boy-eunuch. With me, on the other hand, he castrates himself and expresses no resentment about my reluctance to get fucked, no impatience, practically no initiative about it (despite the fact that he knows that other, more insistent boys do screw me). He prides himself on the number of times I've screwed him, and in bed he takes on that woman's face, that horrible, fictitious mask; otherwise, he cultivates the most accurate boyish ways, and the effeminate is so strange to him that if he sees a mincing queen in a movie, he doesn't understand that the hetero director is trying to portray a homosexual. I explain to him what it is, but he can't absorb such a disconcerting code.

He lives his nonconformity through a maze of orthodoxies. He thinks he's superior to women and children, pokes fun at the disabled, the physically ugly, morons, the insane, looks down on the poor, is racist, admires violence, wealth, weapons, religion, manu-factured products, spitefully denounces queers who are less in the closet than he is, uses the word as an insult, even to refer to some decent man who's gotten him out of a jam. He needs these ideas, wants them, believes in them, stands by them; they're the only link he has to the group; if he rejects them he falls. Obviously, he'd have better judgment if he were less dependent upon others, less worried, less penniless. In his situation, any variance in opinion condemns him to being banished and destitute with no way out.

At times when his safety and situation are better than usual, his conformity disintegrates, he's willing to learn what you want him to, to turn over a new leaf, and he becomes a good kid, as he is a good person. But such periods are too brief, and soon he has to go back to his island of poverty, where he clothes himself again with the savage values that he currently accepts.

Those days when he claims to be homosexual, the plans he comes up with convey the economic origin of the dilemma. He thinks of leaving his country, having a good job, getting rich; or he dreams of making do with me—a foreign enclave within arm's reach—and he depicts the kind of married life he'd create for me, with him as the wife thinking obsessively of benefits and the care as prisoner he'd get from his top. But the days when he senses that these plans will never come to be, that he'll remain in his city without funds, protection or a satisfactory occupation, at the mercy of his family and fellow countrymen, he's gloomy, wants to get drunk, swears that he can go without boys, and anyway, girls really turn him on, he screwed one the other night, etc. An hour after, he's flat on his belly in my bed, although I haven't encouraged him to and only get minimal pleasure out of it. I tell myself that his life is so unengaged that it would be better for him to go straight. But he likes his body; and after all, his contradictions have only one source: homosexuality is an unlivable form of freedom in the poverty into which he was born.

I wasn't used to a boy I was screwing being as selfish as he is. If he jerks off, he almost always comes before I do, and the atmosphere that results embarrasses me. One advantage of it is that his face becomes normal again; instead of the menopausal star he inflicts on me, I rediscover the boy I like so much. A rather arrogant kid, who's waiting politely for me to finish, and who uses a finger to push back some sperm cooling on his stomach that has begun to trickle down his side. He doesn't want to stain the sheets, he's tidy. The amount of sperm is amazing; usually I want to drink some, lick it, but Francesco spurts too much of the stuff, even for smearing my cheeks with it.

If I fuck him flat on his stomach to protect myself from his hasty orgasms and the vamp's expression, he turns around afterward and masturbates as he chomps on my dick by pumping his anus. He's in too bad a mood to paste on the legend's expression and becomes a thickset teenager playing with himself, a greedy one, with squashed, brutal features, like a dog during fucking, his ears straining backward, the eyes a bit glassy, the skin of his forehead taut. I get hard again.

One morning when we get up, he's mildly challenging; I tell him that I want to jerk off by myself, and he can do the same. The first one to come wins. He claims he'll shoot before me. I know him, and I'm sure it won't happen, his brain isn't uninhibited enough. We start our race and I leave him in the dust. Francesco keeps going, but for a crutch, he needs to toy with images and lose control of things outside of him, which he isn't looking forward to. Impossible to be outside and inside at the same time. Finally, he decides to pull the sheet over his head; protected from my presence, he can get immersed in his thoughts. He comes quickly and reappears red and smiling, as satiated as if he were waking up from a siesta in hot weather.

The act of pulling over the sheet is another thing that proved to me that the vamp face is voluntary; it's the one he chooses to hide behind when he's being fucked; his features take on that expression with a tiny quaver or misfiring, as he luxuriates in the sensations in his "rich bowels."

Talking about races. Francesco was at a man's house with a friend. In bed and totally naked. The man looks, touches, sucks; their cocks are nice, but they won't get hard. The man holds out a new watch and promises it to the first to get a hard-on. And at the very second Francesco sees the object, his cock gets rock hard. He gets the watch.

That's how he tells it. But he really could have reacted in that way. First of all, he's crazy about watches; secondly, he gets hard very easily. What threw cold water on the two of them, as it's expressed around here, was obviously the fact of being together. The shiny object dazzled Francesco, he forgot about his inhibiting partner and immediately his rod sprang up, which is what it usually does without any prompting or any reason as soon as he takes it out. We need other kinds of stimuli, or screens, when something in bed turns us off. But with Francesco (and with most of the boys in this city), cocks seem independent of any sexuality and have an organic life below that of desire. Often when we're eating or chatting, he pulls it elegantly from his pants, fully hard, the way you'd take a party whistle and blow into it to amuse your host; his always hard big prick is a good practical joke that he never tires playing on everybody, a source of perpetual laughter, a mischievous animal attached to his belly that couldn't care less about the outside environment and the human being that lives on it as a parasite; it wakes up or sleeps at whim. Conversely, in an erotic situation, the member and the man reassociate; Francesco's stages of erection follow what he's feeling, and even depict his many variations in mood, minute by minute, with a faithfulness that's affecting and voluble.

Whenever I'd come before him and staying inside him bored me, according to our rules of selfishness, I'd pull out and stick in a finger or a few, instead. He'd squeeze his anus around them to the point of almost breaking the bones and jerk off for dear life. One time, curiosity led me to slide a finger in with my cock when it was kind of soft. He has a roomy hole, and he liked it. He felt very sticky, but not dirty. I explored the area around my member, tickled the glans with my finger and was enjoying it a lot. Francesco sprayed a load on himself as he followed my game.

The transformations of his face weren't reduced to the metamorphosis I've just described. The expressiveness of his features was amazing, and since he was childish, he'd screw up his face for a laugh and make others laugh all the time. He showed me every imaginable face, every attitude, every type of person, every disability, age, feeling, every kind of conventional mugging that women and men consider useful to flaunt their sexual identity. Some of these caricatures make you laugh to the point of tears, others are tiresome, which is usually the case with clowns.

I discovered that his simple, natural, usual expressions were as much a put-on as the others. The teenager I knew who appealed to me was actually only a teenager who was a master at imitating unaffected adolescence. The faith he inspired in me was brief. In a few days of notes of two or three lines that I'd scribbled on a calendar, I can already find my first suspicious or disappointed remarks. But I preferred to forget about them. I liked Francesco's character, he was charming, perfect, very unexpected in this city (nor had I met anyone like him anywhere else); nor would I have called his machinations simple trickery designed to get money out of me. The thousand roles Francesco played, his thousand poses, the thousand lies he spun around me served, as a whole, only to help him live with the least unhappiness possible, given his identity.

The pleasure he gave me, my need of him, helped to make up for the breaches in his character. I avoided interpreting the inadequacies in his amiable funny-faces because I needed them. I was a starving, enthusiastic spectator, and I fed on him, changed by way of him, and if he hadn't gratified me so much, I would never have become free enough to deconstruct the illusion he created.

Since childhood, he'd been able to perfect his affections, good behavior, cheerfulness on a lot of men, learning how to please adults, avoid their violence, coerce their egoism, produce an impression that was strong enough to make them ignore the part of it that was phony. Cheating was his immediate mode of expression, and he was never more spontaneous than when he told a whopper of a lie, never more appealing to see and hear. Unless you saw him intimately for a long time, it was impossible to suspect.

Like a lot of promiscuous types, I'm lenient with those I frequent and don't take a strong line with them; they relax freely with me—but my scrutiny doesn't relax at all. I don't let on to what I notice (it would change what's being shown to me), so people think I show a blind eye, whereas it's my passion for observation that makes me so neutral. I take those who attract me as they come, don't ask them to make adjustments in the direction of what I like about them, which is often very far—too far—from what they think they are and seem. When I observed Francesco, I was underhanded, indirect, like a man who goes into a movie theater not to see the film but, for example, to take cover from being tailed. Then the film fascinates him despite himself, and when he has to leave the theater, he regrets it doubly: for the security he's experienced and for the show itself.

Francesco's act got old quickly; he was aging, turning into an adult, his routine had stopped suiting him, the mask was becoming too tight and no longer held to his face. I'd already discovered that face, was curious about it but didn't like it, accepted it only because of this mask it wore. Francesco was looking desperately for another. He'd tried living as a hetero, then a hippie, a trendy yuppie, a rebel, a drunk, a delinquent, a fairy in a relationship, an honest and determined worker, a good son, a useful friend, without finding anything that worked, that was as rich in resources, as adaptable as the graceful image of an adolescent that he was no longer able to pull off.

Therefore, despite our affair, the boy I call Francesco was the most imaginary of the boys I'm talking about. I created him with what he simulated for me. What I guessed about him, and which the fineness of his features helped him misrepresent so well, repulsed me, and interested me only for the unreality with which the actor, whose previous performances I'd admired, endowed it.

His face of a star during intercourse was a particular failure founded on a misunderstanding. If I'd told him that the face was hideous, he would never have made it again. But if there was only a single chance that it was involuntary, I wasn't going to risk hurting him. So I never spoke to him about it, he didn't suspect my disgust and thought of this "attractive" face as an infallible seduction trick every time he put it on.

Francesco's unsuccessful faces. When the eldest boy threatens that he'd better not play any tricks on him, Francesco lowers a spiteful weakling's face. That expression isn't "his." When he becomes ill at ease as a policeman passes by: no fear, but a kind of shrinking, a thug with a cowardly expression caught in the act and thinking about giving up his accomplice to save himself. His arrogance and foolhardy sarcasm, when he's feeling powerful because he's with his friends, has had a bit to drink and has just gotten what he wanted from me. The victorious laugh of a con man who's leading an imbecile around by the end of his nose.

His hatred for his young brothers, the way his face looks when he speaks to them, are so brutal that he frightens me. He knows about my passion for children, but he underestimates it as much as he disdains them. He doesn't think about holding back, nor that his tone of voice, gestures, features project a grotesque light on the pretty boy he's pretending to be. And yet, although I don't pay much attention to what's being done to me, I go over and endlessly evaluate what I see being done: I've loved or detested my friends, become extremely attached or separated myself from them, not because of how they were with me, but because of what they became with others—and especially certain others, those you can subject without any bother to social and family hierarchies and the prejudices and racism that reigns. It doesn't make me happy to admit that, in France, when it comes to a test like that, I don't even need all the fingers of one hand to count those I'm fond of.

I tell Francesco how shocked I am by his behavior with his younger siblings. My rare reproach surprises him; it had never ever occurred to him that a circumstance so insignificant in his eyes would provoke it. But his concern for pleasing takes precedence. He learned to stifle his hardness when I was there. He knew, besides, that he should gain Pablos's trust, since I was fond of the little boy. The surprising thing is that gradually he himself began to trust the child; and as a result, he even dared kiss and fondle another homosexual adolescent in a very amorous way in front of a totally amused Pablos, who climbed up to me (I was standing) and did almost the same to me.

The letters. During my first time away, he had a high-school friend compose and write out some letters to me for him, in a style he figured was favorable: one blank page, some empty formulas, not one word worth reading. The process was absurd, given the degree of closeness we enjoyed, and after I myself had helped him to write equally formal letters. But he'd forgotten.

My answer reminded him of it and furnished him with the right model. Then I got some illiterate, obscene, snickering scrawling that exactly matched the particular tone we shared. In Paris I got homesick for this city; it was all I thought about, I was in a rotten mood and couldn't stand anybody; I was more bad-tempered and tormented than I'd been during puberty. Only Francesco's letters made me happy, and perhaps more than the presence of their author would have been able to. Likewise, during each of my return trips here, when the plane descended, in the angle of its sun-flooded wing I spotted the city looking vast but tiny, rustic and green, nicely concentrated and round in the midst of an arid countryside, and my feelings brought me to the point of tears, although it was more emotion than a moment later, when I was back in these streets, among these houses, this climate and these men. Because I wasn't smitten with this city for the purpose of gazing at it, but to live there; so I'd forget it the moment it began to make me exist. It was happiness itself that I was hoping to get from it, which it alone gave me, out of all the places I've seen.

The error in tone in Francesco's first letters wasn't really the result of his having forgotten something. In reality, he had qualms about spreading the debauchery we took with each other to that new domain. He hated revealing himself in a raw light, preferred to seem chic, rich, educated, formal, and the letters that I was asking for put him face to face with an embarrassing obligation: abandoning the most proven recipes for seduction and pleasing me by displaying exactly what displeased others. Since he had nothing against behaving naturally, provided the payoff was as profitable as that of a well-played con, he adapted. And the enormous amount of scribbling he sent me, its fantasy, abundance, its ornamentation and the drawings accompanying it (it took him an incredibly long time to draw something; the smallest part of an ass, heart or cock meant a full hour of work) showed how happy he was to practice a form of freedom that, for once, wasn't harmful to him.

The sessions in which I'd help him write letters for his "friends" were harsh. He'd dictate, or explain what was supposed to be said, all the while mocking them ruthlessly; he'd have me string together corny, pompous sentences, with nothing that followed. The finished letter was a caricature of a nice note communicating deep, fawning, bombastic friendship.

"Now I'm going to send this to that faggot bastard," he'd declare with glee, as he sealed the envelope. Obviously, since he was confiding this in me, I wasn't part of Francesco's faggot bastards.

What made him a consummate actor was a quality that was rare among people like him. He was very sensitive to the effect being produced; but for him it was no mere trick, it was also a means of developing a persona. He needed to begin afresh every day; the material results, the gifts, money, promises were secondary. He'd betray himself ceaselessly in order to adapt to others and remain on their favorable side, the most flattering one, like an animal that wants to stay in a sunbeam and follows its path, transforming itself into fish, insect, ox, lizard, bird, human being, according to whether the sun is touching a river, anthill, plow, rock, tree or restaurant terrace. But false notions made him pick the signs he used for guidance, and because his errors didn't bother me, neither did it ever occur to me to point them out to him. Or so rarely that he only thought I was being capricious.

We almost never went for walks, he was afraid of being seen. No problem, but friendships deteriorate when confined to four walls. The boys who aren't attracted to men don't show any such reserve; they go out with me, flaunt it, greet me in public by kissing me, as is the local custom. They're not afraid of damaging their reputation, or they make a joke of it. A friend of Francesco, a well-off teenager who leads an easy, lazy life and doesn't sleep with men, waits for his girlfriend of the moment near me at an outdoor café (he spends his time cruising girls, getting drunk, buying nice clothes). We chat, get on well together. A few days later, he tells me that the girl saw him with me, and since foreigners always have a reputation for bad morals, she treated him like a queer and broke up with him. He laughs about it, showing all his teeth.

His tolerance for me is connected to his being harebrained; he makes a fuss over children, gives change to the poor, helps the disabled in the street, showers his friends with gifts, does a thousand favors for me; he's a hundred percent kindness, laughter, humbleness and generosity. You like him for it a lot, but no one imitates him. That definitely proves that people think he kind of has a screw loose. Passing as queer amuses him because he doesn't see any inconvenience in being that way. It's an attitude common to all straights satisfied by their own tastes; homophobes invariably have sour balls or bitter vaginas, repressed desire, anxious undies, and when they have sex it's on a bed of little scissors. Their hatred of homosexuals is only a form of their aversion and fear in the face of all sexuality, a fear of their withdrawal, their failures. I've never had a problem coexisting with straights, male or female, as long as they like pleasure. And the war of ways hasn't taken place between the two predilections, but between humanity and the insects.

This boy was born happy: his father died before being the cause of more children, he had a rich mother who didn't beat him, a big house in a working-class neighborhood, a future good inheritance of farms and land waiting for him, a pleasant face, an attractive body and the best health. All he lacked was reason.

He laughed at the girl, but he doesn't look down on anyone. Instead, he figures that everything turns out for the best. When he falls for an idiot and it illuminates his stupidity as never before, this also offers him a way to get over her. When he loves a girl who has a temper and she sees in him a chance for more blow-ups, she's giving him the opportunity to stop putting up with them any longer. When a virtuous girl refuses his advances, he avoids the erotic censure that would dominate in his bed if she climbed into it. And so on. His mind goes no further because he meets so many girls he wants. If he likes one of them, it's for the pleasure he gets out of it and not so he can think about it at the office. So he's not very civilized, and neither are his conquests any more so.

Francesco hates walking. One of his former gentlemen, a German police officer, made him get up at dawn for a long session in the gym and jogging field after they had sex. Running eighteen miles, he claims. I bet every yard felt like twenty to him. The man would pay him to exercise. It's a more common way of getting pleasure from an adolescent for those who aren't having intercourse with them, for teachers or parents, rather than for others. But Francesco collected monsters. A one-legged man locked him up for thirty days in his hotel room. A sadist fondled him for weeks, and when it was time to leave, tied him to chair, flogged him to the point of drawing blood and covered him with sperm and cash. Francesco remembers the amount and has forgotten the pain.

In the northern part of the city, there are big vacant lots, high mounds of dry claylike dunes, fields of manure where lean cows graze. These grassless hillocks and this dust, the deserted bends of a road, a giant, tortuously deep ditch full of deep crevices through which flows a miniscule river, all give this landscape a mountain or moonlike aridity that appeals to me. I can only manage to drive Francesco to a small sewer, a some-what verdant brook frequented by donkeys, and where a few storks and some big white birds are pecking. Francesco says they're cowbirds, and one of them is perched on the rump of a donkey. I come closer to get a better look at my storks with their feet in water; they may be another kind of wading bird. They all fly away. The donkeys stay. They don't fly, I say. Francesco looks at me with astonishment.

Of course, he'd rather go to new, modern places, where there are buildings, department stores and posh cafés, cars, cold-acting passersby. He looks down on the old city: according to him it's tacky, dirty, smelly, obscene, everybody does and shows every single thing they do outdoors; he's humiliated by my dragging him toward where he lives, which he thinks is a pigsty. I didn't insist and went on by myself. I walked a lot at night; but not in a neighborhood and park they say is invaded by criminals and which it seems even the police won't risk at night. The thousands of little streets with their high-risk atmosphere inspired a feeling of infinite peace in me.

Francesco doesn't understand why I do things a bourgeois person wouldn't do: housework, cooking, the dishes, the wash, for example. But I enjoy taking care of myself, and if someone managed the domestic aspects of my life, I'd be deprived. Now I have my sheets washed, whereas, for a long time, I washed them very carefully in my bathtub: not so much to save money but out of my habit of figuring things out myself. Doing chores isn't a burden for me, but I adapt badly to the schedule and intrusion of anybody else taking care of it. This lack of flexibility goes to the point of my preferring to fast on certain days rather than go out and buy groceries; for me the street isn't neutral territory, nor are the shopkeepers or their hours, and I don't start doing rounds without sufficient reason. So if tearing myself away from my cave seems more of a disruption than staying hungry, I just look for something to nibble on, like sugar or a crust of bread. I'd be a lousy wolf, but I've everything that makes a good hermit.

Except for my crotch. If I were thrown deep into the forest, I'd be happy and wouldn't live differently than I do in the middle of a city. But they'd have to castrate me first. I need cities because of the boys. I only become civilized for their sake, it's only to find them, have them over that I discipline my days, shave, wash my behind, fill my cupboards, buy and rent some comfort, think about money. I know how to survive when my pockets are nearly empty; but then, my bedroom, my bed, are also empty, and that's the only deprivation I can't stand for very long. In order to avoid it I inflict a lot of others on myself. For Puritans, sexual pleasure is a withered treat, separated from everything else in the world; but for me, it's my social life and my nourishment. And this despite the state of my income, because I don't have the budget of a minor wage earner, the kind established by government agencies or philanthropists. What good would it do to forgo an existence that makes me prefer being alive rather than dead? I'd just as soon be forced into being a panhandler or a manual laborer as long as I could satisfy my homosexuality. But in a society like China, for example, where apparently they now distribute manuals that go so far as to condemn masturbation in the name of Marxist-Leninism, I'd tell myself that I wasn't human enough for such happiness and exchange my share of freedom for a rope to hang myself. And since I don't have the wisdom of certain intellectuals—who come back from this country and marvel on the radio that our sexuality is "behind" theirs, then trot off to their usual gay bar to see what young French behinds there are to fondle—if I leave for China one day, I'll just go to Hong Kong.

I like brooms, sponges, detergents, bubbles, wax, dust, grub, stains, hammers, pliers, saws, screwdrivers, paintbrushes, needles and thread, rakes, spades, cake molds, turpentine and plaster. As long as fairly fresh cocks are right there under my nose; they're my carrots, without them I won't keep going forward and you won't get a thing from me, I just won't budge, shiftlessness and grime will be enough for me. However, I've been better at fiddling with the fine mechanics of my bicycle than I am with the balls of any boy; I talk to it when I'm on the road; I even had a secret name for my first adult bike; and when

I'd put up my tent in the evening and hit the sack for the night, I was very unhappy about leaving my machine all alone outdoors. That was a long time ago, and with the second one I'm less sentimental; however, we still haven't made any serious trips.

As far as Francesco is concerned, you only make yourself do manual tasks when you're too poor to assign them to others. Obviously, when I become fat or old or burdened by visits, duties, national honors, that's what I'll do. I'll have to say goodbye to myself, and I'll miss the intimacy that we had. In the meantime, my hermitlike habits remain so stubborn that when I get sick, I curl up somewhere safe and don't go to the doctor unless I'm really not getting better or until the pain is more than I can stand, which is a lot. And there's still my habit of getting dressed only if I have to, meaning when I expect to be disturbed. If not, clothes feel too heavy. I always write completely nude, and I don't wash myself before.

Don't think that such nudity encourages me to question my penis about whether or not a passage that I write is any good. When my level of inspiration declines, it's true that I sometimes fall back on my pubes; but it's like a schoolboy staring dumbly at flies. I'm more apt to look to verify that the night before hasn't left me with crabs, until I remember that my most recent partner was prepubescent and that the creepy crawlies could have only moved from one head to another.

I can't get excited by what I write. I was very good at it at fourteen or fifteen, and the floor under my table was moldier with come than an old piece of wreckage eaten away by salt. My attraction to it didn't last. The kind of texts I was writing without masturbating were what made me continue to write, and I composed them long before trying any others. They sucked all they could out of that novelty, but they didn't cede their place to it. My jerk-off porn was only the way they lost their virginity.

Since that time, I'm only enthusiastic about pornography in pictures. The photos give me the freedom to see hundreds, thousands of desirable boys whom I'll never be able to see in the flesh. I don't get used to it any more than you grow bored with beautiful days, pleasant landscapes, the return of the seasons, the flavor of your food, repetitions with which we identify happiness. It brings to hand so many visions created near me, which is the opposite of the world moving through our streets, where human beauty always disappears, enclosed forever in bags. Films, on the other hand, frustrate me: they're moving; they take back what they give and even what you must extract in the end from the perpetual movement that is yanking everything away from your eyes. It's true that forms arouse me more than actions. So I hardly ever go to the movies; I come out of them depressed, famished as I am after some lousy walk among the shutdown figures, welded lips and fleeting bodies of the capital.

Pornographic images captivate me as does the sexual intercourse I have, which is another kind of experience. Boys, kids, the pleasures that they represent have a life with no material equivalent. The snapshots you take yourself never acquire enough autonomy, strangeness. The image has to come from nowhere. Nor is this kind of life based on photos one of fantasy; each of these unknown boys surpasses my imagination. It's not comparable, in fact, to voyeurism, in which you spy on the ephemeral, the animate, the extensible, and where you choose completely on your own to have an orgasm only with your eyes. Our body slips between the feeling of reality procured by the photos and their conclusive unreality, their strict limits, the untouchable part of what they form. The irresolute permanency of photography, and nothing else, offers this experience.

Pornography adds to this what our society is organized to hide—yet which seems the least ugly among the images that humanity is able to show itself about what it is and what it does.

Those who, through some strange infantilism, see nothing but transgression deal with pornography puritanically, in an excited or censorious way, rather than being sensitive to its object—the faces, bodies, genitals. And transgression is a period coming before, which by itself has no value; pleasure doesn't come from smashing prohibition but in inhabiting the territory that it was protecting, which is the most populated there is. Because the other world on which pornography opens is the one where we are, and it's toward ourselves that it leads us.

I don't reproach myself for my obsession with images. If I believe the arts in every continent, nothing has ever seduced man more than the look of his own species. But to get off, I have no need of any art. I don't even approve of the fact that these photos try to be artistic: when they're brutish, flat, ignorant, basic, done with a low level of skill, they are more faithful to their real power. I detest those geniuses of film who shove their fat back between us and the boys they're photographing.

The puritans claim that pornography is tiresome, that it always shows the same thing. I fear they overestimate the variety of everything else. I open a magazine: every week I find mugs of the same politicians, scenes of the street, the office, school, factory, war. I read novels: couple, family, money, work, war. This diversity is accentuated by the originality of the literary approach. The bottle's the nonreturnable packaging, the drunkenness filtered water. But an infinitesimal difference between two portraits of people in ties, two stories about marriage, is enough to satisfy the customer. Me, too: the littlest amount of posturing that differentiates one photo of the same cock from another seems like a universe to me. I imagine, then, that when puritans know how to look at crotches closely enough, they'll be fewer weighty politicians and silver-haired castrates of the Church yapping against the resemblance that there is among human beings. *Seen one seen them all* is a maxim that even bigots who pass judgment on the hats of those around them at every mass don't apply.

The ten thousandth kid who undresses under my eyes will shake me up as deeply as the first. The millionth photo I buy will be enriched with the capacity for interpretation I developed by gazing at those that came before. The ten millionth boy's fly I see buckled by the cock it's crushing, like the cheek of a kid crooked with the piece of candy he's stuffing down, will continue to seem to me the best thing worth opening your eyes for.

Pornography and the photo were born almost together. Now that today's obscene images are no longer reserved for wealthy connoisseurs, there is quibbling, haggling, price-fixing, coughing up of coins, fighting. But I'm thinking of the only serious fact. Armies of acultural photographers have created what has never been seen on this planet: a gigantic academy of every form of beauty, and even ugliness, that human beings of every generation, every race have had at one age or another in their life. The earliest of these photos have become better than tempting, their evocative power, their aura, the ranges to which they carry us are even those of art. Like those objects of civilizations that had no "artists"—medieval, primitive, savage, prehistoric—their goal was short, to give pleasure, produce an effect, conform to an order, etc. Then time passes and they escape it. I'd find it amusing if, in a few centuries, the only thing that our descendents condescend to retain of our artistic production, the only thing in which they'll see worlds to admire, to penetrate, the only thing that they'll show off as precious in immense museums after having flushed down the toilet all our acknowledged masterpieces, the only thing that will give them nostalgia and love for us will be our porn.

Obscene art is made for anyone who comes across these images and consents to be compelled by a particular boy or girl who is now wrinkled or dead. The humble impishness of a lazy ball in the snapshot of a kid from 1900 already seems like an inspired, incongruous detail to me, as extraordinary as the rarest historical fact revealed to me. And the innumerable correspondences that are developed in the image of a boy—between his face and penis, for example, his eyes and erections, his radiant skin and retracted foreskin, his gesture of jerking off and the shape of his buttocks or edges of his lips—are so many silent, barbarous, complex, indecipherable and self-evident phrases that, ages after they have been written, will continue to move us.

But no one knows how to read the body; those of us who are less blind discover only that an unknown language has been traced on its surfaces that yards of mud have buried for such a long time.

This is also the reason that literary pornography doesn't do much for me. Neither those texts nor mine reconstruct those who inspire them. A few suggestions, a few equivalencies, a tiny fragment that's transmitted, drowned in the stammering of a language armed against the flesh and unable to reconnect with it. I won't reproduce this nose, this chin, this texture of skin, this sphincter contraction forming a smile, this glazed globe moist with urine that produces looks, these glands, these casings dangling in front, and their vegetative life. I'll recite them in common colors, and rambling on from cock to cock, I won't even understand the confusion I'm feeling—just as we can't understand why we'd call a head this dented tubercle punctured with holes, sullied by patches of hair, with its jutting skeleton, its flaccid meat, its unsavory, sticky cavities, bristling with misshapen, distorted appendages like an old sprouting spud, and that for us its numberless appearances on earth are an object of contemplation, analysis and love that no glance can wear out.

Smutty photos, as much as, and in conjunction with, smutty people, know how to say this, how to solicit and fulfill it, whereas literature is powerless in the face of it. That's the reason why I don't jerk off while writing and only get hard to it by chance. When I learn that my books sometimes have a less mediocre effect on others than they do on their author, that you can read them with one hand, stick together their pages a bit, I have trouble believing it and it would make me conceited.

Once Francesco took some new underwear I'd brought (we're the same size). He left the dirty pair with me. A little dirty. I washed it with my stuff, without any reservation. I gave it back to him when he returned. He made such a strange face that I had the impression that I'd committed an error, an injustice.

Nevertheless, at my place he likes working, like Andrès. He wants to do everything, in fits and starts. He cooks the local dishes with patience, talent, an adroitness that's surprising. Preparing fish, chicken, takes him three or four hours. His appetite is small, in just a few mouthfuls he's done with his meal. He's proud of his culinary aptitude; doesn't exercise it often; never tries the same recipe twice; lets me eat without looking for compliments. These moments of married life enchant him. Last fall, I was out of money and none was coming. Francesco managed to borrow a very small sum for me from a friend who had a shabby shop near him. Then, since he knows things that I don't, he went hunting in obscure marketplaces, wouldn't let me go with him and day after day brought back a bag of food for a few francs. He prepares them, we eat, sleep, the next morning he does the housework and grits his teeth if I help him. Never has he seemed so happy, so hard-working, so friendly and attentive. He'll often talk to me again about those five or six days as the best we've ever spent. I liked them a lot, too; but I would have liked them less if I hadn't known that they'd be over. Kicking back together like this was like a cure for sleep, with wonderful, sluggish dreams. They refreshed me completely so that I could begin to live again.

I'd met Francesco before dinner the day after the first time I arrived. Night was falling. It was beside a park that I wanted to enter so that we could fondle each other. He said that the place was dangerous. He pretended to be in high school, played it shy and too docile. A few hours later, he gave up on that lie and burst out laughing at the idea that I'd believed it. The appealing thing about this laughter was that he was more familiar with it than he let on. His strategy was using the lie as the approach, the confession as an attack, and the laughter as the conquest.

From what people said, I knew that in this city you occasionally met boys like he seemed to be: curious about foreigners, appreciative of pocket money, tolerant of males without desiring them, able to fuck asses without being turned off or on. We're walking under the trees of a side street and since he's very easy, I push him into the darkness. He's too timid to do anything out-doors; this will be the only time he has consented to doing it with me. He kisses me and feels my cock with such warmth for a straight kid, and he has such a nice cock that I very much regret our not being able to go somewhere private. I don't yet know about what's available in this city; he claims ignorance about it. However, after the meal, he takes me to a small hotel in the old quarter; it's a cool, attractive house, with a patio and mosaics. We don't have sex there either, but I want to live there and decide that I'll move the next day. No one has explained to me that it's a hotel for turning tricks.

When morning comes, I bring my possessions. Francesco comes over. I have a door and a bed, which we get into. Since I've thought about what I'd like from him, and that he himself is probably looking for, I expect to be plowed. But we've barely started to touch each other when Francesco, who is on his back, flips around to position himself just the right way against me, grabs my cock, spits, wets and pushes it into him. Or rather, gulps it in the blinking of an eye. It's a relatively copious nourishment: neither a single course nor something from the land of plenty nor a fast, and it's not very often that it's gobbled up the way Francesco is doing, without any grimacing or effort. Yet his anus isn't the distended type: it's a novel hole, very active, small and muscular, which he knows how to open up as much as necessary. I'll find that the other boys from this city who agree to take it have the same control and, rather than opposing pricks with a ring that needs forcing, they spare themselves any pain by opening up like a mouth. I was surprised that I myself was nearly incapable of the same mastery; an effect of my education that I figured was not irremediable but would require time.

Francesco, then, can actually rape someone with his ass. Then he eats: being pounded by a cock doesn't make him move his loins, but squeeze and relax his anus. Such gluttony is another talent I envied.

In fucking Francesco, I discovered I was a butt-boy to the last degree, a superstitious person who violently impaled himself on symbols. I've done a good job curing myself of that—as well as of an infinity of other things that, to simplify my life, I would call "bourgeois." I reconstructed my own orgasm strategies on the customs of the boys of this city. I had an idealistic body, rotten with mythologies, padded with values. I stripped and recovered it another way. That peeling away of myself was so intense, so abrupt that for a time I felt I was being voided, eviscerated; I couldn't even jerk off any more; my arsenal of images was barren, scattered with old fantasies gone flat. These shredded husks were my means of desire. Then slowly, a new kind of flesh was put in place, worked out, it covered my bones and a new system of images came into being. This regeneration is a strange thing to talk about, impossible to describe any better, perhaps difficult to believe. It is not, however, an illusion. Nothing was more concrete, more conscious. In talking with other queers in this place, I discovered, as well, that they'd experienced the same situation. They had felt the same corrosive power of popular morals on their desire, their fantasies, their fascinations, their pleasure apparatus. But they had reacted to it as a kind of frustration, a danger; they saw in it no opportunity for freedom, intended to keep themselves as they were and not allow themselves to be ravaged by these invaders. My attitude was the opposite: I wasn't asking for anything better than the destruction that I was having so much trouble accomplishing on my own; and whereas the others were enduring attacks, I was receiving help. Now the change is so complete, so stable, that when I go back to France, the queers that I meet for sex seem like churches on legs, guarded by ferocious beagles, where an inquisitor is saying the mass in front of an audience of bailiffs, policemen and old devotees. And I don't want to enter.

During those first days, Francesco insisted on raping me with his ass. I only succeeded once in making him come in my hole, which I had, however, indoctrinated for that. Useless lessons, Francesco has no cock. It's something other than him, it doesn't follow him, and when it's in my ass it's not he who's coming. Whether it was a new or unknown cock would make no difference to me, a dildo is good, I'd loan him a messenger bearer who looks like me while I fucked with this phantom. As it becomes familiar, this rerouting becomes impossible; but I can't reattach it to Francesco either; there's no circuit running between him and it. So I'm indifferent to it. Sometimes I look at it afresh for itself, isolate it, and it interests me for a moment, so I suck it, knead it, try to put it in. Then Francesco comes back, and I have the feeling that I've had an orgasm with a dead, mummified organ, as if I'd stolen a piece of him that he keeps in his pocket, in the way that someone operated on would keep at the bottom of a tube of formaldehyde his appendix, finger, a fragment of bone that a surgeon removed from him. I've never had that feeling of a divide between a boy and his member, or seen my appetite for a penis ruined because of it.

I met Diego (Pedro's older brother) a while after I'd left my trick-turning hotel for the little modern apartment that I have described. Francesco would come over spontaneously, he found Diego there and was jealous. They hated and avoided each other.

However, I only saw Diego from time to time, as was the case with his little brother and all the others. That's what was convenient for them, there was nothing about their lives that could be blended with mine. Their families kept track of them more and left them less penniless than Francesco's did. They went to school or had a trade. Homosexuality wasn't in their future. Having sex entertained them but didn't arouse them. They approached it coolly, with the calm ease of boys who leave school in the evening to play tennis, or go to the pool, meeting up at the playing field with their basketball or football team. Their relations with girls were just as relaxed. They liked to come, but no feelings were taken advantage of and the mildness of their customs found an advantage in doing it.

It isn't that they're indifferent. They willingly boast about their city, claiming that everybody in it only wants to have sex and does it better than anywhere else. I don't know. But it's impossible to take your pleasure more calmly. No superstition, no fever, love is seen as a well-rounded summer day, a form of leisure no more important than their youth, which is this carelessness.

They didn't need me, they simply wanted a few bills to buy trinkets, amuse their friends, spruce up their outfits, date girls. I was a sort of distant relative, void of interest, whom you come to see and then put up with because of the small sum of money you get in the process. And I began to take on the habits of forlorn old codgers who expect such visits, get ready, set aside a few bills to slip to them without embarrassment, choose drinks, treats based on the age and the taste of the person who was coming, a particular chocolate with pistachio nuts, these fruits, that kind of fruitcake, a hearty roast. The pitiful profession of the uncle, a name I knew before having practiced it.

They discovered that I wasn't miserly. It suited them, but they also distrust someone with easy money. Some, however, didn't see it as on the square—like a kid working in a service station who's disconcerted by a big tip, and just in case rewipes your windshield that he's just cleaned, and you flash him a big smile through it. The generosity of such impulses left me feeling unhappy. My usual youngsters were sure to find what money they needed at my place without my having to throw them on my bed each time. They were understated about their taking advantage. This taste for giving without compensation didn't come quickly to me. Then it grew to the point that the role of business became minute. I felt relieved, despite some undecipherable sadness that had nothing to do with money.

Hence, only Francesco was really free; alone or almost so, he was fanatically gay. He wouldn't have had to fear competition from Diego. But he had hoped to win me completely; he surrounded me with manageable friends so that my desires wouldn't leave our circle; he organized his reign without guessing what a mistake he was making, like those drowning people in comic strips who think they've come to an island and climb onto the back of a whale. I was the wrong territory to conquer, I didn't stay in one place.

Diego gave him other reasons for being vexed. He was younger than Francesco; with his small size, his muscles and nice proportions, at sixteen he looked like less than fourteen. Diego wasn't one of those semiwhore bad boys; neither was he the kind of dazzled slave who gravitates around you. He wasn't from the old city, didn't set foot there, lived in an apartment building. Diego was going to school, as the dunce, but conscientiously so; he never hung around where he wasn't supposed to, conducted his love affairs discreetly and rapidly; his loyalty, honesty were irreprehensible, entirely devoid of imagination; he just didn't know how to fabricate a lie. His family was a little poorer than Francesco's; his absent father sent money. Diego wasn't trying to charm, he pleased without really knowing why. Diego wasn't homosexual, didn't put himself in that situation, had small flirtations. And finally, Diego was so handsome that, next to him, Francesco—snickering and tense, all his ploys and games ruined like a tart's make-up is by a downpour—looked like a rat, and smelled like one.

Diego, on the other hand, envied the glibness, ease, adroitness of the other; hurt for some obscure reason, he'd pull a sour face and not say a word. But he was neither a gossip nor someone who taunted: I never found out what he thought of Francesco.

Just as in the northern countries, where brunette boys are preferred, with their curly black hair, in the south, people admire what's rare, paleness and blond straight hair. Francesco, who was obsessed with appearances to the point of idiocy, thought less of himself for having dark skin and tight curls; he displayed total contempt for those who were darker than him, made fun of me if I liked a boy who wasn't light-skinned enough. I'd answer him sternly. Sometimes, when he got undressed, I noticed scratches and red marks on his body; he'd admit having violently scraped himself in the bathtub to make himself whiter. His inferiority complex and the values it made him revere appeared in all his actions and life choices; his prejudices about color, however, spared his friends. He was the only one in his family who'd turned out dark-skinned; he was miserable about it, though he knew that pale-skinned types were only trying to get browner. He didn't link the two, and while I was getting a suntan, he'd exclaim in a delighted tone, "Wow! Really! You're getting so red!"

Nevertheless, his attempts at cultivating a white-skinned look made him seem pallid and gray in the light of summer; then he took some sun and he himself thought it offered a big improvement.

Otherwise, having this skin color humiliated him—especially in front of Diego, who was blond and white. Diego wore his hair at half length, with large curls; it was actually a soft chestnut brown in which gold, beige, tawny colors, mahogany were closely interwoven; the highlights were blond, over a deep, velvety color background, with clashes of chiaroscuro. Diego cared for and styled that hair guilelessly and with flair. Its lightness flattered him, pure and simple. His body was smooth, of a delicate amber and scented in certain folds like an orange-tree grove under the sun, his skin plump with luminous flesh, without the hardness of a lot of boys. These signs of lushness upset Francesco endlessly.

He was upset, but troubled. Diego attracted him. The somewhat gruff, taciturn or thuggish behavior of the kid, his dull voice, his not very mobile face, its paucity of expression, his stocky, tight body, his delicate features that blurred between the solid mug of a boxer and the ravishingly sweet face of a little guy with big eyes, awoke the old Hollywood broad in Francesco, who's wild for blokes, biceps, narrow bottoms, the movement of shoulders—and in me, the lover of children, amusing children, little brutes who smell like milk.

So Francesco's tenseness and jaundice when faced with the other expressed all jealousies and all desires. It was difficult for me to decide between the two boys, whom it was impossible to keep together. Once, when Francesco is there, Diego happens to stop by; I send him away, Francesco is too sensitive, you have to keep your dates with him. Diego leaves and doesn't hold it against me. Another time, he's there at the expected time and Francesco arrives without advance notice. Diego immediately gets ready to leave, as if he's respecting an implicit hierarchy; and Francesco settles in as the master, pretentiously and mockingly. It's the end of the afternoon, Diego doesn't come often and only stays for two or three hours; so I have him sit down and tell Francesco to come back later. He reddens all the way to his ears and slams the door. He'll reappear a week later, dead drunk, contrite, sentimental, ridiculous.

Then he gets accustomed to what I will not compromise. He'll give up his place at the table, in bed, when Diego or another sleeps at my place, during school vacations. But he'll slander every boy that I see, although he doesn't know any of them (because I meet them very far away from the usual places). One of them is a used-up slut, the other only goes after fags to rat on them to the police, another is syphilitic, another attacks people with a knife, another just came out of prison or is a drug addict, another is spreading the worst stories about me, another has an butthole like an airfield radar system, another wants to have my eyes poked out and to have me thrown into a cell, all of them are rotten, ugly messes, ridiculous, thieves, liars, and they smell bad. His nasty, nervous, snickering face, his spiteful little phrases that pop up about anyone at all, even a child, the moment he's seen him with me, the pitiful quality of the accusations he invents (several of which only stigmatize his own life) will, like other things, cool my friendship.

I feel that this text has to be given a bit of freedom, if not I'll quit after two more sentences—yet no reader can put up with as much as I do. I often see these long paunches dilating my books, when I get closer to the middle; whereas a well-formed stomach seems to be composed above the navel of blocks of muscle side by side, like flagstones, kitchen tiles, cobblestones, mosaic. But almost all books have flabby centers, hammock concavities. It's probably like the hollow that you see in beds, chairs that have been used for too long. The springs need changing.

Or this lap transformed into a fakir's board, with narrowly placed nails sticking up. But let those nails be so many stiff cocks. The next chapters, to return to what's going on.

Diego is fucking me.

When I met him (I use the word *met* as freely as I breathe) he wasn't alone. It's the time when, getting out of work and before dinner, people stroll past the lovely, brightly lit shops. A calm, varied, cheerful slowness as they come and go. It was already night.

Diego's friend is a taller boy, square-shouldered, thickset, very ugly. Young males often go around in pairs, at the least, and also these couples are often composed of a frightfully ugly one and a handsome one. Diego called his friend *the monster*. He said that this fright attached himself to him against his will. They go to the same school, the ugly one's Diego's foil, and Diego is his powerhouse for meeting people.

Diego is so well behaved that I'm hesitant to approach them. If I'd known that everyone thought he was the most beautiful kid in the city, I would have been even more timid. His trousers, which fit well, are decent in front, less so at the behind. He seems like a child. His eyes don't avoid mine very much and that decides it. I'm greeted cautiously. All three of us sit down on a cement bench off to the side.

Diego is silent. The *monster* takes possession of me immediately. He bogs me down, is glued to my right side, leans and twists against my shoulder to speak right in my face and stare at me with his squinty eyes. He wants to prove to me that he's the best friend conceivable. He even shows me a school certificate, his monster pedigree: imperturbable, incapable cretin, deserving and servile. The more I pull back, the more he advances. He'll gobble my nostrils until I've admitted that no one is as worthy as he is. I try with difficulty to speak to Diego, to look him over. But it's as if the monster had an extendable neck, he manages to stretch his head in front of ours without budging and, with the help of raucous remarks, banana smiles and a drizzle of saliva, he shuts our traps. It's a horrible scene. I'm grimacing. He takes that to mean that I have a migraine, which only makes him lust after me at closer range. He has a low, sunken, hairless triangular skull. While his snout roams to within a finger's width of my cheeks, I'm wondering if he laps or crunches.

I've never seen someone show off his face so insistently. If it were attractive, it would interfere with me just as much. He wants to unload his educational future on me. I don't question his capacity for success. I don't question the rest, either: those gargoyle lips, a big pug nose, two or three eyes that I thought had been ripped out of an ox or pig and stuffed into his sockets to fill them; prominent cheekbones like thin shoulder blades; narrow, receding cheeks, a chin like a chicken's rump; yellowish skin completely overrun by black down. But he's hoping before long to change into a monkey—like the Beast in the fairy tale, who, moved by love, becomes a man.

He'll show me a letter that he received. The author is a Norwegian father. He had come here with his wife and children. He fell in love with the monster. He writes that he keeps his photo over his heart. He admits that their love was impure: he likes something, he says, that the boys find humiliating. He congratulates himself for not having committed it: *I was right to respect you.* But he talks about it endlessly, out of fear that the other won't understand what he should answer. The Norwegian hopes to come back. Bizarrely, he ends the letter: *Sleep well, my little one.*

So, the monster thinks he's handsome. Diego has never received any letters like that, which certainly proves it. His beauty isn't powerful enough to catch the eye of a daddy.

A strange letter, certainly. Impossible to read a self-portrait that is better written. A queer ravaged by shame and lust, feverishly cultivating family values, kneeling before the petit-bourgeois myths of Childhood and Adolescence, Purity and Self-Control. Married for twenty-five years as a "cure." Wrenching his guts year after year, hatching three daughters with noses like a pelican's, legs like a crane's, new ideas. A practicing Christian, in order to thin out his marriage duties. One bamboozled person, one frigid wife, three coituses, three virgins and God; and nearing menopause, a little trip, a zoophilic crisis that opens his eyes and compromises an entire life of retention, the tortuous desire to pollute the ample buttocks of a monster: impossible love. A desperate effort saves him from the abyss. The Impossible Teenager is disappointed: he damn well wants to be hit on the palm with a tidy sum, was expecting a subsidy. A touching misunderstanding. However, he should have informed the Norwegian, who comes up with two or three saddened sentences about the beautiful friendships that money dirties. A clear and simple refusal. A cryptic allusion to his ass—which stands for the word *respect* in alchemical language. Tender slobbering, some blub-a-blub, some complaints and then, Sleep well, my little one. He must have been weeping as he signed it, this Norwegian. We all get off the way we can. On his moist heart, that photo's going to rot fast. The wallet will stay in good shape: Death in Venice isn't written into the family budget.

I'm not surprised by the fact that if a monster takes a portrait out of his pocket, it will be one that gives you the willies. What's really excruciating about this nightmare person is his stupidity. I like cretins a lot, but innocent ones. They're light and soft like little clouds, just a little bit disturbing when something disconcerts them, but blowing on that shadow makes it disappear. Whereas halfwits like the *monster* weigh a hundred tons, and their weightiness comes from the social and moral normality to which they adhere. One of Francesco's older brothers has the same heaviness, the same stupidity, the same orthodoxy. But whereas the others have class, he simply passes for a nut and they make fun of him. They're wrong, he's a decent boy.

There's no question of my mocking the monster, these messages are too evaporative, his ears have the impassive, pitlike openness of a ditch for pachyderms, you need heavy food brought in by trucks.

For a month, and even longer, he insists on disturbing my evenings, when it occurs to him. The first day, I manage to separate Diego and bring him back alone. But ten minutes later, someone knocks: it's the impossible teenager, who's been tailing us. I send him away. No explanation will dissuade him from returning. Once and for all he has got it into his enormous skull that he can be loved by me, because he made a Norwegian cry and because I go with Diego.

Impossible to extricate myself amiably. Francesco (the monster will also end up disturbing us when we're together) will end up threatening him with the police. The monster feels he is the victim of injustice that surpasses human comprehension; he'll resent me until the day he dies. I didn't even dare offer him a cigarette; if he knocks on my door when I give him the cold shoulder, he'll carry me off under his arm if I'm polite. At the same time, such bestial stubbornness charms me. Remaking the world so that the most obvious and elementary signals don't function, where nothing that we learn is assimilated. I'm like a test a chimpanzee can do, but that's too difficult for a gorilla. The monster hammers at the cage; though we've spent the last thirty days showing him where to press to open the gate, he just keeps shaking the cement walls with enormous, furious gestures.

Diego, who has not a grain of nastiness, uses the word *monster* laughingly. He has accepted this parasite with indifference, or fatalistically. When he goes to my place after school, he uses ruses to keep the imbecile from coming along. If not, he finds it altogether amusing that a boy so hateful, so manifestly repugnant tries to gain entry to the same place where the kindly ways of all others gain them welcome entry. The clumsiness of a bear that ruins its snout on some wire mesh when he has seen a fox cub or cat slip by.

For vengeance, the monster dreams up telling whoever wants to listen that he fucked me and caught syphilis. When

I learn that, I think about some brutal reprisals. He's finally succeeded in getting me interested in him. The reprisals won't be necessary. Everybody knows he's a cretin; at school, Diego has spread the story of his unfortunate love affair. The moron with the brain of a bear is ridiculed. Boys have a keen sense of irony; their ridicule doesn't kill, but it's victorious.

Recomposing this episode by putting myself in the place of the monster.

I'll think about him often. Perhaps because as a child this happened to me almost invariably; at the beginning of the school term or after, I'd come across an oaf of this type who took me to heart and whom I went through hell to get off my back. I keep their portraits in my mind, opposite those of the boys I was seeing—just as there's a permanent memory of the monster between Diego and me. It's not the only time that situations from children's lives have reappeared in my life as an adult, and although the characters may be different, all is familiar, returning cyclically as if my presence had eternally to reproduce the same phenomena, regardless of my age, the circumstances or the place.

Diego enjoyed imagining that I'd said yes to the monster and that he'd gone to bed with me. How he'd kiss, etc. Diego would awkwardly distort his features to imitate that banana smile. This superimposition of the two boys confused my heart. But pervert that I happen to be, to the extent that Diego recounted them, I'd experience his fantasies about the monster intensely, try them out. There are some disturbing dolts that make you giddy enough to want to go to bed with them. In this case, I didn't find a way to become enchanted by the disgusting image: that lopsided face, twisting to look at mine, those gargoyle lips speaking to my nostrils, those squinting, porcine eyes that searched mine with the passion of a dog's muzzle in another's behind.

This is the foundation of my fakir's plank. It's what's stubbornly there and never touched. Behind the pretty silhouettes of Diego and other boys who visited me during that period, the nightmare at my door, in the street, in the shops, is this twilight prowler with big paws, who hunts down benefactors like other half-wits strangle little girls.

Lying completely naked as I usually do, and immersed in a good book, I distractedly scratch my anus with a large knife from the kitchen that was lying there. I notice a white thread on the point of the blade. I dry it off and, by pricking myself a bit, I collect one or two others, which hang gently from their heads. I understand why my hole itches and swallow some worm powder. Buying this medicine gives me the instant impression of being a father, because they ask me how old the child is; it felt sad to admit that it was just for me.

These worms, whose eggs I may have ingested as I sucked a scamp's anus (although my youngsters are very well washed), are nice-looking, amusing, and I could let them live a bit, especially since the poison will make me vomit two nights in a row. But they tickle too much, and if a boy fucks me and collects two or three of these threadlike little guests on his knob as if he'd just fucked the rotten shit of an old corpse, I fear he'd have a bad opinion of me.

Another disgusting ailment I had for a week was an abscess that appeared—I don't know why—in a lymph node in my groin. It came to a head, lengthened, swelled into an apricot and was very painful. I had trouble walking. Then a movement I made as I sat down squeezed it, making it burst. That explosion provided me with a strange, graceful, pink-and-round pleasure, like an orgasm, but without any waves. The hole was symmetrical, a bit smaller than a cigarette burn, was pierced at the side, almost near my balls; and I would have believed what I saw was coming from a testicle: a brownish puss, followed by creamy white, which flowed out thickly, slowly, calmly and continually, like toothpaste. Later, having my hole, which had lengthened and oozed, I identified with those hermaphrodites in Renaissance medical drawings who exhibit a vulva flanked by male organs at the base of their stomach. I had those organs and that opening, in the exact same positions. Walking back and forth at home, always undressed, the movements of my steps made me feel my vulva, and I'd begin to get hard.

It wasn't the illusion of having a woman's genitals that excited me, but the reality of that slit, which because of the defect it created in the crease of my thigh, gave the feeling inside me (in the space of the sore lymph node) of something like the impress, or negative image, of a cock, a new cavity that I found disturbing but welcome, and that doubled my body such as it was, yet didn't feminize it.

The abscess healed. I also caught scabies several times, but only the first case was bothersome, because I didn't know what it was. For a month, I scratched myself to the point of drawing blood, and I imagined fleas and bugs everywhere. Infected crusts formed (I'd often taken care of similar things on the feet or forearms of the boys), and finally I had a name for it. I had to disinfect my entire room, my clothing, myself. Afterward, when I got scabies again, a few closely spaced soapings were enough to stop the invasion. Strangely, I haven't had the itchies for at least six months, although I rub shoulders continually with a little world of vagabonds in tatters that I wasn't frequenting at the time when I caught scabies.

No venereal disease. Not more than in Paris, moreover, where the usual age of my partners, I suppose, saves me from the scourges that the shameful pricks of adults rain down upon the world. As a consequence, in my life, I've only had one brief case of syphilis; I got it from a young straight who spent an hour in the opposing camp, doubtlessly because he simply wanted to dump his treponema there, the way you go to a stream to drown a litter of cats.

Francesco gave me the gift of crabs; I loaned him some insecticide. Good-humored moments when we powdered our bodies together, crotches and rumps floured in white, Pierrots, carnival time, *fêtes galantes*.

Never any fleas. And I've only had one case of head lice. I'd gone into a vacant lot, in the evening, with a very small beggar boy. After we finished, I went back to the avenue and a young policeman in uniform approached me. He's an attractive-looking boy, shy, full of smiles, but very boring because he likes abstract conversations; he asks me what I think of homosexuality. As he speaks to me, he gently picks a gray flea from my shirt collar; we study it; he throws it away. I explain to him why I was harboring it. He laughs, but he's not interested in children.

Pablos thought he had lice. I took advantage of this by fondling his hair and covering him with kisses. I thought I saw a few nits. I came back after running to some pharmacies—I'd been looking for a lotion that was fairly pleasant and reliable. I wet his head, massage it. He's content. His older brother confiscates the bottle, as it's his habit to hijack anything that enters the house. Francesco comes on as if he's liceless; lying on a bench, his head on the lap of his sister, who's seated near him, he lets her caress him. She's a childish, pretty girl, clever, a virgin, with a penchant for sarcasm; she often pretends that she's supposed to marry me, and recounts what happens next so crudely that I would almost say yes. Like a lot of other girls here, she talks about her period with the boys, to her brothers, without any more embarrassment than they complain about the corns on their feet. As for marriage, she'd really like to find out what my cock is like before deciding definitely (she's sure that Francesco is taking molds of it and could clue her in). This freedom in language is common but doesn't interfere with the modesty of their mores. The advantage is that boys and girls don't need abstract lessons to understand how they're made. Pablos, that prepubescent pipsqueak, knows a girl who bites his cheeks to gall him, and he punches her; she has also offered him a ring, then a second—and what else, I wonder, since he enjoys depicting her vulva to me with his hands, and he slides in a finger to show the clitoris. This kind of science is a delight; Pablos's face doesn't light up like that when he describes his prick or—always using his fingers or mine—creates anuses. (And in passing, it occurs to me that, in the sex education books we had as teenagers, texts and drawings hid from girls even the existence of the clit. As for the butthole, no benefactor of youth has ever understood how to talk about it. They already have enough to do when it comes to the genitals, poor people.) The difficulties in sexual conditioning, the trouble they have imprisoning the proliferations of the body in a small, hygienic hetero organ, remind me of the puzzle confronted by a prince in a legend. In front of a palace that he wants to enter without being seen or heard, he has to bind the hairs of his horse's tail; if a single hair unfastens and strikes the wall, it will resonate like a gong struck by an enormous weight, and the evil fairy who lives in this palace will capture the young man, betrayed by his poorly bound tail. I no longer know if the story is French or Hungarian. But those charming fish-faced princes who claim to be selling schoolchildren's development so they can manhandle their genitals, obviously have the same problem. If the least bit of an urge escapes them and doesn't remain shut up in the pee-pee pipe, the entire body will vibrate to those forbidden things our hideous libido adores and that deliver our souls to it. It is to this ingenuous example that I resort when, at the exit to a sex education class (my coat half open and my trousers at my ankles, my member turgescent and my eyes bulging), I explain to the boys why males, even prepubescent ones, also like someone to make them a baby—despite what dad or his rubber-gloved associates and nickel-plated philanthropy have been able to claim.

After Pablos's gesture had attracted my attention, I noticed that the presence of the clitoris in the boys' depictions of girls is as frequent as the absence of breasts. Their love objects aren't very "matronesque"; these girls are, instead, poorly idealized and asexual—and they want them to be round and plump, fulsome. It's interesting to compare the drawings of the older boys with those of French youth. In our country, the *naked lady* is a doll with big boobs, a strangled waistline, enormous lips, thighs pressed together, glued together (women, those extraordinary mysteries, wear a skirt because they have a monolithic pedestal in place of legs). The genitals aren't even depicted; a triangle of hairs is as far as it goes—pierced, however, with a rudimentary hole if drawn by the perverted. The boys here construct a completely different kind of woman. The build of a young man, a chest with no breasts, an ordinary mouth, no waist, hips that don't curve out, but legs parted as if they were squatting, and a collection of little circles or ovals descending like a line of buttons: navel, vulva with clit, anus. A few hairs as decoration. Very often, in a corner of the page or under the heels of the girl: a stiff cock seen in profile, pointing toward the holes. No man on the end of it. This arrangement, according to Francesco, is in line with reality; the boys, who aren't very concerned with the missionary position, enjoy it when their lady climbs on top and does all the work. Me too; my preferred method of being poked is sitting on a cock. No other position more freely and heartily exploits the member that you're consuming.

Strange orthodoxies, in any case. It doesn't surprise me that these kids go to bed so willingly with men: they're too materialist and, when lured by a hole, pass up that arsenal of rubber, knives, plugs, ligatures, eyecups, cramps and conjugal counseling needed by the young people of the bourgeoisie to protect their equilibrium.

But I'm forgetting my story about lice. The older brother empties the rest of the bottle on his mop. He'll find a pile of creepy-crawlies that have kicked the bucket when he later combs his hair. Pablos, none; he shrugs his shoulders with the half-hearted smile of children who are cruelly disappointed but want to look satisfied. He combs his hair again. I like this scene, which takes place as well when I arrive at the house. Pablos welcomes me joyfully, gives me a big hello, opens up his nice, sparse living room for me, seats me next to him, laughs, babbles, and suddenly remembers that he isn't pretty; so he runs to the television where he keeps the brush in a basket of artificial flowers. And standing in front of the old mirrored closet to the left of the set, concentrating, his little nose tensed, smoothes his short hair, and as a finish twists the front into a curl and, arms dangling, the brush in one hand, comes back to me with a delighted face. His interest in his appearance is limited to that. At my place, the messiest kids spend a long time carefully combing their hair after they shower. The flatter it is, the better looking it is. When it's well arranged as they've been taught, still pomaded and shiny with water, there they are again; I compliment them obediently; they laugh with pleasure and, forgetting their exemplary beauty, they are again ready to mess up their mops in my arms.

Diego styles his hair less awkwardly. He came to see me at a place where I had a tub, and I liked bathing him, giving him a shampoo. Such a toilet wasn't necessary but like everyone else here, he had a vice that French teenagers, too tormented by the ideal, rarely cultivate: a taste for washing himself. No convenience pleases my visitors more, whether dirty or clean, than a bathtub, a shower. Some of them linger there longer than in my bed. I listen to them splashing about, gasping, singing, whistling, clinking bottles; and then the long silence during the time they do their hair. I rarely bother them. Only Diego and his little brother have endured my penchant for being the master bather almost every time. While washing them, I could admire and touch them without their reacting; if not, they'd start kissing me and hugging me, friendly enough actions but interruptions to my pleasure. And then I didn't have the gumption to put them back at the distance necessary for watching.

Diego, who's rather shy, was originally embarrassed at the idea of my accompanying him into the bathroom. But he didn't put up much of a fuss and was laughing. So on the first day I forced him, before we had intercourse, and washed his back. I was hoping to plunge my hand all the way to his buttocks, but he didn't want to stand up in the bathtub and dried himself while he was still half underwater. My shampooing conquered him, he moaned and sighed with closed eyes. The following times, I remained standing and watched without bothering him. He acted as if he were alone. But when it came to washing his back, he finally looked at me and, with a gentlemanly smile, silently held out the washcloth. He was also willing to get up and be rubbed all over.

When I'd separated him from the *monster* and brought him home that first day, I'd felt ill at ease, overwhelmed. For months, or even years, I hadn't met a boy as handsome—that was the impression I had, I don't indulge in any soul-searching in such situations. I had no idea what I'd obtain from him. Obviously we'd go to bed, but then what?

He'd had his first man at the age of twelve. He tells me how this young man on a bike, riding by a movie theater in front of which Diego was waiting with some other children, started winking at him. Alerted, a bit anxious, but interested, Diego slipped away quietly from the group. The bicyclist met him farther off and arranged a get-together.

These precocious sexual experiences were far apart, sensible, secret, almost chaste, with very few people, who had a lot of consideration for Diego; he doesn't even know how to kiss yet. At the beginning, his kisses are simply an opening of his lips, which feel calm, comfortable. They moisten gradually. He lets his teeth be licked, then his tongue, and during this time, his warm eyes, so very white, and such a soft brown, stray toward the ceiling. It's as if he were patiently tasting an exotic dish to get an idea of it. It's an effect of his lack of imagination: disturbed by seeing my eyes so near, he tries to refocus his and it doesn't occur to him to close them since mine, which serve as model, stay open. The only open path is up: and rather than daring to lower his eyelids, he stares at the sky. As soon as I can endure closing my eyes, depriving myself of a ravishing vision, he'll imitate me and will be relieved of my face. He'll also learn quickly to kiss like an expert, either delicately or in a smutty way, mirroring everything I've done to him that he has conscientiously assimilated. He's a docile, sensual boy, despite his ways; he sensibly learns what's shown to him, as long as it doesn't disturb the state of middle-of-the-road thinking and behavior that is his method of succeeding.

At first he fascinates me, and I immediately prefer him to Francesco and his clique. I'm hoping to make him attached to me, and I fantasize abducting him. Luckily, he's not the type you can associate with. He doesn't speak much, keeps up his guard, remains well brought up, and his company is banal, dismal, although without any annoyances, and with rare flashes of whimsy. In his loutish poses I detect some pleasant, agile traits, self-confidence, an independent mind, depths of straightforward kindness, so many things that Francesco lacks. But it will obviously be a long time before Diego manifests them. His very infrequent smiles are extremely attractive, as are his tokens of affection and his sleep, his grouchy sign language for drinking or smoking, his full, childish lips sucking on the end of a filter. His easy laughter goes just as well with his face as his withdrawn moods, or the empty, steady expression he has when he fucks.

Like the little boy that I see in him, he undresses. Sturdy little curves, white purities, pretty buttocks, ideal proportions, soft skin, a strong fragrance. None of this matches his cock, which isn't very childlike at all. When it's soft, yes: it's a modest, sweet blond apricot under a very short preadolescent bush. But then it gets hard, amply and infallibly, and becomes a large fat, long member, with a simple, regular shape, a well-formed head that is smooth and silky, pale in color, and of an incredible hardness that is neither bony nor flexible. Stretched across the most beautifully molded stomach. So much academicism is almost disappointing. It's why I was so smitten, given my imported superstitions. Diego, who has a head of hair that falls all the way to his glans, from his neck to his buttocks, from the lyre of his hips to the roundness of his knees, is a perfect pederast's stereotype, a masterpiece of aesthetic and sexual clichés. There's more than enough to set you trembling a bit, as long as you believe in it. I believed in it. It won't be he who'll deliver me from it, in fact, but opposing things. He'll begin to bore me. And as he'll stroll completely naked through the house, this Beaux Arts model in reduced form, with his model penis for the office of a sexologist, though in too large a format, will even stop seeming to be alive. However, he has no affectation, he's not studied, he's canonical despite himself.

He was very curious to compare us and didn't do so to his advantage. Being little and having no body hair bothered him. He takes hold of my dick, matches it to his and, putting his nose close to it, decides mine is more developed. Untrue. But he appreciates the thickness of it, and I give him the illusion of being more tumescent. I estimate his length, and he has three finger widths more. Since his balls are relatively small, he says that, in the past, they were big, but they've shrunk—due to his jerking off, he thinks. He thinks that having sex devours your glands. I explain to him that the opposite is true. He believes it, always listens to me without discussion, the good news I give him about life suits him.

What does he know about venereal diseases? When you fuck certain women, your member rots and falls off. Such a perspective doesn't entail any fear of girls on his part, he's a fatalist.

His story about balls shriveling up has a follow-up, because I saw him a few months ago, which makes more than a year after we met. He doesn't live in the city any more, but he comes back to it alone often. For a night at my place—a pilgrimage. And his balls have taken on a lot of volume—the true volume of balls, not the result of some invasive liquid or inflation of tubes. His cock has also continued to grow; he verifies with satisfaction that mine hasn't changed, and that from now on he is by far the better endowed. I'm distressed by this, of course, but my bottom will draw some consolation from it.

I've got a very keen taste for big cocks. That's a lie, because little members inspire me with the same interest. But it's difficult to love a big cock for anything else than its size, whereas the attraction of the little ones comes from less explainable charms. What is certainly very tempting is the disproportion between the height of a kid and how big his penis is. A defect that is more charming, certainly, when what's too big is the member. But a few more years of perversion and maybe my opinion will change. If not, I'll never succeed in understanding why queers run after certain mountains of muscles serving to support, like an immense oak table, a dinner of soft-boiled egg, in other words, laughable penises. I have the impression, and I might as well write it, that such a thing is already beginning to tempt me. Tall, strong and stupid, with a cuckoo's prick; an especially decadent variant of all little boys. I should hunt it up. I'll get fucked to the point of ecstasy. Oh, big guy, big guy, give it to me hard with your tiny knob. Do the ass-to-ass chicken dance, and some sucking. I'm capable of it when my prepubescents, who are embarrassed by nothing, decide to fertilize me. Would I refuse the same service from a superb stallion who was a bit atrophied?

(Laughing inside when I was in the hospital a few years ago, and the time came for taking temperatures: I saw my roommate—a young, starchy teacher, with spectacles and a humanities major; an arched noselike prey; a lantern jaw; a stuck-up way of speaking; long, fluttery Christian hands; and pallid pajamas—put Vaseline on the end of the rectal thermometer and shove it in with some haughty grimaces, full of captivating dignity. At the same time, I was offering that miniscule dildo to my vacuum-cleaner anus—that fetal, sucking mouth—and swallowed the whole apparatus. When you're confined to bed with a fever, a sweating butt works as a fine lubricant. The difficulty was in keeping a bit of the thermometer on the outside so that it could be pulled back out. I would hold it between two fingers like a slingshot: if I let go I'd lose it. A fascination with chasms, the silver undulation of mercury through my entrails, infinite spaces, drunken boat. As for the gentleman who confronted the horrible ordeal of the breaking and entering of an anus—give me a break. And that gruff, offended mimicry inspired solidarity in me, nothing demeaning, nobility in humiliation, medicine's terrible violence. And afterwards, I'm mocked if a brat of eight or ten fucks me. Yet it's more meritorious than absorbing a tank of thermometers. You'd say that that thermometer was a finger, besides, a sensual one, nimble and gliding; no fingernail or bone, a single bulge just where it should be. When the elites who practice fistfucking— getting a fist and the rest up their rectum—are sarcastic about my bed partners, so be it. But those straights clutching their anal void with two hands, those hypocrites who push turds like an arm, but then, in the other direction, would put Vaseline on a fly's eyelash, well, that really disgusts me.)

The novelty of Diego's cock has to do with his erections.

Speaking about Diego puts me to sleep. For how many months did he visit me? I could have discovered him in the centerfold of a porn magazine, and I wouldn't have lost that much. I would have wrung out my cock to furnish a sperm bank for an entire year. (What gorgeous babies would be sacrificed, what wonderful and talented spermatozoids shat back out with my exploits, or the ones that died malnourished on stomachs, in handkerchiefs.)

Diego is nothing more than an image, perfect and flat; all I can do with him is a tiresome inventory of physical perfections; and if I'm patient, find minute indications that he's less insignificant than he seems.

His erections themselves have the fixedness of photography. Solid and impassive, they take a long time to arouse by the usual means, but once there, they stay, and nothing can discourage them. Exhausted from too much sex, he lets himself be stroked or sucked for more than an hour without coming and without his member becoming even a tiny bit flexible. Squarely affixed to his groin, the organ is there, stays there, like a fake one. When he has come and pulls out of me, he goes to wash, combs his hair again, looks for something to drink, and comes back with his cock as stiff as it was before; he walks it in front of him, useless, magnificent, like those feathers, humps, decorative antlers that certain animals have. His pipes cleaned out, he has the time to set the table and cook an omelet before his cock goes out of commission.

After the first times, he was too lazy to get hard. I disregarded this and fucked him from behind, between his thighs and against the hole (where you don't enter). And yet, as soon as he felt my cock striking his anus and his balls, he got a ferocious hard-on. This made me conclude that his refusal to be fucked wasn't a serious one, and that his body was more disposed to it than he. I saw another boy react like that. Around fourteen, I think, smaller than Diego, with the same kind of pleasant expression and a svelte, fleshy body; this boy only spent a moment at my place and didn't do much. He refused to get screwed; even so, after several kind actions on my part, he allowed himself to be turned on his side and I tried to enter his behind. He doesn't tense up. By applying gentle pressure, I can feel it giving way, relaxing, widening, and I pass through to the other side of muscle. Immediately, the boy stops me and pulls away; he has just shot his load on the sheet. He wasn't jerking himself off, it happened all by itself. Because of the tinkering with his behind, or because he was participating intensely in the act of fucking; or did he imagine himself in my place, decipher with his buttocks a history of ass-fucking? At the exact moment that my cock entered him, his sperm came out. This kid as well was convinced that he hated being fucked, and that I was a big queen. His coming embarrassed him; it's the very kind of situation that boys "forget" a minute after. He thought only about getting dressed. After he left, I jerked off while sniffing at the spot of sperm on the sheet, a small spot (he hadn't entered puberty very long ago) with a nice fresh scent to it.

When it comes to Diego, I only remember our first session of intercourse with any emotion. The evening of the monster, the shy soaping, the eyes looking into the air. This childish Diego disappeared quickly enough from my mind—and subsided gradually into his personality. A season later, Diego, who hadn't changed in appearance, was nevertheless not as brusque, spoke more, dressed better, was more male, and certainly now knew he was a handsome young kid. To put it briefly, he was no longer a child, except in his brain. Which is something I can do without in those who no longer are the age to make use of it as only a child can.

I'd gotten his cock hard, I'd put up with his resistances to being fucked, and then he'd fuck me. Such works in progress on the part of these little men always bother me a lot. He did to me what I do to Francesco. But Diego, if he's curled up against me, puts his face on my shoulder or tit. He's on my left. He drives in his cock under my thighs, without hesitating to determine the placement of the hole. He enters it calmly, placidly, his eyes glued to my genitals. I take him in with less pain than with Francesco, whose diddler (which, as I've said, doesn't excite me) is not only bigger, but flatter, more massive. That day with Diego my butt yawns open with desire. He brings his loins nearer in order to be exactly in line with my guts, and only sticks in half of his cock; he fucks by pulling his member out completely and driving it back in with each thrust, in rhythm with a rather lively little gallop. This lovely member drilling my anus pierces it spongily, pulls back, gets some air, is shoved back in, hurts at first, then gets interesting and, finally, fills me with enthusiasm. Diego's previous conquests at least taught him that—which he carries out without worrying about me, like a decent lad who threads his annular beads with care, enjoys them, and sauces them up to his liking.

When he has come, he drives it in to the hilt and I jerk off.

My chest is his pillow; he doesn't move his face away. He watches my hand. I'm going to shoot my load on his nose, lips, I feel as if he's waiting to snap up my come. At the last second, entwined as we are, I move his head, out of fear of getting it wet.

He doesn't have time for us to begin again. It was night, time to return home. Reign of the mothers.

During the times together that followed, being fucked excited me less. I have a go at his buttocks. Lick them a lot, come between them. His anus, oval and cute, with folds like the striations of a spiral shell, is tawny light with chestnut brown hairs. No colored ring around it. The tuft of hair surprises me, because Diego is smooth, but under his arms he has this same bouquet with the whiff of flowers and fruits, an odor that the bath dilutes. Invariably, I try to force my way into his hole. A purely amiable ritual: the unspoken convention is that Diego has to accept and that I mustn't insist. Give a few pushes with my cock and then avow, "It's true, your hole's too small."

If I push too much, he grimaces and mutters barbs between his teeth. Barbs into a void, not intended for anyone: his humor is always easy-going, despite the rarity of his smiles. A very sensitive crotch to frequent, and I drench it often.

I have my mouth fucked; on his knees over me, Diego has intercourse with my face. He presses his hands against my shoulders or the wall in front of him, and contemplates the action with the eyes of a young cat, lips parted and moist. I like to feel his cockhead poking against all the hollows and all the flat areas of my face. He fucks carefully; I shove it all the way into my throat while taking hold of his buttocks.

I ask him to masturbate. I watch as if at the movies and masturbate as well. This doesn't bother him, he's not the type to pull a sheet over his head. His face remains bland. Impassive, with a nice regular movement that follows his penis and descends to his balls, he makes a shoe-shining gesture. The first time I wanted to see that, he was actually surprised, but didn't hesitate. His surprise was because I was punishing him for no reason, depriving him of an anus. He didn't deserve my condemning him to *Mrs. Five Finger*. Next, I took advantage of it; if I come between his thighs, he wants to fuck my hole afterwards, and that annoys me. So he can only jerk off. More patient, I lend him my crotch, or I suck. I give up my rear less often. He demands it with naiveté, sweetness, caresses my back. His awkwardness delights me, I turn over on my stomach, he feels me up from head to toe, soon I'm trembling so much that he senses I'm ready and climbs on top of me. This ass-fucking from behind is less subtle than when he's curled up against me: he fucks hard, strong, deep. But he isn't brutal.

He was more likely to employ those caresses starting in the summer, when his mother was away and he could sleep at my place. And it was at dawn that it happened, because I sleep on my stomach and he would wake up before me. The nights were very warm. I'd pull the little bed onto the balcony for him, lie very near on the ground in front of the French windows. I'd admire him for a long time, then doze off myself. When the sun began to shine, he'd join me there on my blanket, his cock hard, give me shivers between my shoulder blades, murmur things, smile, spit softly in my behind and lie down on top of me. I didn't resist in the light of these summer dawns.

If, despite everything, I refuse to be fucked, he implores with a silly patronizing face, full of giggles and contrite cupidity, as if he were imploring a yes-means-no kind of girl. He diddles them standing, between their thighs, anywhere at all. He has certain trees where he does it.

He doesn't suck. He jerks off pretty well, while continually examining the tip with a look of curiosity, as if something that he's never seen before were going to spurt out of it: pink sperm, a tiny snake, a shower of gold pieces, mayonnaise, jumping trout, a brood of mousies.

Secretive as he is, I'm amazed that he doesn't avoid me when we're outside. One time I even saw him with one of the girls he knows; they were on bicycles and riding gently down a street bordered with orange trees covered with fruit. I didn't linger, I'm too compromising for a young boy engaged in a come-on; but I was wrong: Diego tried to catch my eye, and as soon as he saw that I'd seen, he smiled, shouted a hello, waved his hand. An imprudent kind of loyalty (or, if he simply wanted to show me his conquest, vanity). I don't know what he could have said to the girl; in the new city all of them know about this kind of relations and spurn or reject boys with a reputation—even if it's false—of engaging in them. No question of being suspected of having a sexual imagination, if you want to be authorized by these ferocious victims of the male order; they impose their lifestyle with blind intransigence, something most boys managed without. And if you asked these future male chauvinists where the obligation to be orthodox comes from, in good faith they'd point to those kindly and merciless virgins, not to their parents or the law.

It's thanks to the queers that the penniless suitors of these "copettes" are able to invite them to the movies, pander to them, offer them treats, something to eat and drink at quality cafés, a walk in the country, English cigarettes, trinkets of jewelry, a little record with songs. Such an afternoon of next to nothing represents, at their age and in this city, seven or eight days of salary. Which already allows these girls to skim off the best from their lady-killers. Boys like Diego, school kids from poor families, ought not be able to approach females—except for a few francs for old whores with the faces of abortionists. This, then, is how he distributes my generous sums: first to dress spiffy, then to court little chicks who aren't turned on enough by his sweet little button face. Since he never asks for anything, I put my donations in his pocket, whether we have sex or not. Solidarity of the sexually exploited. He regularly tells me about the flirtations it has allowed.

He only spoke to me about money once; he wanted to buy a bike. He shows me his savings, in five-franc bills, which he again counts. He's in a very good mood, thrilled to have saved all that. He doesn't dare suggest that I add to it (he needs twice the sum). I don't offer it, either. We change the topic of conversation, and take care of my vice. Then, just as Diego wants to leave, I tell him that I need his bills (which is true, because such change comes in handy on the street), and I buy them back from him, using a daddy-style rate of exchange: each for a ten-franc bill. I don't have enough of the ten-franc bills. So then I buy them back, as well as the five-franc ones that are left over. Diego leaves with funds in good shape. But now I possess this bundle of five-franc bills, some old, some new, some wrinkled or smooth. I'm happy about it. I usually never end up with something belonging to the boys. And if the rate of exchange seems ridiculous, it wasn't entirely: I really have purchased those bills that were accumulating over a long period in Diego's trousers, just as I purchase what his underpants contain.

Buying, as I've already explained enough times, is a uselessly unjust and spiteful word. It's part of a futile form of bitterness. But in the long-ago time when it happened (as my awkward rate of exchange shows), I hadn't yet revised my money system. With that as well, it wouldn't be the Diegos who'd help me do it, but all my rascals with their clipped heads, fidgety pricks and blackened rags.

My progressive inconsiderateness toward Diego. The way I speak to him is barely friendly, I'm selfish in bed, have bad moods; space out the dates far apart, make him clean what he dirties, cook what he eats; I'm not welcoming if he comes over without warning. I'm tired of him. A funny situation occurs when, out of money and waiting for some to be sent, I explain to him that he doesn't need to come over, because I won't be able to give him anything for about two weeks. Advice that he listens to gravely and follows to the letter. Pedro, his little brother, will behave the same way. They'll reappear at the opportune moment. It's not greed on their part, but, yet again, lack of imagination.

They're efficient in the way they spend their time with me. Eating, drinking, smoking, hanging out, talking as little as possible, grooming, furnishing me with their nudity, taking off; the part of this schedule that's devoted to me is minimal. In the long run, it bothers me. I was hoping that our fucking would produce a little intimacy. That's not their concern. Pedro's visits remain unchangeably brief and cold; Diego's, moderately civil.

A cycle that's almost mechanical. I fill the refrigerator, cut the fruits, clean the bathroom, make the bed; they come as arranged, empty the refrigerator and the fruit bowl, take a bath; we go to bed, carry out procedures that are tolerable and then get dressed; they look to see if there's anything else left to empty, and go. I have the impression that when I take my pants off, it is also one of the duties of the host that I carry out mechanically. Plates bottles soap ass cock money leave, arrange the furniture, remake the bed, clean the bathroom again. Then think about the microscopic variations there are between this visit and the ones before, the way you'd compare several prints of the same photo.

I don't hold it against them, I understand their reasons; but I'm disappointed that, as justifiable as the limits that they impose on our relations are, the weeks and months are accumulating without their strict respect for antihomosexual (antiforeigner, anti-adult?) protocol wavering. It's why I'll pay exaggerated attention to the most modest deviations they deign to carry out.

Once I said to Diego that if he really wasn't going to let me fuck him by our next date, I wouldn't see him any more. He said nothing.

But he comes over and seems to be in a good mood. He's decided to hold onto his place. I enter him from behind. It really hurts too much, he's not used to it, and because the conquest has become stale, there's the risk of prolonging his suffering—I won't shoot my load quickly enough. Besides, I don't even want to. These circumstances don't appeal to me. A silly kind of blackmail, desire that has passed its use-by date. I pull out my cock.

My bad ways have a strange effect upon Diego; I find him softer, friendly, more trusting. You'd think he was waiting to come out of his shell until he knows me better, but that knowing an adult, in his eyes, is merely learning the worst there is to be endured. My roughness reassures him.

One summer night, he had fun locking himself in the bedroom—I no longer remember why. Annoyed that he was prolonging the joke heavy-handedly, under such tiresome conditions, I slapped him as he opened the door. He didn't react in the slightest. We passed the night each on his own side. I'm ashamed of having struck him. And yet, he bore no grudge. Coming from a man, this seems run-of-the-mill to him, ordinary and acceptable. After that, Diego acts friendly and relaxed as never before; he's disinterested, confiding, tender in ways my good behavior was never able to provoke. Maybe he sees me as more normal, more approachable than before the slap, which has put me back in my place.

Subsequently, at the final stage of our relationship, my desire is reignited, and I remind him that in the spring, I'd screwed him. He puts up with our starting again. Same result. The goodwill that he displays proves that his pain isn't faked. Also, my cock can recognize new anuses, which wrap themselves around it, sheath it differently than holes being squeezed together deliberately. Diego seems to be in agony. We try different positions. On hands and knees it goes well enough, and from then on Diego, betrayed by his body, puts on an act. He's evasive and promises that we'll succeed the next time. Then we discuss it: he claims that I'm doing it wrong; I should have pushed it in with one lunge. He also suggests squatting over my belly and impaling himself gradually. These ploys had the effect of increasing the constant involuntary contractions he couldn't get the knack of controlling, which made my careful pressure on his hole more pronounced. But since we have managed to overcome this, because anuses loosen their rigidity once they've been bypassed, provided their owner can stand a minute of moderate pain, Diego's suggestions, I think, have only been aiming to ward off a difficulty that isn't physical.

When it's time for our next date, he remembers his promises, but isn't too keen on keeping them. So, in the bedroom, he suggests I forget about them; in their place, he'll suck me. An unexpected substitution. I thought that disgusted mouths were more insurmountable than resisting anuses; and if I sometimes lay siege to the latter, I don't try to oppose the former. So I'd never asked Diego to suck me, from the moment he told me he didn't want to.

In the end, the bargain suits me. We get into the position for sixty-nine, I'm going to suck him at the same time and devour his asshole; I eat cocks at both ends, swallowing the balls on the way. He gets very hard. And he really sucks. Is it because he's coming to the rescue of his anus? He goes down on my prick with conviction and dexterous lips, a warm tongue that amazes me. And he gulps it all the way into his throat. His penchant for imitation must be responsible for it: he kisses like I do, he'll suck like I do. He even copies my small strokings of his anus, testicles, the hollow of his thighs. When I lick his hole, his mouth stops cautiously near mine and grazes the edges; the limit of his copying.

I wondered why he didn't know how to kiss, since he went with girls. Then I found out that the practice of French kissing was not very widespread for such flirtations; they kissed, pecked each other's faces, but no tongues. The kisses seen at the movies changed nothing. It was the queers who spread the new ways of doing it—through the boys. Those poor girlfriends.

Nothing came after sixty-nine with Diego; I went back to France a few days later, and our relations in the bedroom wouldn't start up again. When I got back, I sometimes saw Diego in the street, and (except for the night of pilgrimage that I've described, during which our pleasures were perfunctory) I lost my desire to invite him over. Now that he's seventeen and his family has left the city, his life is better. He's free to do what he wants, he travels here regularly, where he uses his talents superbly: a foreigner, a hairdresser for ladies, takes him to bed, feeds him, dresses him, styles his hair. His prosperity is a pleasure to see. His hair, less so; the hairdresser realized a secret dream of Diego by making his hair blonder. The unusual shades have vanished; now he's an insipid blond, and it looks vulgar, like a salesgirl on her night out. The work is perfect, the hair stylish, but it's a shopkeeper ideal. Diego no longer has any real hair.

I prefer that long-ago spring when the *monster's* timid friend came to my place. After the bath, I cut his toenails. If I touched his limp member, he'd push back my hand and murmur, "It's sleeping!"

I liked to see him sitting in the middle of the bed. I'd gently spread apart his legs so that the best part hidden by his thighs would appear. I'd bury my face in it. Diego, embarrassed, would laugh. I took a piece of broken mirror, a big triangle, from the closet. Placed it between his thighs and showed him what I was admiring, so that he could appreciate these secret wonders himself. He doesn't look away; his cock rises a little; he studies his crotch with a hint of squinting fascination: his nice set of balls with their delicate parallel creases, the plump little half-moons that cup the hole and that the underside of the buttocks form under the top of his thighs, the ingenuous luminosity of this youthful landscape with the fullness of drowsy cheeks.

At the time, Diego had the odd habit of asking me about all that was being used or consumed (a can opener, lighter, some cheese, tissues, beer, a pen, a fork, aspirin, a map of the city, some chocolate, a grill for meat, shaving cream): "How much does that cost?"

His tone of voice was dull, flat, without curiosity. But the question was indefatigable. I'd answer. His features betrayed no reaction. A nod of the head and his slightly lowered eyes stared at nothing: he had to learn my answer by heart. In this way, he built a strange catalogue of household items. Usually, the figure wasn't enough for him and he'd immediately ask another question: "Is that a lot?"

As if a price didn't indicate the worth of an object—or rather, as if Diego wanted to know both the price of things at the home of people he thought were rich and the opinion that the rich people themselves have of these prices. In the same way that if I heard a man tell about how he had lost one hundred million in the stock market, I might ask him: "Is that very much?" all the while knowing as well as can be what a sum like that would mean to me if I had it. The strange thing was that Diego had that attitude about the most available products, and was determined to know if it was "expensive" or not that a newspaper cost one franc.

I started to become disappointed when something new, a canned food, an illustrated brochure, eau de cologne, didn't inspire the famous question and he'd eat one, thumb through another, put on some of the last without asking how much they cost. His questions seemed to be the expression of a private preoccupation but stemmed instead from a lack of finding what to say, or because an object that he hadn't noticed before suddenly attracted his attention. For example, there was a low pinewood table in one of the rooms; Diego used it for dozens of days before finally asking me how much it cost. I didn't know. I told him that it was a low-priced piece of junk, like everything in this furnished place. He nodded, memorized *low-priced piece of junk*, but he seemed convinced of the opposite.

Now he no longer goes to school. He kept repeating years he'd repeated. His hairdresser was maybe going to take him on as an apprentice. An unhoped-for turn of events. I don't think Franceso will get out of his situation that well. At the beginning, Diego wanted to be a movie actor, in other words, a millionaire. And he wanted to go north, to France, for example. A few months after that, his ambition didn't go any farther than wanting a job with the railroads. And France? It rains too much, snows all year, he's been told. I was almost worried about his becoming so reasonable.

Thus, it's his hair that will have chosen his profession, not he. It isn't the worst guide you might have to worry about. Diego doesn't speak much about such a future, which pleases him immensely; he has hopes concerning his hairdresser, but he doesn't really trust him yet.

Strange hairdresser. Because today Diego doesn't know him. In his old photos you see the sudden emergence of this man. Diego wasn't yet fifteen. Up to that point, he'd worn his hair short and shaggy, boyish and charming, on a kisser to die for. The man added a Joan of Arc hairstyle, and with early adolescence helping, Diego's face would darken as a result, look anxious, sensual, intelligent, wonderful. These photos made me sorry I hadn't come along a year earlier.

His fear of parents prevented the hairdresser from going too far with his art. Even with his father gone, Diego may have combed his hair less childishly, but didn't touch the color. There are battles with Mom. I saw an episode of that when, at the end of that summer, Diego came over with short, mutilated, atrocious, rural-looking hair; his mother had made use of the scissors during the night. I already knew he was a heavy sleeper. When I would go to sleep long after him, I'd discover his cock hard and it would seem bigger to me than when he was awake. The savagery of this cudgel sticking straight up from a dozing body. Roused, I'd sit on it, drive it all the way to the navel and jerk off. That only woke him up one time; I had started to do it too soon after he fell asleep which I figured had occurred as soon as his member had slowly stiffened. He showed that he had woken up by rocking his hips; given the depths to which I'd lodged his cock, he was tearing at my intestines and we readjusted our position. But my initiative had been well rewarded. There was really not one boy here whom I awakened to have sex who didn't go in for it immediately—with an eagerness that often made these sessions of sleepy-time sex warmer and more passionate than the others. I was caressed, embraced, kissed more. Obsolete sensations, touchingly long ago. In the morning they awoke and were just as noticeably kind, cheerful, benevolent, sylphlike. Those times with Diego were delightful.

His mother's short haircut accentuated Diego's boxer's mug. The way he held his shoulders, arms, his funny faces adapted to it. This little tough was completely new, and I caved in. One more obsolescence. Cemetery of decomposed myths, I haven't finished visiting it, the world changes more quickly than faces that have given up on it. What Diego's mother did hadn't angered him; he was laughing about it, hardly embarrassed at having been made ugly. He felt that he'd been deprived of a treasure, a flattering symbol, a privilege.

But in the end he won that battle of the hair; or rather, his hairdresser and his bleaches vanquished Diego himself. For two years or more, the man waited for his time to come, keeping his eye on that hair the way you would lie in wait for the chance to take someone's virginity; and when he finally poured his concoctions on Diego's ambers, honeys, tawny-brown and golds, and used his scissors, brush and hairdryer to change it into a helmet of yellowed paper, it was like a marriage ceremony. I find it odd, in fact, that Diego's clothes, resources were so meager when I knew him, whereas he had been fucking that oxygenator for more than a year. And, in fact, it's significant that the man waited for the kid's mother to cede all power over Diego's mop—and over everything else, besides—before he could treat him better, move him in, dress him and instruct him.

I had asked Diego if he'd go on frequenting men for a long time. Two years, he says, until I'm eighteen. An urgent date. He explains that if he goes beyond it, he'll like it too much and become gay. I answer that if he likes it, I don't see any problem. True, he says, but it's looked at badly. He has no other objection; he himself doesn't want to adopt such a lifestyle, but he's indifferent about others leading it. He never used the word queer when he was talking about those he'd been with—which is the opposite of Francesco, who wreaks revenge on the discrimination to which he's subjected by using irony, gossip and insults to condemn queers who don't have the ability to obfuscate like he does; and for the same reason, he praises hetero values to the skies, another low trick of which Diego is innocent. My question was obviously meant to get an idea of his opinion about homosexuality. But he had absolutely no thoughts about it; it's badly looked upon and he didn't want to be badly looked upon, that's what determined his choice, which had nothing to do with personal preference, but only with public opinion. Not one word about the physical attractiveness of boys compared to girls. The fateful limit of eighteen will protect Diego from the risk of having a shameful sexuality; so what he does before that has no importance, means nothing, does not at all determine an orientation. A sensible kind of magic.

Diego attracts a following of gays of his age. Andrès meets him at my place, showers him with awed praise, always in that bemused tone he uses, and will form a slight connection with him. I'll often get news about one from the other. In this social context, their having sex together is unthinkable; their fear of others' words prevents them. Indiscretion and mockery seemed to be the most effective pillars of the law. They indicated the value of those who abided by it and those who stood up for it.

However, the tone of the two boys is risqué one afternoon in my apartment. Seated next to each other, they display their cocks. Diego's indecency, satisfaction, laughter. More embarrassed—or more excited—Andrès doesn't get hard; he gives it the old shake-a-rooney and manages to show it to its advantage (according to his notion of what gives a human being an advantage).

Out of solidarity, Diego had given my address to some of his friends at school. I had unexpected visits from his friends. There are none that I'll want.

Yes, there were some exceptions. A foolish boy of fifteen with a round face gave me a boost. He was bothering me, I let him in, but I acted like he wasn't there. I would have happily tricked with him. It's a delicate thing to explain, without defaming Diego: his group of friends would think that I was porking him if I porked one of the others. I tell the lad that Diego fucks me, but that he's enough when it comes to tops who do that to me; if I invite another boy to bed, it will be to fuck him. He clucked inanely. *Fuck him*! On another day he came back for money and claimed he'd do it. I had some dates that were more attractive, and I ignored him. I go to pee, he follows me, gives my cock an eager glance, jokes. He really is moon-faced. A moment after, I change my clothes. He feels me up, puts his arms around me, kisses me. Pooh. A few days later, at noon, I make up my mind to fuck him. We do it standing up. He's irritating, a quibbler, awkward, good for nothing, and I fuck him brutally. He has the same sticky ways as Andrès, but a thousand times more imbecilic. I learned that, after this, a foreigner took him to Switzerland for several months and that he came back as round as a wobbly toy.

But the boys around here whose job is to be shagged are invariably insufferable. I'm fucking another of Diego's friends. He's sixteen, isn't ugly, has a pretty body, a nice cock, perfect butt. Talkative and trivial beyond imagination. We do sixty-nine, because he sucks like there's no tomorrow. I get closer to his hole, and I see that it's completely circled by bunches of small warts, very densely, like a ring with two rows of pearls. This atrocity nauseates me, and it intensifies my hostility about his stupidity. I pull away politely. But he sleeps with me. He's very surprised that I don't fuck him. I paid him in advance. While I'm showering, for something to do, he's writing a short letter expressing his delight about being rich (he's happy about the amount) and about having sex with a Frenchman. Actually, it's several letters—some sketches, each of which starts with his name and address and is repeated on the same sheet of paper. It isn't meant for me to read, but he'll forget to take the paper and leave it on my table.

He's one of the rare young boys who don't hide their homosexuality. Instead he boasts about his classy relations, and to hear him talk, there's no one in the city, or even the country, who hasn't had him. The little balls on his anus must be used to count them, like an abacus.

In bed, in the darkness, he twists and turns, can't fall asleep. I ask him what's wrong. He says that he's bothered by my not having done it. I should have. I touch him, he gets hard. I explain that I've drunk too much to fuck, and without asking, I sit on his member. I splatter him with come, and I shit out his cock before he comes. He jerks off; and during it, his face has a horrible grimace, you'd think his head was being boned, the flesh pulled flat and furrowed in front like the edge of a chair being crushed by a rump.

The experience doesn't calm him. He begins twisting and turning again. I ask him what the matter is. He says, really, it's not normal that I won't do that to him. I repeat that I drank too much. The opposite is true—and goaded by pride, I swallow a glass of whiskey. Around ten minutes go by. Languor. I'm not thinking about the pearls any more. Against me are lovely buttocks, soft skin. I go inside him, cover him completely. Ah, he's content. His hole is nice, alive, tense. He lets me pound him very hard, and I come quickly. When I lie back down next to him, he's all smiles and caresses me as if I were a good dog who'd finally retrieved a ball. Nevertheless, the next morning, he'll insist again that it isn't normal that I only did it to him once. He thinks I'm impotent in some way; he's not wrong, I am.

There are certain minute faults of flesh or word I cannot deal with. Others, it's true, don't bother me, whereas boys who are more wholesome than me abhor such things. A lot of worthy fags flee partners who are laughers, jokers, sarcastic, boisterous, brusque or selfish—qualities I venerate. I myself flee those who are sentimental, altruistic, virtuous, speakers of fine words, demanding. Body hair, especially on the buttocks, thighs and stomach, disgusts me. But I had very lustful sex with, for example, a poor panhandler whose hand had been cut off, and who was far from attractive and very dirty, at the back of a vacant lot where we trod on shit. I'm no fan of either shit or filth or infirmities; my cock, however, doesn't care. On the other hand, I sometimes go soft with interesting, adorable, well-brought-up young people, whose only failing is a verbal stink, whether petit bourgeois or not, that asphyxiates me like a Turkish toilet into which my brain has been dumped just like Ubu's conscience in its nightshirt. Therefore, chance has constructed me all wrong; the loftiest signs of masculine, intellectual, civic, conjugal, bourgeois and revolutionary value dispirit me, and atrocious imperfections are my delight. I made a commitment to that helplessness that can't be cured, to that pathological vulnerability (which explains, if not justifies, the flaws in my private life), and I try to couple only with headless monsters. But you're never very sure about it, and there are mental riches that only reveal themselves between the sheets. As for my current cause of unhappiness, I don't dare have the spitefulness to talk to him about those anal pearls, or about his amusing prattle. Having strung that alliance, even when I was anesthetized, seems like heroism that I won't be able to accomplish again. And when he suggests we hook up once more, I say that I'm an unrepentant cruiser—which isn't true these days since I've been copulating faithfully with the same three or four boys month after month, without looking for new adventures and while accepting only a very few who solicit my reluctance.

In addition to Diego's friends, I got visitors that no one was sending. They don't lock their doors here; going into the homes of strangers, having them over, is as simple as being approached outside. Everybody needs everybody, so it's no big deal for two humans to speak to each other without having to put an ad in the personals section of the left-wing papers.

Someone knocks, asks if X is there, I answer that X doesn't live here, our expressions show only mild surprise; if the boy's looks appeal to me, I invite him in, and if mine are OK by him, he accepts. If not, since X isn't there, you can get out of it without a fuss.

To figure out where to go, the boys simply head for the addresses of the furnished places, where they know that there are a lot of foreign transients; among the inhabitants of the city, homosexuality adopts clandestine styles; whereas with foreigners, all of whom are thought to be queens, you take care of business outspokenly.

I got very little from this door-to-door marketing. I had too many boyfriends, and the apartment was almost always occupied. And if it wasn't, not only did I prefer to go out and hunt then to be cruised at home, I also had available hardly any more sperm for these spontaneous partners. Lovely faces, decent youths, shy schoolboys appeared right under my nose in that way.

There was a student of eighteen or twenty who was more like a satyr than a sales rep. He fucked anybody who had a rear, but he preferred boys. Francesco, to whom I pointed him out in the street, said he was a bastard and a notorious nut that everybody avoided. He was a bit thin, of average height, had a tough, pleasant-enough face, and his method for finding tail was ideally simple. One day, there's a knock at my door, I open it, it's him (I don't know a thing about him, and, obviously, I got my information afterwards). He asks if he can speak to me. I can guess what kind of conversation interests him, and I don't feel very talkative; I answer coldly and shut the door. A moment goes by and there's knocking again. I open the door. It's him. He asks outright if I'd like to have sex; he's standing a little back from the threshold, and his fly is open. Hanging out of it is a large, pink member, as thick and long as a forearm, really enormous and as visually appealing as can be. I tell him I don't like that. And I'll say no three times like that to this well-endowed god, meaning: I'd like to a lot, but I can't imagine what to do with a cock like that, belonging to a man who doesn't seem that manageable. I close the door. Another knock. The boy is standing close to me now. To tempt me more, he quotes a price—very low. I deny a second time that such a thing interests me; but my hungry look denies nothing at all. Door closed, a knock, door opened. And since he never stops exhibiting his masterpiece, I find it cunning to hand him the money he wants; he takes it and, shaking his cock, murmurs, "So, that's a yes?"

Third rejection. The cock isn't crowing; he's too perplexed by this customer who pays without consuming, buys some masses and pushes away the priests and the deity. But I react the same way with certain children in the street who offer postcards, chewing gum. I don't need any, but I give them the amount they asked for. They're happy, since if they sell what they have, the benefit is insignificant, and doubtlessly for the profit of an adult. This money will be for them alone. But my door-to-door salesman is more interested in unloading his merchandise than in getting a good price for it. At least he stops insisting once he's paid. I'm alone now; I take a few moments to jerk off while thinking about all of it.

I'll find out later that he's discovered a place for his enormous rod; it's a man who lives below me; round, bald, big-butted, grandpa-like, with an ostrich-egg head. This sexagenarian's abilities amaze me. I always feel like a mediocre kid playing doctor when I think of what a homosexual worthy of his forbears is capable of taking. But between now and sixty, I won't lose hope in imitating such far-reaching examples, and of using ten- or twelve-inch cocks in ways other than in my imagination. I have several degenerate objectives of this kind that add discipline to my life.

There's a happy age when (just like other old folks who no longer wake up except to eat, talk about unappetizing food, and drool on their bedroom slippers for the ten thousandth roast or ragout or even just the boiled lump they've caught a whiff of) you remain attached only to small, ravenous cores of pleasure that are dense, concrete, well-worn and sturdy. In fact, indifferent to the beauty or personality of a boy, you're content with appreciating his strong cock and powerful erections; you wolf it down like the aged gobble up éclairs, coffee cake, cream puffs, and having experienced the easy release that such stimulation favors, sit back and wait for it to be time for dinner. Boys like my door-to-door salesman are perfect partners for the old; I know a lot of young people whom I wouldn't go near today, and whose look-alikes will be my lovers tomorrow.

Francesco was willingly imagining his old age and mimicking it. He pretended to be skinny, dried up and stiff, with a cane. He saw himself as married, a patriarch. He says that on his deathbed, he'd summon his oldest son and tell him, "I'm going to die, go get me a boy. A *very* pretty one!"

The son obeys, the very pretty boy is there, and Francesco demands, "Fuck me."

He shows him his buttocks. The boy takes out his member, looks at that old tail and shouts, "How am I supposed to screw you? You don't even have any more meat on your ass!"

"Fuck me!" orders Francesco. The boy does it. And, says Francesco, my hole is so big, so wide that it's as if he's screwing the wind. After that, Francesco as an old man turns around and fucks the respectful boy. Then he dies, surrounded by his sons.

Such a nice way of imagining old age coincides with mine. Aging doesn't cause me any apprehension, and I'm shocked, in France, to meet so many adolescents, young people, for whom being twenty-five or thirty means falling into a decline to the extent that some of them, when they think about such a future, simply say, I'll knife myself.

But they won't kill themselves. Their scorn for other ages will have only prepared them for becoming anything at all when their turn comes. To submit to everything, to make do with any intellectual, religious or social servility, any kind of conformism at all, to endure any kind of defeat; and this is how they'll become exactly what they hate today in those who are older. Knife themselves? They'll be dead people, yes, but the kind that smell bad.

I have the inclination and the need to connect to all the ages of my life, past or future. From my childhood until today, I don't see those sections, those famous stages, that all normal men go through, each time denying and forgetting the age that came before. I slip inside myself as if along a river that you can travel up- or downstream; I rediscover and am in harmony with myself wherever I am. As for old age, I was very unhappy at the beginning of adolescence because two-thirds of life seemed to be spent in withering and dying (real death was nothing but an insignificant corporal formality at the end of another interminable death). I'd send feelers, images, in the direction of these future years. And it is only when I was able to live, to feel, for example, like an old queer sucking off brats (and had foreseen, worked out what I would be in that situation, as well as an infinite number of others) that I finally began to live what was left of my youth without too much apprehension. Such fancies certainly have little to do with what I'll experience; but they take in hand the difficulties of the future, sketch out the tactics I'll use to survive there as I do elsewhere.

My movements toward childhood are favored by my having chosen everything I like, everything I do, everything I will continue to do from the beginning. My first literary scribbling (which wasn't obscene) dates to when I was seven. Then a lot of plagiarisms, then nothing at all; then, around the age of thirteen, this began to increase. I was very secretive, and anything others found out about filled me with shame. As for boys, my first butt-fucking sessions date to age nine or ten. First of all, I got raped by a kid who was at least a year younger than me. We would jerk off together often. One time, he suggests I put mine in his hole. I angrily refuse, reel off all the objections. But a few moments later, I was lying on top of him blissfully and was deep inside. He gave it back to me right away. My immoderate taste for music, the kind that annoys, is even older; but the start of practicing it actively also dates from the age of nine or ten. As do a multitude of other pleasures, curiosities, behaviors, sensibilities, reactions, fascinations, follies. Let evil tongues decide whether I developed too early, or if I've remained undeveloped to this day. The two are similar, because a life that is constructed early on includes those things that children don't want to eliminate from their lives but that must be renounced, apparently, in order to mature in a true sense. How I envy genuine adults, who polish their vestigial stumps every Sunday.

I took to music like bread, played it ceaselessly. In the past I even pretended to write it (especially some pathetic twelve-tone scores), like a kid plays at being a doctor, a grocer, a Picasso; I know that people are musicians by profession even if they don't do any more of it, but this doesn't console me very much.

The majority of our contemporaries feel glum and foggy, stunned into silence, when they endure that obscure art. Then there's the blathering, stupid, clammy and smug superstitions of the competent music lovers and other discophiles. When all is taken into account, I prefer the company of the deaf to that of lovers of sounds, just as I never dislike an illiterate, whereas my threshold for enduring literary types is low. But it's useless for me to get worked up over subjects as depressing as this. Once, in Paris, I found a mass by Palestrina that I didn't know, because it was so infrequently recorded; I forget that such music is aggressively exotic for the average buyer of industrial noise, and when I met a friendly apprentice baker an hour later and brought him home, I could neither put off listening to the work nor having sex with the kid. He was kind of tall and robust, excited about men's cocks. He was shy and wanted the light turned off. I didn't. He came up with a compromise: light those candles, over there. We fucked, the boy relaxed with me beside him, the candles burning, the mass playing.

"It's like a funeral," murmurs the kid. But it amuses him, he dozes off, doesn't ask for any other record, he enjoys being dead. The two of us, naked and unmoving, lying on this bed like two recumbent statues. Polyphonic music is no longer associated with pleasure. When I was aware of the situation that had been created, it wasn't its funereal aspect that shocked me but its aestheticism. Getting off with masses while doing it with a baker's boy in an apartment with veiled light, jeez, how degenerate. (A German choir of young boys to boot, boobless sopranos.) Doing it on purpose would already be ridiculous, but, involuntarily, it really takes the cake.

First wrinkles and hair loss; wizening; the crumpled, veiny pudginess of my declining cock, beginning of my first infirmities (severe rheumatism in my ribs): I've already been carrying around these stigmata of aging for a long time, have been forming them inside me. But I'm still ahead of the worst, don't get to any age without having arranged my place in it. That's why I feel OK about it and don't make pronouncements about the years depriving me of whatever it may be. I like life too much to refuse an hour of it, no matter how sad it may feel. I'm oversensitive to every annoyance, but if they can't be avoided, I soon grow comfortable with them and am struck by impressions and feelings that are stronger than they were in the state before, I explore them the way others "take a trip" with a hit of drugs (except that the drugs are used to escape the very places where I put down roots). That's also the way I adapt to illness, inhabiting my fevers and leaving them regretfully to regain the platitudes of health.

The boys here who are accepting of queers often have peculiarities like those of the kid with anal warts. Subjected as they are to a rigid system of popular values, they need to have been made to feel inferior before becoming resigned as well to the social censure awaiting recognized homosexuals—something a person like Diego, who finds great prestige in the code, refuses to do, despite the fact that he's capable of becoming the most genuine of queers; he just has too much to lose.

I find a boy who's beautiful, very warm, very civil, extremely attracted to men, whose large cock, unfortunately, suffers from hypospadias (meaning that the opening of the urethra, instead of being positioned in the center of the head of the penis, is located on its underside). Another, whom I fuck on a dark street, has phimosis. He didn't even lower his underpants as far as the stomach; he wouldn't let me jerk him off and left without coming. Another couldn't shoot during the three or four hours in bed we spent together. Another had only one testicle. Another, a handsome, strapping little fellow, gets fucked by anyone; he can't get a hard-on. And so on. I understand why there was a medical legend going around that claimed that homosexuals "lapse" into such a lifestyle as the result of a physical defect. It actually could be that such was the case in the past, when the social context had burdens, pressures, drainage systems, lines of flight that were different from today's. Nowadays it's easier to hide sexual infirmities if you're straight, by marrying a virgin, by adopting rigid principles. Among queers, on the other hand, ways of doing things are so crude that the slightest defect in an organ exposes you to horrendous humiliations. And the wholesomeness of flies and backsides that subscribe to a conscious homosexuality in French places where cruising goes on is a sign of the insane intransigence of the reigning values. Those in a sorry state will only be able to take cover in Catholic, Arcadian, right-of-center homosexuality, or on the side of the vicious heteros of the patriarchy. Meanwhile, working-class homosexuality over here remains a refuge.

One evening, I come back from having a lewd time. A long, lovely walk to my place—the old city now. A bicyclist keeps following me. He passes me, looks at me, keeps going, comes back, passes me. It's annoying, I finally come up to him and, in a harsh tone, ask him what he's looking for. He was already smiling. If I hadn't had sex before, I would have been more polite, because he isn't unattractive. He's terribly taken aback by my aggressive question (something boys who don't like boys never do). He disappears, murmuring an excuse.

Another night, another cyclist, same circumstances. He's probably about twenty. I'm even more worn out than the time before. But I'd like to get fucked good, it's missing from my evening. I figure this follower is one of those monstrous perverts who hangs out in the streets at night, and brings down weak men with his dangerous, pestering glances. After almost a mile, I slip into a perpendicular street and wait. The bicycle joins me in the shadows. The boy is relatively appetizing. But for the only fantasy that's tempting me, I want some low-down information. So I explain to the boy that when a man's cock is larger than mine, he's the one who does the fucking; and if his cock is smaller, I fuck him. Such insane talk doesn't surprise the boy. But he makes me repeat myself two or three times. So, he stresses, with a dejected expression, if the other person's cock is smaller than yours, you fuck him? And is yours big? I say that it is—but we don't show each other anything. He hesitates, fiddles with his brakes, his handlebars, then, with a sheepish voice, suggests, "So … you do it to me?"

Horribly disappointed, eyeing his fly to figure out, despite everything, whether it might be redeemable, I tell the boy that I was explaining my principles; but as for their application, I'm too tired, it's late.

These situations always bother me. I'm bad at getting out of them. I'd enjoyed the cyclist's naïve behavior; but the image that I've gradually created of the young homosexuals in the city make me sick.

In a park in the afternoon, I'd chatted with a teenager who was completely different than my nighttime cruiser. We were standing, cocks exposed to the air, and his member was cute and brown. He took hold of mine politely (he doesn't like boys), and with a thrilled smile and widened eyes, declared, "*Ours* is so big! You people, *yours* is so small!"

My cock, which he was touching, could have served as a case for three like his, but that didn't count; the general truth that he was pronouncing, very widespread among these boys, put things in their proper place, and the dimensions of his member or mine became exceptions to it that confirmed the obvious truth of the law. I quickly agreed. I was worried that, unconsciously humiliated, he had flung back his truth at me to produce a bit of a smokescreen and mitigate what he considered a confrontation. My acceptance of what he said pleased him, and he jerked me off with great goodwill. In any case, he wasn't the one that the reasoning I'd insisted upon for the cyclist would have compelled to offer me his butt.

Speaking of which, I haven't yet noticed that the males of one country have, on the average, a more developed penis than the males of another. It isn't, I should add, impossible, but I'm not the kind of person to draw universal conclusions from several random experiences. It's significant, at the least, that the clichés, the images we have of the peoples of the earth invariably include ideas about their rods. Apparently, monkeys are less attentive to these differences in phallic value (or of tail length, among those who have that fifth or sixth member) among species, packs or tribes. Animal stupidity, no doubt. I don't mix with them: first of all, they have such scrawny dicks, you can easily see that they aren't *sapiens*.

I was hanging out at an old square with a number of outdoor stands. A lot of them were open evenings, and the stalls selling fast food were open part of the night: there's a bus station where travelers stock up. I knew an eighteen-year-old boy who worked alone in a clothing store. But I didn't want to have sex with him. His boss wouldn't let him close before midnight. He'd obey, but there was never a customer. Nice-looking, sweet, mild-mannered, reserved, generous (despite his lousy salary, he'd offer me something to drink, smoke or snack on); I enjoyed his company. We went to the very end of the stall and lay on the ground on top of a bed of rags, old clothes, cushions, goat skins. We talked. Easygoing, relaxed evenings, with no ulterior motive. I was delighted that these relations were so different than those I was forming elsewhere. They made me as happy as a lot of my dissolute pleasures, though it's true that I didn't have to give up one for the other.

The boy asks me if I'm thinking about marrying. I say no. He says me neither. He says that he doesn't like girls. I ask why. His answer is vague, he has nothing against them that he can see. In such prudent language, one negation is worth one affirmation. Who wants to understand will.

When I was leaving the shop at closing time, he went with me for a moment—and without daring to say it, he would have liked to follow me longer. But I was dying for sleep (it was during a period when I was getting up early). One evening, however, he closes at eight, and I invite him to dinner, then to my place. He's happy, very well behaved, more formal than in his shop. His life is sensible; he gets up at dawn, goes to lift weights in a gym, takes care of himself, opens the shop, works and eats there, closes the shop and goes to bed. He has few friends, doesn't speak much, doesn't wave in customers, spends nothing, dresses properly in very masculine jeans, wears the insignia of the pacifists hanging from his neck and is waiting to do his army service. He bought the insignia, made of a metal openwork design on a black cord, without knowing what it represented. He has no family in this city, lives with the family of a friend. His melancholy tone, subdued voice, shy amiability match his situation. He shows me photos of him with his brawny companions from the gym; his face looks so handsome that I don't recognize him. It was before he was working. Working out hasn't thickened his body, which is magnificent.

I haven't explained my ways to him. With sad bemusement, he speaks about an old man who came to the stand and began nosing around. When the boy tried to find out what he was looking for, the old fellow spun abruptly around and shouted, "No, nothing, nothing … Ah! my love, you're what I want!"

The salesman was sorry, but he wasn't for sale. Disappointed, the old man left without even responding to the kindness of the refusal by making a small purchase, a real one.

The boy's visit to my place continues with perfect propriety. A week later, another dinner, another visit. A storm breaks out, a very violent rainstorm. He asks if it would be possible for him to stay. OK, I say. He takes a shower and comes back almost naked, in ultra-brief weightlifters' shorts, which are obscenely packed. I think that, actually, I'd really like him to fuck me. I'm getting these butterflies in my stomach announcing that my head and behind are in agreement. Such inner harmony doesn't at all procure me the serenity promised for similar cases by those who peddle mental stability. Who's lying?

I still doubt his intentions a little, and by adding a touch of mischievousness, I want to let him make the first move. There we are side by side in the big bed (I claimed I didn't have any sheets for the other, we'd have to sleep together; he keeps his shorts on). Trustworthy and widely separated, like brothers. I mean, not all brothers, but most. The lights go out. I'm smoking in the darkness. From the window, lightning from the storm and the scent of the rain on the garden flood the room.

The boy doesn't move. Except that, sometimes, he turns around with a brief, muffled movement. I'm waiting. I get hard, wet, the end of my cock is like a bib slathered with frothy saliva. It's ready to lubricate holes, it seems. Nature is provident. Go ahead, slut.

About two hours pass. The boy still isn't sleeping. His breathing is quiet. I'm really too hot. I get up, go to the balcony. Big sighs. It's raining. The thunder is far off; beautiful blue flashes of light persist. Behind me, the bedside lamp has been turned on. The boy is having a cigarette. Can't sleep, huh? No, he answers, with an embarrassed smile. I get back in bed. Lights out. I've helped him a bit by touching his forearm, shoulder. My mischievousness doesn't amuse me any more, my anus is in turmoil. I work my hand under the sheet. Feeling up cautiously, for a very long time. Electrified fingertips, an unbelievable sensation. Such slowness restores an old, painful, rending pleasure to me, one I'd forgotten: desire.

The boy is lying on his side, and his back is to me. Round, fleshy, unexaggerated buttocks, well defined. I caress them. He doesn't react. Gently, very gently I lower his shorts. He doesn't react. I touch the crack with my cock. I spread apart the crack and put the head into it. He doesn't react. No movement. So that's really what it was. Oh well, I readapt. I look for the entrance, find it, push, push hard, I'm in. My boy twists around, seizes my neck, kisses me. That contortion obliges me to decork.

We get aroused, enjoy ourselves, he gets flat on his stomach. But his hole is squeezed shut now. He must like rapes. OK, only needs a bit of K-Y, *the ideal lubricant for easy insertion of rectal thermometers (etc.), a widely used lubricating jelly, greaseless, water soluble, sterility guaranteed, contents 2 ounces*; I've never counted the number of fuck sessions that gives, two *ounces*. The boy protests that this is the first time a boy has done this to him. Could be, but it's certainly not the last. His hands folded under his head, he seems very happy. I fuck him boldly; unlike what usually happens, this anus doesn't want to get even; I'd like to jerk him off; he has a thick cock, short and massive, but he won't let me make him come. He goes to church and only drinks water. He doesn't shoot his load. He gets up, goes to the head, comes back dressed (his clothes were in the bathroom) and since the rain has stopped, forgets he was sleeping and leaves. He even refuses the money for a taxi. Smiling, excited, alert, in a hurry to not see me any longer. Sometimes I'll go back to his shop, but the conversations will lack verve. I must fuck badly, or my member is too thin.

I don't have much opportunity to pull a fast one, put a boy in my bed whose intentions I'm not certain of, hide mine. Enticing double game, but one whose conclusion is rarely worthy of the preliminaries. There was one situation, however, in which I kept up my sham right until the end. I still regret it.

Just after dinner, I'd met four boys whose ages ranged from twelve to fifteen or sixteen. They weren't from this city, were spending a few days of vacation with an uncle.

They're decently dressed, two of them have long hair. They seem less rustic or provincial than the average teenager from around here. It's the smallest who interests me. His face pleases me enormously. He laughs, comes on like a little animal, gushes freshness, and his eyes have a hint of flirtatiousness, a minute squint that adds to his high spirits. Already quite tall, well proportioned, twelve princely years with lovely flesh. He's wearing a cowboy hat of thin leather.

I'd like to separate him from the others by walking past him, giving him the eye. The three older boys are attractive, but I only want the youngest. It's the older boys who respond to my advances. I was afraid they'd get rid of me. Here we are chatting, on the sidewalk, then at a café. A friendly conversation. I don't talk about my tastes. They don't make any reference to them, either. Encounters without ulterior motives, as I've explained, are common, motivated only by curiosity, or boredom. I've seated the beautiful child in front of me at the other side of the table. I want to eat him. He is truly a good-looking person, with his dumb eyes, his laughter, his awkward, flippant ways. He says that he has a job in a workshop that makes hats like the one he's wearing. I didn't know about the use of such hats, because nobody wears them, and what they're made of makes them too expensive for children. Except for this one, who makes them. One of the other boys also has a job in a workshop, the others are high school students. The smell of early puberty overwhelms me, those voices, gestures, hair, glistening skin.

The handsomest of the bigger boys eyes my beer, he'd like one but is afraid they won't serve him: only I (and they) see these big guys as big. I announce that I have something to drink at my place and that it isn't far. I'm hoping to bring them together, because the child isn't separable. But they intend to separate him—in the other direction—by sending him back to their house; if not the uncle will be worried. I discuss it, I need the kid also, or no one. I take him by the neck, he slips away, rubs against me, consents, laughs, escapes me; oh I like this, I'm thinking, little beasts like him. I don't come up with any complicated thoughts when I'm not planning to write them down. The boys understand that I'm sticking with their pipsqueak. White cheeks, pink lips, an amber gleam to his neck, colors that merge into a fruity radiance. They decide to send one of the bigger boys to tell the uncle, we'll wait. And I'll starve. But everything is OK, the uncle says yes, the gang goes with me.

They drank hardily, wine, beer, hard stuff. They were polite, fun-loving, talkative, with nothing equivocal about them. I was cruising the kid intensely, and he noticed it, but didn't have the audacity to believe it. And he didn't drink any alcohol. At a certain moment (everybody was already very drunk), I grab him and kiss him hard on the mouth: I'm less patient than I was with the weightlifter. Is it because I'm less afraid of getting socked? His mouth is wet, open, with beautiful, twinkling teeth, big lips. The child pulls away, but not hastily. Another moment and I would have had my prey. We talk about ages, and someone says that he, the little one, still has no hair near his cock. The youngster protests—he has a high, even voice, the smooth, delicate forearm of the beardless. We decide to find out the truth. Suddenly he's unzipped, his belt undone, pants down, being grabbed, tickled, strangled, chuckling and giggling, underpants lowered to his thighs (I wanted to see his tush); and like old ladies with spectacles confirming someone's virginity, we all bend down together over his groin. At first, he looks like a very clean child. In addition, his prick is long for the young age he appears to be. And, at the groin, there are about twenty shiny hairs, curving inward. His pants go back on, and despair sticks in my throat, my jaw, so barren does my mouth feel.

But the child has come out of his ordeal victorious. The chaperones are quieting down. We eat something. He's kind enough to help me cook. I love his manner, his personality so much; and his size; and his tiny big dick; and his round little bottom; and all the rest. I think about it, he has to be separated from the others. One on one, he'll be ready for anything; with all of them around, I'll get nothing out of it, or almost nothing.

It's almost enough for me. There's no other option. It's very late, they stink of alcohol and beg me to keep them at my place for the night. I agree to it. Two of them, especially, are drunk, the one I was saying was handsome (a rather long, oval face, long, black hair that makes him look a bit like Andrès, but more child-like) and another (male face, hard expressions) who intermittently flashes aggressive looks at me. The third one is playing at being the model schoolboy, has been drinking moderately, behaves well, has intelligent, plump, friendly-looking features. I have a large bed and a small one. The three bigger boys will sleep together in the large one, the small one will share the little bed, which is in the other room, with me. No one says a word about that arrangement.

The first incident occurs when the kid goes to bed. He's accepted the dangerous role that his cowardly elders abandoned him to, but he's afraid of being plugged. It's hot; he pretends to be asleep at the edge of the bed and is bare-chested. We were right to take his pants down on the balcony; when he's inside he refuses. We stretch out, turn out the light. If I'd had less to drink, I'd wait for him to fall sleep and I'd do what I could. But after these hours of feeling him up, these teasers and pranks, I can't stand it any longer. I paw his torso and everything that's uncovered, kiss him. He puts up with it. When I touch his belt, he jumps to a standing position and rejoins his buddies.

I go in there, too. The boys in the big bed remind me of the older brothers of Tom Thumb in the ogre's chamber: side by side on their backs, their arms, legs and heads neatly positioned, feet wriggling, figures posed anatomically in their underwear as in the tale by Perrault. The kid's reticence is a bother, somebody has to be sacrificed, there aren't four places in the bed, it's normal that the one given up should be the smallest. But there's nothing they can do. So the one I call the most handsome suggests himself. Such a bargain depresses me. It's back to the little bed.

Darkness, silence. The boy isn't avoiding contact with me—on the contrary. Sick of it, exasperated, I put on a sour face and pretend to sleep. The alcohol helps.

The other isn't sleeping. My snoring is very loud. He touches me, gently shakes one of my shoulders. No danger, I'm terribly sleepy. But the situation is beginning to interest me. He touches me again, and makes up his mind. Since I'm facing him, he moves to the other side of the bed and pushes me to the middle. Positioned three-quarters of the way onto my stomach, I won't be easy to fuck. He looks for my anus, wets his cock and pushes it in. It's quite a small cock. He's a vigorous top, with flexible lower-back muscles and a hard cock. For a moment I would have woken up. Keeping my hands in check is the most difficult.

The boy comes quickly. He gets up and goes back to the other room. Murmuring and low laughter. Endless discussion. And a second boy comes to see me. He explores the field, lies down, then a thick, solid rod pushes into me. But it's an impatient one, the boy moves too much. He slips between my thighs, stays there and shoots a load. He gets up immediately and leaves. A new confab, more smothered laughter. With my finger I catch the sperm that tickles as it dribbles out of me.

The third boy takes his chances with the ogre. Clumsy as the one before, a pointed penis, he sometimes plugs my hole, sometimes misses and kind of spurts—wherever. Leaves.

Until I sleep and, deep inside, laugh more than they did. But a final visitor approaches with a light step: it's the child. He's no longer at all afraid, and his deftness will be different from his elders'. He glides against my back, adroitly finds a way to fit there, despite the uncomfortable position. I feel the end of a penis and a fist, then the fist vanishes and the penis plunges straight in. Forgetting the rules for this kind of thing, the gallant little one presses affectionately against me and caresses me as if I were a big bow-wow, while the wee willy I saw on the balcony stirs inside the viscous hole of come that the big guys have prepared. I can no longer control my feelings of affection, nor my hands. I send an arm behind me and take hold of his behind; the child lets out a cry of surprise, shoots backwards and disappears.

I get up, smoke, wipe myself off, put my pants back on. An uneasy silence in the other room. I have a wicked idea. I enter. They're still lined up on the bed, but Tom Thumb is squeezed next to them. I growl with anger and indignation. I explain to them that I wasn't sleeping: ah, isn't that nice, treating a decent foreigner like this, raping me like a girl or queer; fortunately I was pretending to sleep to see just how far they'd go, ah, I'm wise to you, you gang of dirty pigs. Etc. My little act disconcerts them. Francesco has told me stories about boys who were butt-fucked in their sleep, for the express purpose of making fun of them in the morning. But you don't force your way into holes. My boys exonerate themselves just in case, and each claims that it's another who went in there, then returned a second, third, fourth time. I fiendishly describe the intimate details that these defilers by themselves revealed to me; it's hard for them to keep from laughing and finally they acknowledge their sin. They're going to leave, and anyway, they can't sleep, and the uncle won't be a problem, they've sobered up. They get dressed. The intelligent boy apologizes profusely on behalf of the others.

Someone has pinched a new bathing suit and some sun glasses that were lying around. Meager booty, if I compare it to mine.

I can't get over my disappointment at never having seen that child again.

Then I moved to the old city. Located some distance away from the main highways and intersections, it's a maze of piled-together residences through which cars have a hard time driving, and where the shuttered houses rising from narrow lanes; the squares of sunlight, clouds or night above these walls; the covered arcades and their ceilings of round beams; the asphalt or earthen roads; the recesses, the cul-de-sacs, the descents, the archways, the narrow passageways, the detours; heavy, low doors; strange, ruined arcades; skies dusted red; tufts of plants stirred by breezes—all compose a moving and savage landscape.

I had a lot of trouble finding a lodging hidden away enough. When Francesco was in a bad mood, he claimed I wouldn't be able to; or, if I succeeded, I'd be ostracized. My neighbors would avoid me, no boy would dare enter where I lived, the children would stone my door; people don't like it when you come in and upset their neighborhood. Francesco was lying. He would have preferred me to keep living in the new city and it's fawning dog pounds for johns. He offered to help me look, but he did nothing and collected false information. In the end, as I was about to give up, one of his friends—the affable skirt-chaser—took things in hand and, bringing Francesco with him, found me the place to live that I no longer hoped for, at the very back of a dead-end street.

The neighborhood is poor and opulent looking at the same time, the houses are solid, large, very old, with massive walls; they have big, open-air patios, mezzanines, terraces, tiling that's cool and quiet. You live there in moderate ease. The lifestyle brings to mind the petit bourgeois eighteenth century of the common folk. Even in the evening, the men spend less time in their homes than in the streets around them, corners with fountains where stands are squeezed together—some of them very small, just lean-to's, the others made of a large niche in the street with a counter or stall to stop at. These shops, and their shadow when it's made by the sun, are a rallying place to take a break, have some conversation; boys, children gather around them or sit beside, settling into all of the niches, all the surrounding structures.

At the corner of a street with the lane where my cul-de-sac ends, there is a tobacco stand and, in a deep loggia, a very lowly fruit-seller—who acts so lordly in such a fierce way that I don't dare buy anything from him. He has the sturdy face and the bare neck of an old man from Antiquity, his head shaved, his short half-moon beard white, without a moustache, a big nose, round cheeks, deep wrinkles. A disability keeps him prostrate; a straw mattress in his loggia is enough for him, and he puts his goods almost level with the ground. When I pass, he watches me with a hard face and eyes like hot coals. Few people I've known have intimidated me to such an extent. He is, however, peaceable; all day he pets an orange-haired cat that sleeps on his shoulder, and he has adopted a poor yellowish-white dog with wild eyes that the brats of the neighborhood were torturing; he also lets the boys sit on the edge of his crates to chat. Lying behind a rampart of melons and watermelons, or sometimes, if the sun is mild, on the sidewalk where they've pulled his straw mattress, he makes you think of Diogenes; I get the impression that his pale, moist, sparking, intelligent, circumspect eyes, powerful with contained rage, are reproaching me for the hatefulness and crimes of all of humanity.

Closer to me, opposite a plain-looking chapel, is a bakery. This is where people bring in dough kneaded for cooking, as well as homemade pastry. Set some distance below ground level, it offers the warm, aromatic pit of its door, through which you see, on plank shelves along a wall, the entire row of round loaves. I pass little girls with the bearing of women who hold on their head with one graceful arm a tray covered with a cloth, under which is the bread they're bringing in to cook, and metal sheets with rows of little cakes made of yellow dough. These load-bearers, their hair pulled up coquettishly into a headscarf to expose their neck and its brown ringlets, their small ears delicately pierced with a tiny golden ring, have the incredible softness, the capricious ease, the ravishing, casual, sensible countenances of those who appear in the ancient paintings of Venice.

There are ugly ones, too, but I'll talk about that another time.

The flat is one of the four sides of a large square house, buried in those next to it, with no façade but the narrow, high wall that forms the end of the cul-de-sac. On the ground floor, a door with a knocker; very high up, a small window with a wooden marquee and a forged grill. I push the door, enter with my head lowered, and I'm in a dark corridor that, beyond a bend, joins the patio and the landlord's house. I'm not going that far. I open a second door at the entrance of this corridor, go through it, close it: this is where I live. First there's a staircase lit by a window looking onto an adjacent property; you're blinded by it halfway up if you've come out of the shade. Above, three rooms in a row. Very old, and perhaps built for a bourgeois or merchant of the past who wanted a flat with some pomp (since the rest of the house is ordinary), these rooms are laid out like those of an old palace. One has the little window with the marquee that overlooks the cul-de-sac, the others have larger windows that overlook the patio. The top of the walls are decorated with ornamental paneling and stucco; the high ceilings, covered with illuminations, have slender fake beams contained in recessed casing. The encrusted colors of this joinery, its sheen, with figments of brown, gold and greenish. No hallway, the rooms communicate directly; the two on either end are raised a step in relation to the one in the middle, whose extravagant ceiling calls to mind the dome of a chapel; the rain comes in there. Monumental doors, decorated with paintings on both sides. Each of their leaves contains another door that is as large as a child. I thought of Pablos when I saw that, imagined him going through it. They're taller and wider than him, he gets through them easily, whereas I have to slow down and stoop. In the evening, or if it's cold, I close the large doors and only use the little ones; and merely by the rhythm of their steps as they walk from one room to the other, I'd be able to tell the age of my visitors. Little musical doors full of caprice, glidings, a filter for children.

Walls of bare plaster. Decorated wooden cupboards. At the back of my bedroom—a rather narrow room where I write and sleep—behind a pediment of woodwork and color, is a deep alcove with a slightly raised floor and very low ceiling, cut in the shape of a trapezoidal prism and supported by a frieze of innumerable little capitals made of sculpted wood, painted in a floral motif, accentuated along the walls by woodwork with russet illuminations and other finely worked molding. My amateur attempts at sleep, some of which are alcohol-induced (but I only drink in spurts, these days, very spaced apart, because I hate getting drunk alone), my reading, my editing of rough drafts, my jerking off, my sessions of sex, my beautiful visions of bellies, thighs and faces take place on that big bed that this alcove presents like an altar.

With its strong walls, its austere luxury, its windows pierced high in the walls like those of a dungeon, but full of light, this place has a powerful subdued atmosphere, which is striking, welcoming, encompassing.

Then the bathroom, constructed at the back of an adjacent passageway, reduced to a faucet without a drainpipe and a hole for shitting. The flat lacked independence, I was living there with the owner and his family; but the rooms located below mine were junk rooms, while the thickness of the walls cushioned the noises coming from the patio. The bend in the corridor protected the comings and going of the boys below from anyone who might be watching. On the sides, no neighbor could be heard; and in the house, no one was living above the ground floor. The apartment's character, its inconvenience, prevented anyone from sensibly choosing it. I moved into it the day after it was found for me.

I had my suitcase and a bed bought and delivered that afternoon. It was as if I were camping out in a historic chateau after visiting hours; but I wasn't afraid of ghosts. The nocturnal light that fell from the window on the cul-de-sac, the moonbeams and starlight were startling; and, being a ghost myself, I'd wander endlessly in that darkness invaded by shadows and glimmers. Everything seemed immense to me, and mystery created spaces.

It has shrunk, become commonplace since; I see my refuge in its actual size; I've built, measured, explored what's around it. It's no more than three rather small rooms, half broken down, overloaded with décor without artistic value, the kind of thing a new-money storekeeper, a canon with a good stipend or a prosperous madam must dream of; and the day I leave this place for anywhere else, I have no idea whether I'll miss it.

About a month after I moved in, I received some money I'd been given, lent. I had a toilet put in, as well as a shower, hot water, a washbasin, a hotplate, and a few pieces of furniture, some dishes and sheets I'd bought. The rooms were filled in successive stages; now that they have things I can use, they're nice to live in.

What to make of this strange refuge, this piece of the old regime, which you'd imagine as a sanctuary for sophisticated Old-World types, devotees of Sade, vampires from horror stories, the exiled, the living dead? Why this secrecy, these premises, these expenses, debts, this work? I know. But the effect of this place on my life is that it has eviscerated everything from it, and I've given up what I was expecting of it. I have no desire to describe these mental changes, these changes in my actions, desires, plans, ideas. I feel as if this metamorphosis is negligible; it offers only myself to recognize at the end of these incarnations. Naked, empty, paralyzed, but gifted with ease, alacrity, movement.

I never hoped I'd be such a convenient object between my own hands, so uselessly obedient to myself.

Among the crude intentions I had in moving, the most important was having boys stay with me. The kind of thing that required countless ruses for the impoverished people I was encountering when I lived in the new part of the city. Letting one or several of them live close to me. I didn't want to make them captives, I wanted to be a welcome stopover. This was materially, financially, socially impossible.

A preposterous idea, a badly chosen place, a freedom that no one had any need of. My home was only a retreat, a prison perhaps; in the evening, the big and little boys who went with me were full of precautions, whispering, furtive ways, the sharpened attention of convicts who were escaping a fortress; but they were coming to my place.

I'm a bit ashamed in recalling this period, the errors in thinking I was amassing. My horde of kids themselves healed me of it. The way they glided in before disappearing. The way I'd find them so different, so preferable, in the street—schoolboys or panhandlers, almost always fatherless (the others are watched more closely, and have less of a reason to seek adventure). It was in contemplating these flights of birds that I renounced taming any of them.

Now here they come again, these birds; I have writer's tics, you'd say.

Therefore, I won't be hosting any children—no more than I'd know how to be a father, mother or teacher. You aren't taking care of children when you avoid the society to which they passionately desire to belong, or when it avoids you. Not that this is an obstacle that stops those who procreate; the last of the social outcasts produces his brats just like others do. But I don't procreate the children with whom I copulate; as a consequence, I maintain the kind of considerations that parents don't worry about. Stupid considerations; the demand for order and education, norms, butchery, come from the children themselves, from where they're from. Because they want to become as human as us, the monsters.

When I'm older, perhaps, I'll have less scruples than I do. And if my worst tendencies endure obstinately, if I resign myself to everything as I age, I'll take a prisoner and play the father thing for him. Apparently it's normal to welcome that decline as a benediction. But I'll make love with my pupil, and I'll impose a sacrifice on myself that asexual parents don't: I'll prevent him from resembling me. I like my life, I'm committed to it, I prefer to live in my head than in any other; what I am, what I do, however, is no better than the opposite—and has the inconvenience, sometimes palpable, of keeping me apart from everybody. The first duty of human beings, they say, is to be happy. I chose the worst path for achieving that; it's not that I regret it, but I don't dare bring anyone else along with me.

First of all, I'll encourage everything for this child that can render him normal, ordinary. So he'll have the most popular tastes, the blandest leisure activities, the most common reactions; he'll learn to read by deciphering ads in magazines; he'll reflect little and think nothing.

From the youngest age, I'll seat him in front of a television. The rest of the time, I'll put him in the company of his little peers, who, under the influence of respectable adults, will tell him the correct slogans and endow him with an exact awareness of what he should want to be. Whether he becomes sanctimonious or a Communist, a follower of gurus or the rules of calculus makes no difference to me, because he'll be on the right side. Since I won't be capable of restraining myself, I'll at least show him how ridiculous and harmful what I've chosen is. I'll encourage him to make fun of me, to turn up his nose at the least thing I touch or admire. And by being a living example of the unsightliness and anxieties that come with a lack of discipline, I'll make a more normal, more average man out of him than any normal, average father would know how to do with his children.

He'll have no vice, peculiarity, curiosity whose consequences he can't observe in me, and that doesn't inspire extreme repulsion in him. Each time he shows a tendency to veer from the norm, he'll think of me, my problems, my failings, what's said about me, my filthy books, the kinds of happiness I'm deprived of and my disgusting obsessions. He'll learn not to confuse my depravities with freedom, my mental abnormalities with intelligence, my pleasures with pleasure. In this way, he'll become the child of my neighbors, my concierge, the policeman standing on the corner; the child of radio broadcasts, pop songs and mainstream magazines; the child of doctors and teachers, grannies and the State; the child of the other children. And that combination of favorable elements, while positioning him right in the center of average values, will open for him all doors to happiness.

If he grumbles, I'll force upon him the kind of development he may not have had in a real family: I need absolution for my pederasty, and I'll do it by demonstrating how it can transmit and instruct norms better than paternity itself. That is because normal people are so convinced of the universality of their vision of the world that they sometimes do too little to contaminate their progeny with it. My own parents were like that. If they'd known what relentless structuring produced balanced, mature, adjusted adults, they wouldn't have left me alone so often. Because I followed my whims, obeyed them, starting at the earliest age, I became attached to a countless number of things I happened to discover, and I learned to enjoy them, remaining deaf to what could have saved me from them while turning my base curiosities and obfuscated pleasures into irresistible vices that the best therapists would, as a consequence, have difficulty eliminating without destroying me as well. Obviously, I don't at all reproach those who educated me; their system was rigorous, conformist, and if it had been applied relentlessly, it would have produced the best effect. But it didn't even succeed in making me buy a car or love hashish, things that even the clumsiest of fathers know how to get their sons to do today. There were just too many blank spaces, too many unsupervised hours; I knew too well how to take an interest in myself; and since I was by far the youngest of the children, they unfortunately credited me with an innocence of which, on the contrary, I was the only one deprived. The result, for example, was that just when one of the older ones was being humiliated each night at table by being forced to imbibe drops meant to cure loneliness, I, beyond suspicion, smooth-cheeked and prepubescent, was jerking off only on days when I wasn't ass-fucking.

Once this habit of perversion was established, I gradually understood everything that attracted me, always choosing the crooked path, and not even for the purpose of winning any prestige from such lack of convention so that I could later ascend to the dominant class; it was, instead, purely for pleasure, because that was the only thing my poor head ravaged by orgasms was still capable of feeling. This was the effect of the good opinion that people had of me, the times alone I was allowed, the withdrawal of my isolated family that avoided others and their excessive confidence in the order of things.

What can I do with myself now? Even my adult reasoning strengthens me in the choices made for his own use by the child I used to be. However, his age deprived him of all judgment, and anything he could do was wrong. If I think like him, it's because he has twisted my brain. He made me into a maniac who reproduces his actions and cravings, a sexual retard, an unmarried man who'd rather fondle brats than father any, a blind person who has never known the beauty of breasts, beards, homelands, factories. Until my last hour, I'll be the puppet of his ideas, fixations; and if there's an autopsy, they'll find only this deformed, imbecilic, insatiable gnome, who has been tyrannizing me for more than twenty years, and whom no sensible observer would consider human. He was mistaken about everything: not once did he find out how to become attached to something that everyone appreciates or approves. Actually, there was only one normal object that he made me love—boys—which half of humanity seeks and desires, and I certainly wouldn't be able to say as much about other things I like. Except, when the child I was took on a worthy object for once, he forgot that it was recommended for a gender other than his; so he only knew how to be normal at the expense of an anomaly worse than all of them. This is the monster who was allowed to become me.

It's true that, during those years, society wasn't yet so calcified, so totalitarian; it was hovering to a small extent between old bourgeois notions and progress; we were applying prewar rules to a time that was the beginning of today. Obviously, such lopsidedness will be what will make certain educations so ineffective. But there's nothing to worry about now: our new society is coherent, there isn't anything about it that it's not aware of, it's in touch with all its parts and knows how to control them. It's enough to dunk anyone at all into it for him to become like everyone else—with the happy illusion of being only himself—and for him to behave exactly like all of us—with strictly personal reasons for doing so. And it's only in families that are too indrawn, anachronistic, authoritarian or poor that a few abnormal types are still being produced. The open, well-subsidized family of tomorrow won't experience such failures of reproduction.

That is the reason why, if I educated my brat, I'd try not to shut him away but would instead make him ubiquitous, not restraining him but granting him every freedom, provided, obviously, that he practiced it in the company of his most conformist peers; and I'd surrender him to all influences, with the condition that they were like political propaganda on television whose importance is proportionate to the number of individuals who buy into it. The only thing I'd forbid him would be to seek isolation, to prefer himself to others, to cultivate a predilection, desire, a demand, a dream, a rebellion, an eccentricity that wasn't part of the majority. And if I noticed in him the strength to conflict with others—having come from I don't know where (unless from some early psychosis)—I'd go drown him immediately.

The most serious consideration of all: his chances for being happy. In the name of that, I'll believe that each peculiarity of mind or behavior, each whim that is not in demand, each initiative that hasn't been provoked, each hesitation in the face of practical certainties, will be equivalent to a cancer, a plague, paralysis, a canker, the atrophy of an organ or member; all of which would build up in my pupil until he became disfigured, deformed, repulsive, oozing pus and teeming with viruses, and be thrown out with the trash. When someone suffers from an incurable disease, it's just, if he wants it, to give him death. My student would be incapable of knowing what hell awaited him, and how that makes euthanasia that much more worthy; but I'd kill him, anyway.

Contemporary education confirms this as well. In a democracy, it explains, each can develop his personality freely, but if you want to be happy and truly become adjusted, it's better to be like everybody else.[1] A faulty brain like mine, of course, sees bizarre insinuations in such a principle. If a man who's different from others is rejected by them, it's because well-adjusted individuals who resemble everyone else enjoy persecuting those who do not. A strange proof of being adjusted. It leads to the conclusion that the essential element of happiness resides in crushing the other; and that, the more balanced, normal and adjusted you are, the more intolerant, nasty, intractable and stupid you become. Therefore, must you be like everyone else because the majority actually do possesses happiness, or simply because the majority dominates so aggressively that, if you're not a part of it, you suffer more than you would if you were a part of it? Teachers don't have the answer. But they use the words equality, health, justice, freedom, wisdom; they tell on which side all these virtues are located; they say that such a side has the startling distinction of being unforgiving when it comes to the other sides. However, they do not say that the key to human happiness, in whatever society you happen to be, is being a part of the

---

1. See *Good Sex Illustrated.*

most imbecilic, yelping with the wickedest or backing up the strongest; and if they don't yet dare to put it all in black and white, their students understand quite well without needing things spelled out.

Besides, the ferocity of this lucky majority is obviously just a legitimate protection of its happiness against the rabid few trying to cause it harm. Our suffering comes from a defect in consistency of taste, behavior, appearance, age and state of mind; and therefore, everything that can level differences is good. Extensive conditioning, of course, identity in the acts that all perform at the same moment, including thoughts, resentments, admirations; laughing together at the same things, adopting the same values, eliminating conflicts and resolving revolts, suppressing those incapable of adapting, rehabilitating those who don't produce; prisons, asylums, old folks' homes, community centers and hospices for the old; prison camps for the disabled; places where immigrants can rot; penitentiaries to hold orphans; throwing into permanent institutional limbo every person whose race, color, age, past, activity, health, morals, opinions, habits or dissent would sully the harmony of normality. We do this, and only underdeveloped nations aren't yet in possession of all these instruments of happiness. The only thing that's imperfect is our conditioning: some manage to escape the forge and fall through the cracks. If we can remedy that, unity, tranquility, the certainty of things will finally be established; future generations will inherit a perfect society, and the five billion years that separate us from the end of the world will move forward without a jolt.

If, some night, an irksome individual keeps me from sleeping by making a racket and I complain, and he tells me that this racket happens to be the most beautiful music on earth, I'll reply with every right that it is time for sleep, not for beauty. Even though happiness, when it comes to him, is like sleeping forever. Nothing is more legitimate than protecting it against those sick people who are stricken with insomnia.

I can therefore clearly see what separates the happy majority from minorities: the former only suffer from the existence of the latter; whereas the latter suffer from themselves and—mere handful though they be—prevent unadulterated contentment from reigning. This is why you have to resemble others to be happy, and hunt down differences to stay that way.

What I've been writing also proves that I underestimate myself, and that, when I want to, I'm capable of reasoning as well as the next person. Could it be that, in claiming my vices are incurable, I'm only looking for an excuse and actually could straighten out and get back on the right track, even without help? I don't dare answer that question. Instead I have the depressing impression that among my number of perversions is my tendency to imagine myself normal, and that if I'm not correcting myself, it's because I'm sincerely convinced that I already resemble whomever it could be. But why am I so often the only one with that opinion? It will take years before I understand it.

My bad morals, to limit the discussion to those, seem infinitely commonplace to me, and I can easily conceive of a society that would impose them under the aegis of the average values and the majority ideas that are currently condemning them in our society. Even slight alterations would not be necessary.

In this average, petit-bourgeois homosexual society I'm imagining, common sense would affirm, for example, that since man is superior to animals, he must free himself from the instinct compelling him to fornicate with the opposite sex the way animals do (the lowest toady from the Church or some professional organization can understand that argument). It could be added that restraining sex to procreation is simply absurd, since no one has ever totally devoted the entire sixty or eighty years of sexuality he has available when born to reproduction (as is commonly claimed in this society, I may add). Those who put pleasure into the sole category of procreation are, consequently, idiots, or out of their mind. And this immense reservoir of sexual desire with which only humans have been provided (though no one knows why) must serve a higher, more extended kind of relations. It is also said that copulation lowers woman to the rank of object and victim; that we're abusing her when we make use of the morphological features she inherited from our bestial past; that it's monstrous to inflict penetration on a human being who won't be able to do it back now or ever. This is ethical thought, without any exaggeration or the addition of novel, specious reasoning. The rest is, of course, a matter of social choice. One comes to the conclusion that the way to emancipate man and woman from the inequitable horrors of coitus, and to divert our too abundant desires to the benefit of social unity, is to impose homosexuality en masse. It follows that a law founded on these principles will curb the crime of *bestiality*—in other words, heterosexual acts. (After several centuries of the death penalty, psychiatry and relentless agitprop, we're becoming a bit more liberal, as we should.)

Moreover, if we may borrow the aphorism of a famous biologist, we can say that the adult is only the form that the child is forced to adopt in order to reproduce himself. And although hygienic practices have created a situation in which, instead of dying a few years after having become adults, we live as such a lot longer than we do in the previous stage, we ought not forget where the high point of human perfection is located (be it intelligence, liberty, invention, sociability, a communal spirit, good cheer, kindness, courage, spontaneity, generosity, sweetness, mischievousness, emotional richness, solidarity, loyalty, beauty, etc.); namely, in childhood. All individuals of less than thirteen or fourteen are thus the model of what one should love after that age. It's allowable for adults of both sexes to infantilize their person, notably, by bleaching and curling their hair and making it soft, silky and luxurious; using makeup to create large, expressive eyes and long, delicate eyelashes; employing rouge and lipstick to give the impression of an infant's coloring; removing hair from the face and body and exfoliating the skin; scraping or massaging flesh; tanning it and slimming it down; washing throughout the day to smell less like an adult; using one's voice at a higher register and changing all its timbres; stamping feet or yelling shrilly; copying the literalness, innocence and energy of childish gestures, their postures, their ways of climbing into bed, sitting, eating, looking, answering, laughing, crying, hugging; getting into the habit of making faces that are excessive or trivial, candid or contrary, stupid or dreamy, sensual or rebellious; in brief, caricaturing childhood, like only women are forced to do in our society.

(And we know what object of desire they are when they've done a good job at it; yet how feared or neglected they become if they seem like adults.)

Reproduction is to occur by planned schedules of insemination, homosexuality being (no scientist would deny this) a way of controlling births that is infinitely more convenient and reliable than Western pills or the Eastern hammer and sickle. Children belong to no one; adults who agree to supply their sperm or loan their uterus and then keep for themselves the children that result are accused of infanticide and put to death. Animal stupidity illustrates that no mind can advance in a sphere as small as pater-mater. Therefore, if you want a child to raise, he has to be free to go where he wants, speak to whom he wants, get organized as he wants, learn what he wants; and, through his hundreds of encounters, chats, associations, initiatives, risks, experiences, sleepovers and friendships with people of all ages, cultures, places, races and professions, he can match his mind to the yardstick of society. Refusing him this is to murder him, to turn him into a cretin who fears others and doesn't know how to control himself, who doesn't notice the links among things, has no light to shed on the life of the social body and won't be able to furnish any apt solution to the problems it poses. He'll become stultified in the miserable occupation to which he clings, and every difference, every novelty will render him nasty, every object, possessive, every desire, withdrawn and underhanded. This is why we liken to assassins those adults who indulge in the crime of the *reconstitution of family* (and a child who undergoes this is worth even less than a corpse).

Once such a civilization is effectively in place, it will allow a minority that is incapable of being raised to practice pederasty the freedom to look for hetero pleasures between adults, without it being considered a crime. Of course, it will be necessary to hide it. But it's easy to spot heteros: you can sense it. When they look at you, their eyes contain a mixture of guilt, dissimulation and sexual craving, something dishonest and shameful. When they're with men, they only watch the women going by—and if they're women, they stare at males exactly like a male would, but with a slimy, pathetic expression. We don't condone these depraved individuals; if they accost you, denounce, execrate them, put them right; if there are two of them together, mock them, reprimand, threaten and separate them, put them in quarantine, exclude them from the group. Whether treated that way or not, they seem ill at ease; there's nothing frank about them, nothing clear, nothing natural; no relaxed, open and trusting relationship with others. They aren't a part of anything.

When they get together in their particular enclave, they do grotesque parodies; the women, by feminizing themselves, imitating the coquetry of tarts; the men, by acting virile with the clumsiness of gorillas. They need these transvestisms to be desired, because they aren't even convinced of being attractive to one another. It's also their pathological hate of homosexual norms, the panicked fear they feel in the presence of people of their sex, that compel them to take on these disguises and twisted expressions, without which men and women would resemble each other too much; but *hetero* does mean "other," referring as it does to the Greek term *heteros* (they help themselves to Greek), and it's one of their ways of fabricating differences for themselves so that they can be sure they're really practicing their vice and not normal love.

You can imagine what sexual, affective and intellectual deficiencies create this obligation to tamper with themselves so that each becomes the fantasized opposite of the other; like crazy people who decided to associate by using only the left leg and arm of one and the right leg and arm of the other, despite the fact that each has all his or her members.

These disabilities make them incapable of understanding other people (they claim they're heterophiles, but the *other* always seems frightening and faraway to them) and of carrying out most collective tasks, since they divide everything they touch. Among objects, ideas, feelings, acts, even the sickest people still do distinguish the part that is to be reserved for one sex and the part that is destined for the other. A few undetected heteros in a group are enough for the homosexual organization of labor to fall apart—to the despair of everyone—until the cause is discovered and the divisive influence expelled.

In general, they demonstrate great contempt for children, and some bestial reflex makes them want to dominate them and appropriate them for themselves. They don't hesitate to order them around, and even hit them. Such offenses, such influences render the young incapable of acting in a responsible manner in society; those who were once the victims of heteros will demonstrate now and then certain deficiencies, which include servility, ignorance and aggression.

In compensation, their disabilities are an aid to early detection. When a doofus who likes nothing and feels nothing tyrannizes others or obsessively tries to obey them, or a lass who acts scatterbrained and makes spelling mistakes or a blubberer or affected little girl who never has sex with anybody is spotted among children, a psychological exam immediately reveals the reason for it, which, fortunately, is not always as dreadful as hetero-mania. Because the latter is incurable; electric shock or a frontal lobotomy supress it, but these cause permanent mental decay; the sick people become slow-witted rather than true homosexuals.

To prevent inveterate heteros from contaminating normal society, they're allowed a few bars or clubs where they can meet.

However, the police and neighbors harass them enough to make most of them—except for the wealthiest or most debauched—afraid of going there. There are dragnets at the meeting places they've improvised for themselves in the city: parks, railroad stations, shady hotels, carnival fairgrounds. We've had to destroy a number of public toilets because male and female heteros, taking advantage of the anonymity and rapid traffic, see in these facilities an efficient and risk-free way of meeting, recognizing one another and exhibiting their sexual organs to each another, and even a place to satisfy appetites they've curbed for too long. What normal citizen would choose to take refuge for his pleasures in a place so disgusting? But heteros have lost all dignity, any solution at all pleases them, any expedient attracts them and, actually, the more dangerous, degrading and unwholesome, the more they delight in it.

The police send plainclothes officers to loiter in the remaining public toilets, plants who pretend to be heterosexual. This permits imprisoning a few of these perverts; because no law condemns their existence, there's a strong need to invent other means to bring them to justice. Internal Affairs takes care of this.

Of course, they're prohibited from going around in public together, because the example would be too dangerous for our youth. And the sight of these men taking a woman by the hand or touching her neck would turn the stomachs of people passing by. There'd quickly be a brawl, trouble, fighting. Certainly they're allowed to walk around outside, and even in pairs if they really want to; in fact, if they don't look at each other, don't touch, don't kiss, avoid any suspicious word or gesture, they'll have no reprisals to worry about. Such minimal constraint is all that is expected of them from the time they are children to their death; yet even that makes them duplicitous and obsessed with embracing and feeling each other up. They do it without any consideration; and far from practicing that pleasant, tender courtship with which homosexual love so beautifully adorns our public benches, cafés, subways, heteros throw themselves on one another like animals. Thank God, it's away from most eyes.

Starting with the early stages of life, with the first people who bend over newborns' cradles and caress them, masturbate them, tickle their uncontrolled anuses, we instill the habit of homosexual contact. It's necessary to be vigilant, and to spare nothing to make their eroticism overcome the stages of bestial genitality. You speak about their body, their beauty, make them appreciate the sweetness of obscene words, bring them into contact with many individuals of every age to accustom them to plurality so that they can determine for themselves the kinds of company they prefer. However, if they seem too attached to members of the opposite sex, you break off these dangerous friendships as quickly as possible.

Later, they discover that homosexual pleasure is the cement of all harmony and every activity. They are put severely on guard against the exclusive relations of the couple, which is an antisocial vestige of hetero-mania, a narcissistic and narrow-minded vice. You accustom them to blending sexual pleasure with the collective situations in which life places them: work, culture, leisure activities. Each year, we reward (with praise, candy, a crown of roses) those children who've had sex with the most citizens (some equitable proportion of whom should be ugly, infirm or senile) and in this way offer each the example of the perfect adaptation of their sexuality to civic duty. Thus, the sordid idea of privatizing sex, refusing another or remaining chaste won't occur to anyone.

We warn children against the absurdity of virilization and feminization; we tell them what kind of degradation threatens them if they become hetero, what kind of inferiority and isolation. We teach them how to recognize perverts and thwart their advances. From the first word they hear until they become adults, all conversations, books, toys, films and cartoons, magazines, comic strips, television shows, advertisements, all instruction in every discipline encourage young people to become homosexual and make them spurn and detest the opposite.

As for adults, sometimes they broach the shocking subject of "sexual minorities." You have to know how to talk about it. Some pride themselves on having hetero friends, but that affectation of tolerance often serves to mask their own perversion. Nevertheless, it is on homosexuality and pedophilia that all human communication still remains focused: books, films, television, radio, newspapers, the university, the sciences, philosophy, sexology, photography, painting, sports, documents about heads of State, the important men and women, interviews, theater, mime, pornography, fashion, games, vacations, stamp collecting, gastronomy, religion, training fleas, official art and marginal research. As a result, members of this society would find it hard to discover in their mind or body the most minute trace of desire for the opposite sex, and are thus unanimously convinced that homosexuality is dictated by Nature—the nature of humanity.

There are enormous difficulties when it comes to showing the mainstream public the brutal scenes of hetero-mania presented by the life of animals; a film in which lion cubs grow up between the paws of their *parents* had to be censored, it so outraged the first people who saw it. Representing the truth to the point of provocation, in fact, is forgetting that objectivity must engender harmony and not disorder. The National Association of Minors with Baby Teeth, a very powerful pressure group, registered a complaint against a documentary: an adult, attractive-looking bird was giving her beak to naked, featherless, toothless, helpless baby birds that were confined to their nest. Settled in advance, the case demonstrated that these images had been rigged, and their author, judged guilty of hetero-familialist propaganda, was given neurosurgery before being executed (sick people are not put to death).

However, scientific minds take a certain pleasure, perhaps an obscurely perverse one (we all retain a vestige of heterosexuality), in the study of the predilections, ideas, habits, pleasures and physical and psychic aberrations of pudendal hetero-mania (considered to be the model for all forms), in that population of pudendal hetero-maniacs who turn themselves over to science. The study is, say these researchers, a kind of plunge into the distant past of the earth before *homo sapiens*—since we have somewhat rectified prehistory and now understand that the appearance of the human genus must be dated from the day when our ancestors renounced the family and coitus between the sexes. In museums, those bizarre little bone needles that were used to practice primitive inseminations are on display, as are the mortars, pots, herbariums and capsules that from all evidence were used in manufacturing or holding the unguent for sodomy; they come from every period and every land and are very gracefully painted, polished, sculpted or carved. Such objects have been found in prehistoric sites and digs, which is sufficient proof that they were used by *homo sapiens*.

We have also corrected history, the arts and monuments, organized archeological documents, literary heritage, travel and exploration narratives, to eliminate what might lead to the belief that other societies or other times didn't have the same customs, or tolerated any mixture between hetero-mania and homosexuality. What sense would there be in letting evidence from the past spread a form of depravity that the modern age has healed us of? Finally, the rare texts or objects that haven't been suppressed are locked in the cellars of museums and the bowels of libraries. No researcher who values his career, no serious scientist, no historian worthy of the name would be able to make use of these documents to qualify or, for all the more reason, upset the official State, erudite and scholarly versions of world history and geography, as well as the travel narratives, which affirm that humanity everywhere, from the time it left the rank of animals, was exclusively and persistently homosexual.

There are more and more works, films, investigative reports, debates, writings related to science, characters in novels, shocking news items that show heterosexuality under the most degrading, odious, laughable light. Other than this, everything should extol homosexuality, idealize it, beautify it, depict its most humble individual nuances by millions and billions. Everything should encourage it ceaselessly, keep silent about its injustices, mediocrities, misdeeds, tricks, failings; we must justify its pressures, honor its duties; and what doesn't conform to the myth of a universal, radiant homosexuality, as the only gauge of dignity and human freedom, is distorted, falsified, and must be minimized or destroyed.

Heteros, who are inexplicably sensitive to these social demands, all lie low, cultivate feelings of guilt and self-loathing, suicidal ideation. They're trying to work out a decent version of their lifestyle and denounce those among them who aren't presentable—those who feminize or virilize themselves too much, those who take it out on minors, who react aggressively to oppression by homos (they think they're being clever in dubbing normal citizens, who have no need to be named, *homos*)—instead of trying to cooperate with society with mutual respect and trust, as they're invited to do.

The boldest and wealthiest flaunt their lifestyle with phony demonstrations of fulfillment: they needn't, because their cynicism appalls most people. These imposters can't conceal the real marks of their vice. Because heteros are unbalanced, immature, enervated and joyless, unhappy, hypocritical, lonely; their dirty pleasures, whose details are repulsive to recount, are furtive and sinister and don't even satisfy them. Their *conjugality* proves it; because when they have intercourse with someone, they get so little satisfaction out of it that they need to repeat it again with that same person for months, even years, at a time—sometimes for their entire life. A pathological fixation, a compulsive sexuality; do they hope that by appropriating a partner and polluting him or her thousands of times, they'll at last experience a pleasure that these aberrant and abnormal copulations will never be able to procure?

We don't know what to do with these wrecks. Here's hoping that we expose their ways; as long as they're not too prestigious or rich, we'll drive them out of their jobs and homes (but usually they go willingly because they're cowardly about practicing their vice and are afraid of censure). Their friends abandon them, neighbors grumble, children are afraid of them. The police bother them as often as they want; it's a kind of social therapy that reduces perversion better than the medical approach, which is very inefficient and difficult to institute widely. We try to make it impossible for them to make contact with each other, and they commonly hang out for hours, looking morose and peering at passersby of the opposite sex while fantasizing that one of them will return their depraved glances, by using their technique for identifying one other. Such cruising in the worst neighborhoods exposes them to the moments of danger that one would expect, and hoodlums, interestingly enough, enjoy setting them straight; there's no reason for us to prevent such aggressions, and sometimes even the police, who want to clean up a park overrun by too many hetero-maniacs (which shocks night strollers and ruins lawns) will set loose on them a gang of hoodlums they've picked up somewhere else. In this way, delinquency is made useful to society, to decency, to gardening.

Science proves that the awful existence in which perverts delight is an obvious sign of their abnormality. Certain writers have created exciting and shocking books about it. They invent theories that explain how a person becomes hetero-manic; but the truth is that you don't become it, you remain it. It's caused by being fixated on an infantile stage of sexuality, which keeps these sick people from developing beyond the dictates of mammalian instincts, and from ever knowing the fullness that we experience when we submit our sexuality to social requirements and sublimate our tendency to pleasure the opposite sex into feelings of friendship, attaching every aspect of our libidinal impulses to our own gender. We know what a jungle society was when humans were prey to hetero-mania; what tortures are endured by children when they're born to pariah couples and live shut up with them, terrified by the outside world, not even daring to go into the street and meet their contemporaries. In fact, every image of honor, contentment, virtue and peace is associated with homosexuality, while every notion of baseness, unhappiness, violence and vice with heteros. We denounce the destruction of the social fabric that would lead to a revival of their mores: moronic, caricatural women kept in thrall to male lust, exploited like dogs; brutal, crass, despotic men, divisive and combative with one another; subservient children, treated with contempt and beaten and turned into half-wits; the atomization of the human community into little cells that resemble animals' burrows, where all that reign are mutual hatred, heartbreak, jealousy, tyranny, moroseness and neurosis. This is contrasted by the immense current of free desire in homosexual society that unites, on the one hand, all boys and all men to men, and on the other, all girls and all women to women, and where peace-loving, egalitarian, respectful and mellow relations prevail between the sexes and among the ages. That being the case, hetero dictates, allowed expression now and then because of an excess of tolerance, have only one effect: they describe to all—to a horrible, nauseating and nightmarish degree—the suffering humanity would experience if it were dominated by the heterosexual order.

I shouldn't have showed off like this; as imbecilic and repulsive as I made that society, it seems better than ours. I transposed all our defects, but in that context they lost most of their effect. And there's still one aspect of this transposition that seems unbelievable: the protests. We can only reproach homosexuality for imaginary failings, and defects caused by social exclusion; on the other hand, in a world in which eroticism was free, who would listen to our heteros defend a sexual order as harmful as theirs?

What is more, it's impossible to conceive seriously of a homosexual society, meaning one that would prevent other kinds of sexuality. Such persecution would be paradoxical, a useless precaution, a form of intolerance without any reason for existing. Permissive and nomadic, homosexuality (except the petit-bourgeois kind, because those queers have been conditioned to caricature hetero norms) wouldn't know how to become a source of public prohibitions. Therefore, such a society wouldn't be "homosexual"; but it wouldn't know anything about our atrophied and cloistered heterosexuality, either. The latter is constructed purely by repelling, severing, attacking eroticism; and only for heterosexuality does permissiveness mean falling into ruin.

This can be seen in our morals. Heterosexuality claims to be based on instinctual, biological laws—and this permits the belief that since it is in conformity with our body's nature, it also satisfies our mind and is thus something spontaneous and sound. But we proliferate to infinity not only techniques of sexual education and correction, but also repressions, taboos, obscurity, lies, censures; we liberally disseminate warnings, medical controls, psychological counseling, people to tinker with couples or to buckle up families, castrators of children, manuals, investigations, journals, compensatory transactions, substitutes, compromises, adhesives, collars, ointments in order to look after or repair this need that nature inspires in us. Have we ever done so many things in order to ensure that we'll sleep or eat? Perverts have a less restive sleep, a less delicate appetite; their sexuality is only a house of cards poorly cobbled together by frightened brains, but they manage without education, sex specialists, matrimonial agencies, dogma, learning, institutions, hospitals, civil liberties, incentives, rules, experts, subsidies, rewards, dignity, spaces, protection, publicity, well-being, security, friendship, welcome—and they survive, in spite of the repressions I described in reverse above, and to which I'd like to see hetero drives submitted in order to assess what would remain of them after a few years. I never stop marveling that nature is so vulnerable, whereas anti-nature is so resistant. That what is constructed in advance is constructed with such difficulty, and that what is only a small undertaking by the disabled seems so resistant to being destroyed.[2]

Can it really be true that official heterosexuality can satisfy nothing of what it claims to fulfill? Degenerate straights; straights who sodomize, suck, fondle; straight voyeurs, porn lovers, pedophiles, zoophiles, enthusiasts of coprophilia; straight couple-swappers, sadomasochists, cruisers, sex freaks, nymphos have no need, any more than queers, of a universe at their beck and call; their sexuality holds up very well without the least

---

2. I read that, during the war in Vietnam, psychologists for the American army had noticed that the recruits who came from the ranks of the socially persecuted (blacks, queers, and all who "deviate" from the correct proportions) resisted more effectively and for a longer time than others when it came to situations of acute *stress*: dangerous outposts, isolation, nervous tension, various frustrations, enemy prisons, torture, forced indoctrination, malnutrition, sensory deprivation. It's a remarkable effect of the training these subhumans received in civilian life from their peace-loving fellow citizens. But that was in the name of freedom. I don't know if minorities with high incomes reveal themselves to be as accustomed to *stress* as those of the inferior classes. Finally, I hope that all this is false; if not, it will be necessary to increase the penalties of prison that, directly or by means of the group, punish the differences of race or morals in our country. Since *they* endure it so well.

social reinforcement. Could it be that their sexuality is enough for them? It is, however, as condemned as homosexuality, and those in charge of sexual development dissuade young people as severely from one as from the other.

Thus, if hetero *orthodoxy* represents nature and satisfies humans, as it claims to do, if a majority of humans choose it spontaneously, as they themselves believe, if they stick with it freely, which is the opinion of their police, and are fulfilled by it, as their thousands of health care workers claim, society shouldn't have to fear other forms of love and be threatened by their practice, their ability to prosper or any unbiased information about them being made available to children or adults. The example of heterosexuality as the dominant orientation doesn't transform homophiles into heteros; their predilections are genuine enough not to be offended by the sight of others' sexuality. But if freedom for homosexuals, their overt presence, their equitable and permanent access to all means of expression available, beginning with those that touch the masses (and that isn't books), are refused because they would pervert the majority—which is, however, so certain of its ways that it crushes whoever doesn't practice them—then what worth is there to these laws, this order, this nature, and what is their relationship to the spectrum of needs that man, by one kind of sexual behavior or another, attempts to appease? Therefore "spontaneous," monogamous, familial heterosexuality, since it rejects the proof of the plurality of mores, is clearly obtained—like the political unanimity of totalitarian countries—at the price of an enormous arsenal of constraints and estrangements inflicted since childhood; it is nothing but baseness, deceit, dictatorship; and it will implode from it.

Look at me, climbing onto my soapbox. Curdled milk quivering in a bowl. The only people who speak in the name of mankind are those who could point a gun at them. I'll never put myself in that situation. Therefore I'm returning to my misbehavior, the account of which is a better match for my character.

The *curdled milk* is from Lewis Carroll, I was forgetting. I still haven't read *The Life of Don Pablos*. The text I was reading while scratching my anus, at the beginning of the third chapter, was Diderot, and is called *Sequel to the Preceding Conversation*.

The family that lives in my house is small in number, and it's a quiet one. The man has a farm close by in the country. Usually he's not there. He brings his food back from there. His family occupies only the ground floor, as I've said. One room on that floor, partly adjoining one of mine, is used as a henhouse. You can see these ladies sticking their beaks out of the window, shaking their combs and feathers through the ironwork scrolling. Right before dawn, the cock sounds very close by; its crowing, a weird yelp, resembles the drawn-out bark of a dog or coyote. Sounds of another cock, farther off, answer it. These cries coming from various distances map the city, placing me in the middle of a star with numerous points of unequal length, some of which are so drawn out that they get lost in the outer edges of the night.

It's the only nocturnal sound except for the crickets in summer. This isn't mute silence, however; it's a vibration so strong that, sometimes, under the sounds made by my body—gurgles, cardiac beats, swallowing, air flowing through my nose, eyelids blinking, cartilage crunching—I imagine I hear an immense river flowing. So either the sound or the silence within this nocturnal calm places me on a vast current that flows through my room, a current whose origin and endpoint I'm unaware of. I spread out, floating on my back into a lyrical interlude.

No boys in the family. A mother and three girls. The first two are women, the third is just becoming a toddler. I imagine the result of a last attempt to produce a male heir. A failure. The farm, the house and, I think, a shop will belong to a son-in-law. That enlightens them as to what kind of husband the girls will have, better than the loves-me-loves-me-not method. The little one is pampered and spoiled to the extreme. She yells, sings and runs wild a lot, for my pleasure. The others are silent and cold, cordial but distant. However, when I was repairing the windows that look out onto the patio (my floor is very high up), one of the sisters went back and forth constantly in the courtyard and each time gave me a shy smile, with a hint of a wink that could melt the glass. Then could I be her glamour boy? No; but I'm certainly not any more disgusting to look at than you. Get your mirror. Later, girls realized that I was crazy and stopped wanting me for a husband.

They invited me to become part of their family life, they'd do my housework, washing, there'd be a place for me at the table, I'd have television in the evening, coffee in the morning. I refused these propositions as time went by; I liked them, but I was thinking about all the things I'd have to sacrifice, the streets, squares, fountains, my social nature, in exchange for this tender world of soap operas and dinner plates. So I gave my work as an excuse, my strange schedule. No one seemed offended. They went out of their way to do a thousand little favors for me, seeing that they thought I was pleasant. Then, without throwing me out, they chose to ignore that I was there; I'd walk up the street into my palace.

An inhabitant of the city would pay three times less rent for this place; I made it comfortable, and I left the issue behind me; a little ruse let them make me pay for the electricity for the entire house. I accepted these disadvantages while imagining what I'd get in exchange. My life is discreet, my guests rare and quiet, my money is sound, easy; people who are more virtuous than me are miserly, and people more honest than my hosts are intolerant. So we were well matched. But at the beginning we didn't know it, and now discovering how much alike we are has made our blood run cold.

Two boys of fourteen or fifteen are facing each other under a tree. Their flies are open. I'm on my knees with both cocks in my mouth. One of them is short and very hard, salty with sweat. The other, which is larger, is half limp and has big balls with such thin, satin, liquid skin, but they're so fulsome and pliant that I've never touched anything like them. I already know this boy, he's been to my place. He'd get very hard but doesn't know how to fuck. When he gets on top of me, he acts like a swimmer who panics in the water while assuming he's learning how to swim. For him, things happen without you, he takes his plunge, and then, *it happened*. I'd help him, but he'd immediately begin to struggle ridiculously, would slip out of the hole, the buns, fall off the bed. During this tumult, I'd be sucking the prick of a nice little boy, a mutual friend. They're panhandlers by profession. This prepubescent has a big, agile knob; on his knees with his stomach pressed against my cheeks, he pounds me so coolly, happily, easily, that the other seems like a muddling simpleton. The balls of this bad swimmer traumatize me because I don't know any form of matter, living or inert, natural or manufactured, with a surface that has such a fluid absence of texture. A bag of limp milk glass.

In the room overlooking the cul-de-sac, if I sleep there at night, I hear the calls of tortured children, or infants in desperate distress. They're female cats in love. These growls have an anguished brutality and aren't like the usual feline noises.

Very rarely, donkeys braying. Little birdsong on the patio, the terraces. A window had a broken pane for a while. In the morning, an impertinent sparrow slipped through it and visited my place. I hadn't yet swept; it pecked about and hopped tranquilly from room to room, a round little thing, it's head very erect, like the bearing of a well-to-do bourgeois inspecting an apartment that he wants to rent. When I appeared, it took off so quickly that its flight barely made an impression on my retina. The place must have been uninhabited for a long time with the pane broken, and that bird had developed the habit of flying down into it, obviously to eat insects; the ease with which it whizzed through the hole in the window and grill was proof of such familiarity. Later, it put up with me if I didn't move at all. It would hop up onto my bed, look at me, jump to the ground and continue its walk. A quick glance, from time to time, to verify my nonexistence. I put some water and bread down for it. It sampled some. It would announce its entrance to me from outside with its rapid call, and then a rustling sound. It was the time when the sun was at its most beautiful.

Some little boys, cats, birds, mimosa a few lines down from here, finishing with some little dogs, and in the meantime, a host of other vapidities: I certainly am an unusual pornographer. I'll only make a few old maids like myself queer. I'd better take another look at my methods for inciting debauchery.

Francesco is carrying a large bouquet. A lot of roses, some mimosa, branches with blue flowers and yellow centers and some snapdragons. I don't know why he's giving me this. It's not even a gift; it's just attached to the end of his arm, and then he puts it down. He doesn't say anything about it. We won't discuss it.

When it was hot, a reddish gray lizard that was a lot more fearful than my bird used a wall of the room to chill out. He'd be spread-eagled against the white background, where the graceful details of his legs, head and tail stood out. No matter how far away I was when I appeared, it made him vanish.

There are a lot of insects in my room, each according to its season. At first there were some little tortoise-shell-colored cockroaches, but not very many. Black insects followed them for a three-month period; they were disgusting and fat as two fingers. They lived in the woodwork ornamentation in my house. I sprayed insecticide everywhere. With their shiny carapaces and petrified pose, their suddenly darting about, a slight shock ran through me each time they appeared. Shoe in hand, I'd crush them, and their bodies made an explosive pop that disgusted me more than anything.

A shy little boy with a crew cut, against a wall, is smiling at me. But as I get nearer, he gets nervous. Speaking to him and stroking his head doesn't reassure him. Touching his fly does. His smile widens. His cock is stiff in a second, his slender stomach is fleshy and cool, and when his willy is in my mouth, he grabs me by the hair and begins to fuck hard. It isn't holes that frighten him, even ringed with teeth, even when wielding his little pencil—white as an egg—in them. My lips and tongue suddenly register an event no other boy has made them experience: along his prick, in the urethra, a pellet makes it way to the head, a lump like an alarm clock in the neck of an ostrich that is swallowing it—or rather, vomiting it. It's the little kid's ejaculation, without a drop. Afterward, he puts away his penis and continues waiting against the wall, a bag of groceries in his hand, his pocket better stocked.

He was so ethereal, and the strokes of his prick so powerful, and his sweet little face so limpid, that the faraway world to which he welcomed me, that unreal and salacious shore, leaves me with an immaculate nostalgia, beyond feeling, beyond desire. I recognized inside myself the place where it exists; it's the one that is the hardest for me to make contact with, the only one that I can't attain without a guide—and I can never predict who'll take me there.

Lady readers of my books who are on their last legs will interpret this as a psalm to their goateed darling, his angels, his little loincloth. (I have another gift to make before I'm finished.)

However, I did experience the alarm clock in the ostrich's neck in my anus, a few years ago. The boy was eighteen or twenty, and when he ejaculated, several bumps passed through him. These urethral knots seem merely to be a phenomenon of the nervous system, because their movement is slow, and my little boy without sperm had them as well. Otherwise, the spasms are less perceptible, whether they drench you or not.

There were some ants: little blond ones in columns, big black ones by themselves. Only two spiders, one fat and pink with transparent legs. An invasion of winged ants; at night you had to close the windows. I didn't always remember to. Ferociously rapid whirling around the light bulbs, a hundred ants of every size, some of them larger than a wasp.

Sometimes a caterpillar or sleeping larva, bright pink and laughable.

Some woodlouses.

A few flies, but skittish ones that irritated your skin.

Crickets, all summer. They would get lost at my place. I'd take them and toss them back out the window. They're hard to catch, their leaps are sudden.

Two grasshoppers.

A praying mantis, so beautiful I wanted to kill it. All I had was white wine. I drown it in it. Soon it stops moving. After a few hours, I remember it, see that it's stiff, remove it, spread it out so it will dry in good shape. But soon it's standing up on my table; it sobered up. I renounce destroying that bizarre beauty; but I imprison it for a little while under a glass and study it. It sees me, as well; and if I bring my face closer, it stands up straight, opens its wings, raises the two hackles of its legs and shakes them as if to claw at my nose. What fury. That eater of little males comes on better than I do. I let it go.

One time, the women who live below me call out to me when I leave; they're afraid. The man brought back a bag of wheat they put in a well-lighted room for junk, and a viper slid out of it. It's undulating on the tiles. It's small and very pretty, svelte, supple. I don't know how it's going to survive; we chase it and it slithers into the place where the cockroaches are hiding, a fissure in the cement. Impossible to get it out of there.

A few years ago, in Paris, in the street, I petted an enormous spider. It was at night. A boy I'd cruised was with me. We see the large animal run along a wall and wedge itself into a corner. So I lean down to pet its back with my index finger. It felt fragile, soft. It leapt and escaped. It was hideous, I hadn't had anything to drink, I wasn't in a sentimental mood, my companion was a pretty idiot, I never did it again.

One stormy evening, I had gone with a boy down to the banks of the Seine. There are a few trees, and we hide between them and the wall. It's warm out, about to rain. The bateaux-mouches go by, and when their projector lights sweep the quay we shrink away. The storm bursts forth; we move to a dark corner, under the bridge. And on every side, stampedes of rats rush out across our path, fleeing into the distance. A bum is standing behind the walls of a cardboard box. He sees that we're sucking each other, but what he grunts is incomprehensible. When it stops raining, we come back out, the bum's digs stink too much. Still more fat rats, countless, terrorized under the blue light. Their pelts are rabbit gray. A big cock shoots near my feet.

Several days before a big meal, from his farm the man brought back a sheep that scampered about. They kept it in a nice room where they'd spread out some hay. The odor of this litter invaded the house. It delighted me. There was a lot of bleating, because the sheep, which would walk around the courtyard, was talkative; and the little girl would answer it word for word. She bleated extremely well, just as seriously, as tremulously. She inserted sharp giggles between the phrases, but the sheep didn't learn to laugh. Or else it learned, and the sniggering I attributed to the little girl was his. These conversations lasted more than an hour; they were so pleasant to listen to that I'd stop my work to open the window. Then the day for the feast arrived. The sheep disappeared. The odor of the litter persisted: but I no longer heard any bleating, from either the victim or the child.

I had announced a gift; that was it. You can't have a real book without one or two passages to serve as dictation or as reading for schoolchildren. As long as the teachers speak highly of my name to their students, I won't ask for any money if they use the story of the sheep—which I've written without thought of any profit, as demonstrated by its decency. They'll even be allowed to change any difficult words.

Francesco doesn't like cheese, except for goat cheese, if it's fresh and made like simple curdled milk and then pressed. Spendthrift that I am, I bought some Roquefort; this moldy rubbish violently repulses him, and its price disgusts him. At noon the next day, we have lunch with Pablos. When I take out my moldy stuff, the older one refuses, so the little one says no, too. But he looks at it, smells it, and suddenly he's curious to taste some. Francesco, stupefied, watches him; the youngster swallows a long buttered piece of bread covered with this exotic and ruinously extravagant garbage, and he munches on it with such voluptuous pleasure that my own slice of bread seems dull to me.

In their house, they tried to produce some red-hot farts for me. At a time when Pablos was so serious, Francesco explained, the only thing that could break him up, make him laugh, was to hear a fart. Francesco farts in my bed, as a joke, and I began to fart, too, to answer him. Like the little girl braying with the sheep. When it's a matter of farts, not brays, it is, alas, the opposite of howling with the wolves. Francesco prepares his rockets, his trills, inflects them and launches them until he feels that his shit, from all the pushing, is going to come out. Sometimes as a prank, he catches one of his winds and releases it at my nose by opening his hand. The more it stinks the more he laughs. You can bet I give it back to him. After our songs we shake out the sheets.

Evenings, an old neighbor lady often comes to their place for the television. She has known Francesco since he was born; he turns around with his butt pointing toward her and launches some gas. The lady shakes her head with good-natured indignation and cheerfully shoos away invisible flies. The mother laughs to high heaven.

So Francesco asks me, "You want a fart?" I say yes, but it has to be a red-hot one. The brothers, the sister mimic the farts they're trying to find in their bowels. Pablos points to some of them for me as they take off. None were the right color.

One time, I have Pablos on my right thigh, we're chatting. And a light, threadlike, silent, odorless wind slips between the crack of his buttocks, which are open deep along my knee. I tell him. Pablos gets up and chases away this bad spirit by beating his hand against emptiness. We describe and describe again the shape of it and how it tickled. Francesco is there, and he can't stop laughing about it.

When Pablos told me his weight and height, together we calculated the weight of a slice of his body having a thickness of one centimeter. It was based on approximating him as cylindrical. He measures 49 inches and weighs 57 pounds, or is it 57 inches and 49 pounds, I can't remember. The weight of his slices amazes him. He studies them along his stomach. Until evening, he goes out to tell whoever will listen the big news that slices of him weigh such and such number of pounds. They question him with wonder. Slices, really?

Between our caresses, or during television, Pablos sends me kisses and parts of himself. He plucks his lips, his cheeks, his nipple, his thigh, places them in the hollow of his hand and blows them delicately toward me. I have to seize them in flight and kiss them. I send some back to him. He chews them while inflating his cheeks.

For cooking, Francesco brings spices in cones made of sheets of written-on notebook paper. The shopkeeper wraps them that way—they don't throw away anything. I read correct addition exercises and poems in violet ink, in big regular letters. Francesco was surprised that these discount wrappers pleased me; he only tries to decipher those that are printed for industrial products. But if I want some of them I will have them: Pablos's notebooks. They're covered with drawings in color pencil. Pablos filled these notebooks during the school year when I was unaware of his existence but had already met Francesco.

He draws very well, with careful, untiring enthusiasm: men, objects, animals, scenes of the city. He copies a lot, invents a bit, creates complex amalgams, outlines strongly, frames things, saturates them with color; expressions are mostly fractured on the page. But these ponderous images have the blurriness and inconsistency of the things one dreams while sleeping. He gave one a big cat's head with yellow eyes, rimmed ears, a nice muzzle, just like his nose. He had also shown me two jagged pitchers he drew and cut out and asked me which I preferred. They were identical. I chose one arbitrarily, guessing the trap he was setting for me. He seemed aggressive and gave me the cold shoulder for several minutes; the pitcher I'd pointed to had been done by one of his friends, Pablos's was the other. Love is based on the same kind of error, except in the positive sense. But Pablos gave me his pitcher.

Francesco enjoys jerking off with my sperm. For example, he's seated on my cock, I'm fucking him; when I'm ready to come, I take out my cock and finish with my hand on his big balls. He collects the liquid to anoint his member and has a long, creamy jerk-off session that drenches my chest.

I had two tubes of depilatory. I showed them to him and explained how they're used. This interested him a lot. We use the cream to remove what down there is on the butt and farther inside, as well as the surrounding areas. Francesco has nothing to take off, but this nothing bothers him. He says that he himself plucks his anus by twisting the hairs between two fingers; he claims that it burns and that they just come off. I've tried but I hurt myself. When the cream has done its work, we scrape it off and rinse off in the tub (I was living in the neighborhood that had bathtubs). The product has made the skin of his butt soft as a baby's prick. Excited, I fuck him standing in the water.

A short distance from the weightlifter's shop, I'm happily talking with a young fruit seller, not very clever but with an open, pleasant face. He gives me nibbles of what he sells, I give him packs of cigarettes. One night, without my being able to remember why, I'm on all fours and go through the door, which is low as a cat flap and lets you enter the place by passing under the fruit stand. I remain on all fours with the stand right over my head and close the door. Dark, except for a rectangle of light in front of me from the shopkeeper's lamp, where his feet and legs are. He bends down with a guileless expression to see me crouching in my corner and is naively delighted, embarrassed. I put my hand on his crotch. My gesture makes him laugh—oh, that. He takes out his stiff cock, which is very nice looking. I touch it, he laughs, gets up to wait on someone, squats again, gives me back his cock and thick balls with their sleek flesh. I suck him. Very surprised, at first he pulls his penis away, then surrenders it to me. He extends a hand toward my groin, but that part of me is too far away; so he caresses my cheek and lets himself be sucked, and a smile floats on the open lips of the distracted kid. A mustached man, resting on a straw mattress to my left, is kicking me with his knee. The two are joking. I swallow, the boy gets up again, I leave my corner. The simpleton, still vacant and cheerful, hands me a fistful of dried fruit.

Among the shopkeepers, there are two more who won't always refuse to fool around. They work together under a boss who comes in but who doesn't linger. One of them is shy, big-bottomed, very handsome, and is fourteen. The other is skinny, blondish, with a nice rascally face, and is two years older. Neither is very tall. The rascal can't resist showing me his cock, which is long and pale, hard as an iron bar. He takes it out, puts it back in his pants, takes it out again, I act indifferent. He's surprised that I'm not showing mine, makes fun of me, insinuates that mine is small. He's proud of his little black book: contacts the world over, men and women, with a special section entitled *Americans* (there are twenty pages but only one name). When a potential correspondent comes into the stand, I imagine how my shopkeeper, as if it were nothing, must pull out his rod to have it appreciated. He asks if I wouldn't like to suck it. Yes, if he pays me. He asks how much. I don't consider my services expensive: ten francs. His work is considered worth even less, and I'd be surprised if he made that much in a day; but he claims he's ready to pay such a price. No deal. This boy is too shameless, too thoughtless, and his rutting has a cool disdain that doesn't attract me. Strange cock, from nothing at all to being stiff. The timid boy interests me more. I feel him up in front and behind. I'm not supposed to be queer. He moves away with embarrassment but good humor. Finally, he's induced to take out his cock. We're outside the stand, and it's night. He presses himself against a corner of the builing and unbuttons while lowering his head toward his fly. I touch, and he says to wait; he's not hard. He's goes to hide against the other side of the corner, but, from time to time, peeks out to send us a veiled smile. His elbow is moving. He reappears and says hurry up. A soufflé to eat right away, or it will fall. Quickly. I touch. Short cock, nice shape, large and solid-feeling in my hand. The rascal is enjoying this. The timid one, satisfied, buttons up again and, as we compliment him, acts like a bridesmaid being congratulated on her lovely pink bow.

The other shopkeepers, big or little, don't misbehave this way. In this austere city, my partners are like a trickle of pure spring water under a mountain of granite. Well, almost.

The boy whose father the mason had hit him with his trowel. At first, I invite him over for an evening, without anything obscene on my mind. He wants to eat. I prepare a quick meal. There's a thick steak. The boy accepts it, but shows me his hand, which is wounded. I hadn't noticed; there are no bandages. I cut his steak. Carefully, I remove the fat and some small squares of meat. The youngster, susceptible to my attentions, doesn't wait for me to finish and takes the caterpillar of yellow fat, streaming with juice, between two fingers, and crunches into it. Mmm! He'll eat the meat, one way or another.

After the meal, I'm sitting in front of him and he must consider me much too shy; he takes my cheeks in his hands and pats them with a sweet smile. Then, a bit later, we have sex. He puts a lot of enthusiasm into it. Despite his child's size, he doesn't mind being fucked. A pit into paradise. I'll wake him up during the night to do it again. He takes my cock in his mouth and spits out the sperm. He fucks me blow for blow. His cock, ample and plump, has no hairs but is almost a man's cock, with chubby balls to rub against my nose.

He sleeps pressed against me and leaves at dawn. I see him again from time to time. Sometimes he's dressed in clean clothes (he's gone home), but often he's in rags. I don't tire of his face, his smile, of the few words he speaks. During that period, he's the youngest of the boys that I'm fucking. His little curvaceous rear enchants me as much as his nice face. He's wild, but his ways are never a burden. He's slender and muscular, with the tenderness of a child, the breadth of a male, the nimble tautness of a boy. I can't imagine a better lover. He's afraid of the place where I live. He has the vice of certain good-for-nothings who get high by breathing glue solvents or rubber solution for tires. This is how the little panhandlers slip into clouds more ethereal than those of alcohol. They rub the product between their palms and, with their two hands cupped as if holding a bird, they sniff the vapors. If they're filthy, this rubbing leaves a large round pink spot circled by black on their palms, which denounces their vice; the more clever spread the glue on a folded rag instead. My lad, certain times, took so much of it that his breath would stink up the entire room. In his kisses, the odor of this solvent sickens me. When intoxicated, he is sleepy and in a silly mood. If not, he's very loving and wakes up cheerfully in order to come.

When I lick his ass, he sucks my cock, pulls at my thighs, puts his tongue in my hole; the strokes overexcite him and he wants to jump on top of me immediately and fuck me. After we've gotten together a few times, I fuck him hard, in a lot of different positions. Our nights are extremely intense, and yet they cause no fatigue. Following these pleasures, I feel as if I've slept marvelously, and my little one is as carefree and merry as if on the morning of a holiday. Both of us come numerous times, something that doesn't happen to me with boys who are older—they don't inspire me with as much interest, and they feel it less. Fucking, sucking, jerking off, every mix of members happens, but we prefer the anus. The boy smokes a little, eats lightly, drinks soda, washes well; he's tactful when it comes to money and wouldn't even steal a match.

One cold evening, I find him covered with a white raincoat two times too big for him, very dirty and crumpled. Little fingers, little grinning muzzle sticking out of it. I think of certain photographs of brats in the United States during the Depression of 1929, or in Germany at the end of the war. But these miserable rags, sported not only by my boy but by the other good-for-nothings of the street, don't have the same meaning here. No one is humiliated by them; you wear them with pride in your body. Tough and cheerful, these cheeky kids incarnate a childish freedom you don't see otherwise; it's the opposite of helplessness. Ragged, mischievous, rounded up by public services—their only torment—which imprisons them, delouses them, shaves their head and lets them go soon after (obviously a sign that their family has been unearthed), they owe their flourishing to others' lack of concern; to the fact that people don't see children as children; to what they hate about being a child; to the fact that their future won't be any worse than that of the poor kids who stubbornly stay in school. Their precarious state grieves me; but I won't be blind to what it preserves in each of these little ones. There's nothing I can do if in our civilization the worthiest destiny for a child, when everything is taken into account, is still this horror.

They don't seem horrified. Playing the role of stray cats, hanging out together, repeatedly getting into mischief, being impudent and self-centered seems to suit them. They're almost never cold; they eat for next to nothing; they sleep in safety almost everywhere. They're bursting with health, their flesh in bloom; and if they didn't pilfer, they would hardly be bothered at all. Besides, practically no one ever goes after them; the police ignore them unless they're following a specific order; they fear no one and their strolls through the good neighborhoods are more peaceable and playful than those of virtuous children in their freshly shined dog collars.

Those whom I'm fond of are often together. I've taken the habit of having a supply of money in a form that can be distributed; during my shopping, I hold onto large coins and small bills and ask for change everywhere, harassing the magazine and cigarette sellers. The problem with my extravagances is that my appearances are irregular, in terms of place, day, time; I'm an enticing windfall but not at all to be relied upon. When I reappear after being away and don't run into anyone, I get worried, sad again, think of each. Then we find one another. Despite their amiability, I have no illusion about the type of feelings they have for me, and I know very well that the impression of a friendship, of being liked, I'm experiencing isn't reciprocal. Which pleases me all the more.

They are familiar with what's in my pocket, but some of them would rather rip out their tongue than ask me for a cent; others, less confident, harass me.

They spend their money childishly, gnaw on crusts but stuff themselves with sweets, go to the movies in the poor neighborhoods, smoke black tobacco. Those who have families bring back something to their parents. This professional panhandling abounds; since it lets outside so many young imps, I don't see any harm in it.

They change their rags endlessly and are never behind the seasons. The little ones round up their gains and share them. There are gangs run by older ones; in exchange for their supposed protection—but really under threat of their strength—they get richer on the backs of the youngest. I don't frequent these boys that copy our ways too much. The brats in my gang, on the other hand, are free from any political system, and I've encountered them only with teenagers infinitely more helpless, innocent or debilitated than them.

My dissolute contacts disturbed me horribly at first. Then they became the best in my life, and I can hope for no universe better populated than by these scallywags with their high-pitched voices and fresh little bellies. Though obliging about caresses, they aren't interested in them, and I don't bother them with my vices. The few that are sensual make it understood, and in some corner away from things or at my place, I find out if they're not wrong about themselves. It's often the case; so I give up on their talents, because I'd be ashamed of embracing children less smitten with pleasure than I am.

There is a small boy with fine features, ugly, cute, amusing, a cross between a mouse and a cat, too intelligent, daring. We make funny faces at each other and laugh at things that aren't amusing; maybe we resemble each other. Our relationship is nonsexual, but that could easily change. One evening, I'm eating inside a restaurant, next to the window. My monkey appears on the sidewalk, alone, deeply unhappy. He notices me, his face lights up, so I leave my table and join him to give him a kiss and hand him his stipend. I no longer care about passersby. The waiter, with my plate balanced on one palm, is watching me through the window. But I dine expensively and I invariably interrupt my meals to dash out into the street, and I leave big tips, so people think I'm a generous nut, and the owners, despite the riffraff I attract to their outdoor tables, practically lie through their teeth in their efforts to be polite. In this way, I conceal my shocking generosities under a veil of being wasteful in general, just as I rewarded Pablos with presents while bombarding his family with them.

All the brats show up. I don't have enough of the right change, so I go back in and ask for it at the restaurant. I'm ashamed, on such evenings, to give less to children than I spend on myself. Apportionment. You mustn't forget anyone, friends or those you don't know. Obviously, I have my favorites. It doesn't show much in the way I handle money, and if I spoil my ersatz brothers more, I don't deprive the others. I'm painfully corrected of that before I can do it. It's exasperating: the least coin you let go of sends a flight of birds beating down on you. When I examined the reasons for my uneasiness, my reluctance, it suddenly burst upon me, like the abscess I'd had in my groin. Once I was in tune with these outpourings, these swarms, I experienced an inexpressible well-being. But I'm not rich, and when I have nothing left, I become a shut-in, take to my bed, stop seeing anyone and live on bread and water. As a result of being gobbled up, I end up on a complete fast for three or four days in a row, near the end of my retreat, and it makes me feel good. Pure, unadulterated sleep, good body, sweet soul and new eyes. I love being alone, I love bread; I love the mirages of plenty and friendship. I leave and go back to all of it without suffering, relieved by having withdrawn to my cave, relieved about leaving it.

My kid passes by the restaurant again. He's smoking a butt. I make a sign at him that says no. He understands my joke, throws away the butt with a comical gesture, tramples it into the sidewalk as if he were rubbing a parquet floor, while sending his skinny-guy laughs my way. Above us, the window is open; I throw him some money for the show. Here's to good deeds. But if I want him not to smoke butts, it would be better to offer him cigarettes; with budgets like his, you don't buy what you can pick up from the ground.

In the cafés where I go, my little chaps assume poses that could move stone, and they hold out their hands. The customers are arrogant, the foreigners refusing and the locals offering ten or twenty cents.

Soliciting people strolling by, or tourists just standing there, is more profitable. You can bother them without risk, you're less easy to chase away. With the difference in size, they don't notice you much and they feel less hounded than when they're seated in front of a beer and some foul-smelling flower pops up: a brat. Unmoving, unshakeable, with the right details to make you vomit: a voice, hands, eyes. Free. Dirty. And asking for a handout without caring for the inalienable rights that Commerce, Industry and Savings Plans have over your salary.

I'm not forgetting that charity is an outmoded virtue; it's social justice that's needed. Happily, whereas the first may belong to the past, the second is for the future, and it's something that dispenses both to us. Faced with these children who have no future, I pay no heed to their present and muse about interdependence: prisons, penitentiaries, orphanages; placement with altruistic bosses or couples that are sterile but right-thinking; using them for medical, psychiatric, pharmacological, judicial, pedagogical experiments; or any other means of rescue that costs a lot more than garbage collection. I'm learning to be indignant that there are poor children without handcuffs on their wrists, thermometers in their holes, ABCs in their pocket.

Alas, in the world there is an abundance of big cities in which you must walk near the muck from which our well-being issues. The standard of living is low, so you go there on vacation—along with the hippies who—like us—are indignant about someone angling for their wallets. It's outrageous that the poor, whose unemployment, scrimping, low salaries create our bargains—a providence for junky boy scouts and vacationing grocers—could exploit us under the pretext that they don't like to work for so little. We're working even so, aren't we?

My city is one of those in which the poor are the most cumbersome: they act as if they're at home. Their city, their order, their lack of consideration, their freedom, their morals. Their sexuality, underpackaged to the retentions and investments of the middle class. Their mouths speaking and their eyes looking. All these children, less groomed than our grannies' poodles. Certainly, schooling is a must: without incineration plants, this filth would be blown around everywhere. When it comes to the good neighborhoods, we find the philanthropists. Those who want only happiness for the human species, provided that it be they who create it and not them; those who venerate the people but see them only as livestock in need of training; those for whom the complex civilization of the masses is nothing but dire poverty, illness, slavery, sloth and illiteracy— as long as the Order of Bourgeois Industry, Western or Maoist, hasn't forced upon it its refinements, geniuses, brand of dignity, progress, sweet talk. And I come to my final mental failing: if I remind myself that humanity already exists, instead of meditating on what it should be, I end up thinking that all its imperfections, suffering, make it less monstrous than the projects of its benefactors. Obscurantism, populism, anarchism, demagoguism: these are the erring ways into which I've fallen as a result of my pederasty. Obviously, it's my belly talking. But it's time to go home, to think again about the Good and, especially, to no longer have to see those who are going to take advantage of it.

The monkey from the restaurant, standing behind a forbidding customer, sticks out his little straight, pointed tongue with a burst of silent laughter; it isn't a starchy child's tongue, but one that wants to be thought of as a stiff one. Or else it's saying: lousy corner, yikes, I'm outta here!

Francesco hated panhandlers. It was part of his conservatism. He treated them like good-for-nothings and thieves, drove them away, insulted them. I insulted him, too; it wasn't up to him to criticize "parasites." A lad of ten or eleven comes up to us, holding a six-week-old dog in his arms. Obviously, for pulling in handouts; but people don't like dogs much better than kids. Francesco says that this one is very nice, we should give him something. I obey. Smiling, with a friendly, placid, resolute face, he was one suspect exception to Francesco's hates. His dog had a pleasant disposition, licked our fingers, wagged its tail, threw out a brow puffy with amusement.

Months later, I invite this child over. He's not unfriendly, but his sense of propriety is impregnable. Completely naked, he's like a miniature version of a perfectly built young man. Sticking out from his silky, prepubescent testicles is the kind of member you don't have at his age. Looking, licking, sucking. I grab him and lift him up to the table. Put a strong light on it and admire it. He's laughing, likes it, gets hard. I tell him to turn around, because I want to see his derriere. He doesn't understand and complacently changes into a top spinning at high speed; I stop this bogeyman shaking my table and bring him back down. He doesn't sleep with me; his mom is waiting for him, he says. He has the manner of a top of the class. He doesn't even smoke. The little gang I like revolves around his virtues. He slips the end of his dick into my ass and gets used to it trembling gently there. This is his only activity. He doesn't want to jerk off. They say he has a family, house. As soon as I've come, he goes to get dressed. I ask him to stay naked. He sits politely on the edge of the bed, as if paying a visit. With my finger I caress the front of his thighs and he begins to get hard, slowly. It's as if at first his prick cocks an ear, from between the thighs that were hiding it; it lengthens, arching in small jerks that seem to follow the beating of his heart; then it rises, straightens, the head very swollen. I stop touching his thigh; the member gently retreats. I caress again; the ear pricks up, and everything begins again. This mechanics enchants me. During this time, the boy says, does nothing; he doesn't even glance at his rising penis. He smiles. It's as if a breeze were lifting his hair.

I won't invite him to come over any more; he's one of those boys that is out of place in the loves I cultivate.

Conversely, it happens that a shy person who doesn't seem to be lewd turns out to be. A brat who has a prick like my index finger sucks my anus to the point of yanking my guts out, has a skinny little tool so strong that it gratifies me, eats my cock, my balls, comes in my mouth, gets on all fours and offers me a ravishing and ready behind. He's not even surprised when, seeing him pissing outdoors, I want to drink his urine; he holds it in, brings his cock closer, lets all of it out as indifferently as if I were a toilet. Very salty piss. That little devil should be something when he grows up. He's not in the city any more.

A pair of swine. At night they take me to the back of an alley and suggest I fuck them. In the darkness, I suck their insignificant pricks. One takes his pants down and gets on all fours: anus squeezed together, a childish behind. I tell him that it won't work. He insists. I push a little so he'll understand. He keeps insisting. I shrug, would rip my way in. Disappointed, he straightens up. His friend claims he can. He's seeing me at close range, he knows what to expect. On all fours, a little ass, the same kind of hole. I talk these braggarts out of it, suggest they fuck each other instead. They refuse, then agree. The one with his pants down lies on the ground, the other pulls on his prick, wets it and, aiming carefully for the hole, collapses onto his friend. While watching, I leave them a sticky souvenir in the alley.

I often run into the child with the dog. He spots me from a great distance, gallops over, flies into my arms. Once he rummages endlessly in the pockets of the pants he happens to be wearing; he says he has a present for me, it's a clean woolen ball shaped like the head of a dog, with the diameter and color of a tangerine. Two drooping, triangular ears and a square muzzle in soft, blue cloth glued to the ball. The ears are big, the muzzle small, there's no mouth. The eyes are two white plastic beads. I put the dog's head into my pocket. We run into a seller of gemstones to whom I usually pay for a crystal without taking it; in order to retail them he breaks them up too much. It's not a handout I'm giving him, he doesn't panhandle; it's a down payment on a larger crystal he'll find for me someday. He's pretty, but a snot. I don't touch him, except for his hand. The bottom side of his shorts distracts me, he can be a slut. When it's hot, he sits on the stairs doing nothing; his pants gape open, and today he isn't wearing any underwear. It's a smutty piece of clothing like women's lingerie from Pigalle, or those outfits of openwork leather they sell to men who are into S&M. But it's a young boy in a pair of worn-out shorts. High in the thighs, low at the hips, little moons running along the butt crack that are sweetly taking in some air. I regret it when I suggest he button up. There are little pipsqueaks that aren't so little everywhere—what a cock!

Diego's little brother Pedro's cock was as thick as my thumb, but was enormously longer, and his balls were plump. He often enjoyed using his prick to poke my foreskin, which he'd stretch into a tube. It was his only whim, and it wasn't very imaginative. He'd caress a great deal, swallow quarts of soda, bananas, apples, cakes, chocolate, cookies—slowly, ponderously, implacably. He liked very long, very expensive cigarettes. He was much more badly dressed than Diego, which I reproached him for. The next time we met, Pedro appeared in his brother's most beautiful pair of trousers, pulled almost up to his armpits. I didn't push it.

Pedro is dark, with short hair and the same blond skin as Diego. He's not as handsome, but he's a child. I have a photo of him at eleven in which he looks exactly like his brother: same features, lips, an expression that Diego didn't have at that age. Then Diego took them, and the little one lost out on them.

I shoot my load onto him from behind, between his thighs. Contact with his body dazzles me. He jerks off. He's at that prepubescent moment when you become a man; and when he comes, a murky spurt, as narrow and straight as wee-wee, comes out of the end. He stops moving his hand and looks at the little spurt with even more interest than I do; lying against his rump, I bend forward to see it better. We only come two times; I tickle him, I carry him, he's nice and heavy, only these tickles drive him wild.

He's violently against my fucking him. Even so, I try. Naked with him in the bathtub, I soap him from top to bottom, slide my finger all the way up his ass without his noticing. In fact, he's very relaxed, but aware that a boy doesn't let anyone do that, he slowly realizes that I've just done it and only then does he protest. He fucks friends at school and recounts it in three words or less.

In bed he's kneeling over me, and I begin tapping his anus lightly with my cock. He doesn't stop me. Stealthily I wet my cock with saliva and push; it gets swallowed up as if it were nothing. Pedro, who's jerking off, doesn't react. With his cherry hugging my cock, I feel everything. Then he finally decides to think . . . oh. And to say it. I pull out gently. He's not angry. But he sees me as unfair; he's a little boy, and he obviously has a hole that's a match for men's cocks, so it's mean of me to take advantage of it and feminize him, it's a denial of all trust. This is what Pedro has internalized concerning anal prohibitions. And (except if he sits by mistake on a cock that's sticking up) it will be enough to protect his rear end.

I can't, don't want to talk about recent lovers; there have been sweet ones, mischievous ones, violent ones—but so close that I don't know where to begin with them. My mind is slow, it takes months before the simplest images become clear. Moreover, the truth of my stories comes from what I write, not what inspires them in me; I ransack so many wonders that if—while rereading what I've written—I weren't able to recall a host of things I didn't takes notes on, but which these sentences are helping to bring forth, I wouldn't dare recount anything.

Pablos had a dog. I was curious to see them together, since the child took every liberty with the animal. He treated this baby dog like he treated me. He didn't hit it, and let it fight; would get very interested in it and would forget about it; rated his tokens of affection by the other's, played without fear and let himself be nibbled on with fake grimaces of pain.

Then he loved him more boldly. The puppy got bigger; Pablos's hands were covered with scabs from bites. In the morning, since he got up alone, he'd make some coffee with milk and bread, place this human meal on the ground, and the little animal would swallow it. When he was surprised at it, he claimed that he wasn't hungry. The dog was fed with leftovers. At dinner Pablos furtively put some pieces in his plate and slipped them to the animal; he didn't dare do anything if the eldest was there (the mother didn't eat with us), and did no more than what he could hide.

Every week we go to the movies. Pablos had never been before, they don't waste anything on the little brats. I inundate him with sweets. Francesco goes with us. If the boy doesn't have a good view of the screen, he refuses to sit on my knees (in public it's an ambiguity that embarrasses him) and uses his brother's. I don't like the movies, but I like Pablos. He holds my hand, distractedly caresses the fingers, the hollow of my palm; he shares his candies, licorice, chewing gum and a thousand bland-colored sweets. Vampires, hemoglobin, brawls thrill him as he sits there calmly chewing away. During the karate films, the kids in the theater burst into laughter; a Dracula movie will give Francesco nightmares, but all the kids are splitting their sides. I myself am afraid. In my hand, Pablos's hand doesn't even clench. But it seems there were never so many vampires, shrieks, tombs, dogs, necks with holes in them, demented faces, bats, chests with stakes through them, corpses and claws. At night, I play vampire on Francesco; terrified, he screams, jumps out of bed, turns the light on, grabs two knives and forms a cross with them to protect himself. It takes a long time for him to calm down and agree to go back to bed next to me.

One time, Pablos doesn't show up to meet me at the movies. Time passes. Worried, I go to their place. Women are there, moaning; the mother's weeping; the brothers look haggard. The eldest is manhandling Pablos, violently threatening him with the police, yelling, pulling him toward his moped like a sack of flour. Pablos is red from crying. I separate them. They explain to me that the little one didn't come back at noon; he went to a nearby park to study with another child, because it isn't quiet at home. But the mother, who strengthens the family order with her frenzied tantrums, and who's responsible for an alcoholic brute, two halfwits and a gigolo before wishing for model sons, had forbidden Pablos to go out. Indignant about the arbitrariness of it all, Pablos spit at the feet of his mother and left. By noon, the old lady had gotten her older son worked up. When Pablos comes back, maternal vengeance is ready.

I pull the little boy's pants back up; from his knees to his ankles, both shinbones are lacerated with bloody cuts. He has been whipped with the thick electric cable, a favorite instrument of the eldest. He's good at his job; to make all that, it takes time, and strength in your biceps. I have some of that, too; I grab the eldest, fling him against the wall and shake him up my way. I find out he's afraid; for a while, he'd kiss my feet to calm me down.

I don't leave until night. I've warned the eldest that if he touches the little one again I'll break his bones. The kid also has bruises all over his head, because his brother, to give his hand some rest, banged it against the tiles.

What is strange is that after that, they didn't really beat Pablos any more. The eldest sucks up to me and chokes back his moaning about money. Week by week, the little one starts to get unaccustomedly cheerful. I'm surprised by this, and I don't understand why. Francesco is just as perplexed. Did we underestimate the reign of terror in sway at home, where I only come as a visitor and Francesco as the guest at a hotel? Pablos is full of laughter all the time. It's an attractive laugh that lights up his features without distending them.

My intervention, that day, hadn't been an example of prying; they'd involved me a little earlier in another family affair. One night when Francesco got drunk with some friends and a whore, he was arrested by the police. Because of the racket they were making, the neighbors had called the cops, and the boys had stood up to them.

Now they're in prison, and they're going to charge them as adults. They inform me of it. Red tape, days of waiting, court, a dreadful parade of kids in which Francesco, looking arrogant with a clenched jaw, is taller than the others by a head. We bring in clothing, things to eat. I hired a lawyer for the gang; in such affairs, it helps to show that the accused is rich or protected by a rich person. The speech for the defense crudely portrays him in a good light. So Francesco is acquitted, his friends condemned with suspended sentences. The same evening, the eldest goes to pick him up on his moped. We're all waiting for him at the house; Francesco comes back in a very good mood, his hair cropped short, covered with lice and rubble. After that, I'm a member of the family.

That was when I began to fondle Pablos.

In one of the games Pablos plays with me in front of everybody, he gives me his nipple to suck and calls me his little one. He lies down and I lie down next to him, and he says we're going to sleep. Pressed very close together. This is during television. I feel good. We kiss each other's teeth, tongues, play with each other's fingers, palms, hair, ears. One evening, he gets up and goes to another room without a word. Since I miss him, I follow. He's lying under a blanket and lets me get under it with him. We begin to caress each other. Suddenly the old lady is snarling at the door. We get up.

At my place, I put my head on Pablos's thighs. I nibble at his fly. He's amused by it, gets angry, pushes me away so energetically that I behave better. In bed, I put him on top of me. That position bothers him, because of Francesco—or the second older brother, when he was the chaperone. I hold onto him, he wriggles out of it; but his face and stomach don't really avoid mine.

My panhandlers' latest prank. A fat granny, the American world-tour type, with crumpled skin, blue hair, harlequin glasses, a tan with old-age spots, refused them a handout. The two of them walk behind her and spit on her back. They double up with laughter, the lady turns around laboriously, like a cow that has been disturbed. Then she starts walking again. The kids spit again, split their sides laughing, wink at me. We watch the gobs of spit dribbling down, feebly dislodged by a flowered ass, with enough meat, fat to represent at least a year of food. No passerby reprimands them; the two good-for-nothings are doing what everybody dreams of doing, and I'd be the first.

A little hoodlum with cropped hair, while he is alone in my room lying on the bed, puts his legs in the air in front of a mirror, studies his hole and balls with keen interest as he yanks at his member. I watch him from a neighboring room, in another mirror.

While I jerk off on his face, a well-behaved schoolboy sticks a finger up my ass. Since his fingers are still quite small, I take his hand to have him put in two; he thinks that I want his whole fist and, biceps tensed, but a bit surprised even so, tries to push it in, knitting his brows and glancing anxiously up at my face. The fist won't go in. I spatter his face. He's a small boy, very sensual and very accommodating, who fucks, licks, laughs, is well brought up, jerks off while lending me his thighs and asks for more in the morning. He bothers me about it as soon as he opens my eyes. His way of waking me up is charming, he spends a long time caressing my cheek and shoulder, kisses me, presses against me, tickles my cock, blows little puffs like smiles into my ear. He sleeps with me if his parents are out. I run into him in the street when he is returning from school. He ignores me. He's chattering with some little girls, and he's almost prettily dressed, holding his schoolbag with two hands against his rump.

In the shower, which has a telephone, he leaves the cord made of metallic rings twisted into a double helix. I like the traces of children after they've left. On the table, the empty bowl of café au lait, the bread crumbs, the fruit peelings (but Pablos doesn't eat anything without running to throw the scraps in the garbage), a knife dribbling butter. Sometimes, my toothbrush is all crumpled because they scrape their little teethies the way you shine shoes. And the shower: always immaculate, well ordered, until the age of twelve or thirteen. Afterward, you become a man, and you leave behind your grime.

A pretty child whom I'll see only one time. Another who took advantage of his parents' absence to try his luck. He has such a good nature that he won't fail at it. Before we go to sleep, I give him some money as a gift; the little ones are never too sure about the honesty of the promises made to them. I didn't promise anything, and he didn't ask for anything: more of a reason. It's a tidy sum. He's very happy, but the money leaves him perplexed; completely nude, he grabs his pants and shows me that there's only one pocket, a small one for tickets. He's afraid that he'll lose the money or that somebody will take it. We think about it. I look for a safety pin, he hands me the money and the trousers, and I transform the little pocket into a gusset that's nicely sealed from the inside. I give him back his pants, he tries the pin, pats it all over, is delighted, and tossing his pants there, climbs into bed. When the lights are out, he looks for the indentation in my side where he can doze off, kisses me, puts an arm around my chest and falls asleep immediately.

The sleep of naked children has a profound effect on me. They go to bed long before the time that suits me. But although I stay up and sometimes go read in another room when I'm with the older ones, I can't separate from the little ones. Their calm, their languidness captures me. They use me to fall asleep the way an adult arranges pillows, looks for a familiar hollow in the mattress, or piles the edge of the blankets against a shoulder or neck; they put their slight legs, supple thighs, soft arms, elastic stomachs together with mine, and they lull themselves to sleep by having their bottoms and hair caressed. That weightless interlacing modifies the boundaries of my body; and their trustful, silent, peaceful, solemn sleep works like hypnosis. Gripped by these waves of serenity, of infinite sweetness, I fall asleep.

It is so powerful that the next day, long after the child has left, I can't get used to myself; I have no more hold over my body. The image, the presence, the eyes, the gestures, the loves of the child have passed through me, loosened some structures, some anxieties, have established the smooth, uncomplicated unity of a lake. There I experience a kind of happiness no one has ever described to me.

When the sun sets, very far from my place, I meet a fifteen-year-old teenager. He has an amusing face that I find attractive. The truth is that he's pretty, but dreadul. He senses my interest, his naïve eyes brighten and he greets me cheerfully. He's thin and rather small. I naughtily touch his fly. He laughs very excitedly.

He picks up a cardboard box and gleefully pulls me behind a low wall, under trees. He spreads out his cardboard, lowers his trousers, reveals a little round, hairless, warm butt and lies flat on his stomach. No explanation. I interpret this strange ritual in my own way. His whole face bursts into giggles. Afterward he groans; his hole is small, small, he repeats. I feel bad about causing pain to such a nice partner. He turns around and offers his mouth. So we take a taxi.

I haven't shaved for several days. I ask him if I should. Cutting my beard seems like a big sacrifice to him. He hesitates, laughs, follows me to the washbasin and watches in the mirror. Such large, twinkling, luminous, intelligent eyes. He laughs, caresses my neck, it's worth the trouble to see that.

It's only after his shower that I notice that he's knock-kneed. Not a lot, a little, but clearly. Aside from this detail, his legs are gracefully curved, as is his body, muscular and smooth, erect, sensitive, the skin tanned and hairless, with a sheen. The short pubic hair of post-puberty, on the softness of a thin, childish stomach. His voice, which is changing, is melodious, inane. My house interests him a lot. Sex, even more. Delicious kisses, warm caresses. For the last few minutes, his hole hasn't gotten any larger; kneeling over him, I fuck his mouth. He likes it, sucks, eats, draws it in, jerks off, gets come on his teeth, lips, tongue. He jerks off while he kisses me. He has a lot of sperm.

We begin again, then he gets up and begs to use my typewriter. The table is about four feet from the bed. I let him. Delighted, he sits down. I put a piece of paper in it, explain a few details to him, and he types with one index finger. My machine is solid and heavy, beautiful-looking.

Finally, I discover that my teenager is not only knock-kneed but half-witted. However, normal people notice such a thing right away. Someone must be taking care of him, he's groomed and dressed well enough.

In my room there are two fans, one on the table, the other on a chest of drawers. They're no longer on at night, it has cooled off. While I rest, the noise of the typing stops, and the innocent, dying of curiosity, timidly toys with one of the fans, then with the other, then with both. There are buttons for changing the speed of the blades.

He sits back down and he types in the humming sound of the machines. I have a camera that someone loaned me, but no film. The innocent, a music lover, plays with the shutter release. He's agile with his hands, I fear nothing.

On the sheet of paper he's typing, there's something to read: in fact, his finger invariably follows the keyboard from left to right and top to bottom, and he writes pages of it. I showed him the capitals and the numbers, but he forgot how to do them.

He leaves his seat only in the middle of the night, in order to sleep. His sleep is restless, he peppers me with kicks, then he calms down, and I feel the youthful body against me.

In the morning, we jerk off. Both of us, once. Then, immediately after, it's his turn, one against the other. During it, when he's about to come, he bumps into me, finds my ass, pushes brutally into it and shoots all the way up me. This rape excites me, and I jerk off to it. Again? Ah, since that's how it is, he begins again, too. We get back in position. He has trouble coming, strokes his cock, which is nice, average and fairly thick, and he practically tears his guts out in order to come. His abdominal muscles are so tensed that they form a thick trapezoid in the middle of his stomach, drawn from the base of his ribs to his penis; on each side, the flesh is scooped out. By jolts he relaxes that beautiful contraction, gets it back, looks at my cock, kisses me, whacks off, pants, drools, tears himself apart, contracts all the way to his toes, puffs out his muscles and comes.

He goes to the toilet and spends a long moment surrounded by the noises of water. He comes back looking very cheerful, fresh, kisses me tenderly on the mouth; his is scented. It's not toothpaste; that sugary, aromatic flavor is my shaving cream. He must have mistaken the tube. Even so, he smells good.

Once more he gazes at the typewriter and sits down in front of it. I fall asleep. The noise of the keystrokes is interrupted; it wasn't fully pleasurable. He goes to look for the camera, places it in front of the machine, turns on the two fans, pours himself a soda, lights a cigarette and, having accomplished that assemblage of pleasures, sits back down and types.

During my siesta, these noises, this ritual bring me a strange pleasure. Little shivers run through me at moments, like those caused by the fascinated caresses of Andrès. But it's no longer a matter of vanity, if it was that; rather, it's the solitary, inexhaustible, blissful aspect of his passion for my objects making me shiver.

I have a hard time removing the innocent from his tasks so he can eat lunch. He has a wounded and infected ear that I bandage. Next, I'll wait until he wants to leave. I like him so much that if he stays, I'll keep him.

But he leaves.

Weeks pass. I can't find him. Some of my panhandlers know him. I'm told that a man has already fallen in love with him and that he wanted to take care of him; but one evening, in the restaurant, the innocent, seized by anger, will take off a shoe, throw it in the face of the benefactor and sweep the table clean. The end of love. I wonder what the man said to him, I've never seen anyone sweeter, more reasonable and more manageable.

At last I find him. He's mostly in rags, this time. He doesn't even have shoes any more. But he's adopted a dog, a funny kind of dog that laughs. The dogs here, members of a minority and mistreated, are fearful and nasty; they growl at humans, get stones thrown at them, and you can see their ribs. But that dog liked humans. Another half-wit.

The innocent plays with him, forgets about me. I buy him shoes, give him money, the dog laughs. Nearby is an old woman seated on a step. The innocent goes over to her, lies down against her, they chat. Then he remembers me, dashes over laughingly, kisses my hand, mouth; I'm a bit shy, but he seems so sad when I half refuse his lips that I let him do it, hard.

Impossible to bring him to my place, he's with the old lady. After that, I never saw him again. I tell myself that if someone annoys him enough and he reacts violently, they'll lock him up. Nothing else is waiting for him.

Months after our breakup, I saw Francesco again. Early one night, on a long, deserted avenue, a moped approaches. There's a handsome boy on it, but his face is hard and his sideburns are too long, giving him a pimpish look. Then I recognize Francesco. I don't know if he recognizes me. But around thirty feet from me, he slows down and makes a half-turn; once he's done that, he turns his head in my direction and lets out a long gob of spit, without looking at me. The moped disappears very quickly.

I saw Diego again. His hairdresser finally adopted him. He's magnificent, a hairdresser, laughs, has grown taller, even has a salary. His work outfit is very elegant. The yellow-paper hair has improved, the darker colors have been preserved. Diego proudly recounts his latest flirtations: goodbye to girls, now he likes little boys. His perverse loves are as stereotypical and boring as the normal ones were; wherever he goes, he walks a straight line. To make fun of him, I remind him of his school friends, their names, what he would say. He answers that that was last year. These days, in order to change his tastes, he allows up to twenty-two years old. He's seventeen; quite a generous grace period. Besides, fucking little boys isn't disreputable, and he knows one that's so handsome, so blond, so suitable, who can take his big cock so willingly, the whole shebang!

My conversation with Diego surprised me; I thought he was too fearful and got too much advantage from the order of things. His prosperity must have helped him. I like his frankness: the little shy hetero from the epoch of the *monster* is as loyal, as cheerful and as nice a kid with his new values, he'll make an attractive man, and that increases my gloom if I think of Francesco.

At my place, the gas bottles are empty. I hate going out when I'm in this book, I ate my meal cold and uncooked. Then I missed having coffee and discovered a combustible: crumpled pages. Those I tear out of my manuscript are more numerous than the ones I leave and the rough drafts. I've already sorted out what I could find in various shirts. All that has lasted a week, with my reserves of food—I only eat right before bed. I burned my writing on the tile floor of a well-ventilated room; sitting on the ground, I held my frying pan, my saucepan over flames and I cooked some steak, eggs, heated up some soup, coffee, milk, several cans of tinned food, refreshed some dry bread. I'll obviously be the first author to be fed by texts he doesn't publish.

I kept the innocent's typed pages. And I'm reading them, reading his finger, his face, his pleasure, his passage. Shivers return when my eye yields to the law of these signs. Is there a law that is so different in the series of words that I put down? I think about the typing monkey who, if he types anything at all and endlessly on a keyboard, will reference all the masterpieces in the world—and also, as long as he's at it, will write his own. If anyone is like him, it's me and not the innocent.

But contrary to the monkey of probabilities, I'm not eternal; and I have a bed, a belly that living on air won't fill. So I have to choose my words; maybe it will keep me from writing masterpieces, but there will be more of a chance that what I type will feed me if I publish it rather than burn it. As for the language of the innocent, I envy it, but few people would read it.

I saw the boy with the dog again. His head was shorn. He had a new dog, white with red spots like the one from last year, but sickly and trembling, with a heavy belly. I told him to feed it milk and not crusts, and to let it walk a little, since he carries it all the time. Later he reappeared with other panhandlers. I'm shown the milk, the dog: the little animal scampers about, is more lively, wags its tail, runs like a puppy toward the hands or feet you shake to entertain it.

In the evening, the dog slept at the bottom of the kid's immense pocket. He woke up, yawned, was brought out to go pee.

Two whores stop, short young women with big bottoms, in trousers, wearing a nice perfume. Polite and polished old gals. They see the dog; the heaviest one bends down and picks it up, raises it to her eyes, checks its sex (female), gets soft-hearted, cuddles it, wants to buy it. The kid paid a franc for it. She offers ten, fifty, then a hundred. My panhandler refuses, very sullenly. The lovely ladies keep talking. Nothing doing. They put the puppy back on the ground. The big pink-and-almond behinds move off toward the lights of the cafés.

An instant later, the little one asks if I want his dog as a gift. Surprised, I say that I wouldn't know what to do with it; I don't even have a courtyard for it to piss in, and I move around too much. He nods. The kid puts his creature back to bed, and it sleeps against the edge of the pocket.

After an interruption of several weeks, I see this little guy again. He's alone, very badly dressed, his face is lean and gloomy, his voice cold, his head completely shaved. He denies that the police picked him up. His dog is dead.

ABOUT THE AUTHOR

Tony Duvert (1945–2008) is the author of fourteen books of fiction and nonfiction. His fifth novel, *Paysage de fantaisie* (*Strange Landscape*), won the prestigious Prix Médicis in 1973. Other books translated into English include the novel *When Jonathan Died* and the scathing critique of sex and society *Good Sex Illustrated* (Semiotext(e), 2007).